Behind the Mirror

Fay E. Simon

Dedication

I'd like to dedicate this book to my Heavenly Father, without whom, I can do nothing. Also, I dedicate this to my mother, Georgia M. Simon, friends Mari Asim, Sandy Katis, and Evie Sanchez.

PROLOGUE

The Wilds of Scotland, 1849

The shadows of twilight danced across the lush meadows, stretching dark fingers out to the Mystic Pool of Aire in the garden of Shylah, the Celtic Seer. A tall, hooded figure shrouded in a black robe glided into view. It wore the hood pulled up around its face, leaving only the yellow glint of its eyes visible. Kneeling by the pool, Shylah disturbed the water when the dark shape overshadowed her.

Shylah cast her dark eyes upward to meet the eerily glowing orbs. Still kneeling, she gathered her robe around her, shivered, and offered the dark figure a seat by the pool.

"I know why you've come. You want to know your future," she said in a delicate English accent. Looking back at the pool, she continued to stir the water. When she stopped, the water swirled into a ghostly white mist reaching out its tendrils.

The image of a young woman in her late teens appeared in the center of the mist. She was dressed in clothes different from their time, a white top with writing and dark blue denim trousers. Her soft, brown hair gently framed her face, bringing out the sparkle in her dark, flashing eyes. She laughed and talked with two other young people about her age, a male and a female.

"How very strange," Shylah said. "For you, I see two separate, yet intertwining destinies running parallel to each other. This woman becomes a major part in both sides of your future." Shylah reached out to disturb the vision, but a skeletal hand stopped her. Its shockingly cold touch sent chills through her body, nearly frightening her to death.

"You want to see more of this woman?"

The dark figure nodded, so Shylah stirred until another image formed. "She comes from another time and space. At the moment, she abides in our future, yet she knows you and everything about you."

The vision in the pool showed the woman and her friends watching flickering shadows on a wall where two lovers kissed. The tender moment was interrupted by a dark-robed figure enveloping them.

"I'm not sure how, but this picture moves, telling your story."

A bony finger tapped the side of the pool. Shylah paused, trying to understand what the figure wanted. Again, it tapped then pointed to the vision.

"You want to know how to meet her?" The tapping continued. "I cannot tell. But without her, your second destiny will be final: one of intense hatred, unrequited love, and certain death." Shylah flinched at the icy, death-like touch of the skeletal hand.

"Do you want to see the second woman in your future?" The hooded head nodded. Shylah passed her hand over the pool. White vapors covered the image and dispersed, revealing a new one. A beautiful young woman in her late teens with dark, cascading curls stood on the stage of a grand theater. With a curtsey and a smile, she accepted the applause.

"They call her Cerise. She is the death you cannot escape. She will never love you." Shylah shivered again and reminded, "You cannot change history."

The shrouded figure stood abruptly.

Standing in the presence of a foreboding creature made Shylah turn cold, and knots of anxiety formed in her stomach. She wanted to jump up and flee into the night, screaming, but the creature's eyes gave her second thoughts.

The skeletal hand grabbed her arm. Its angry, vice-like grip brought excruciating pain, sending her to the ground screaming and pleading, reminding the creature that she only prophesied what came from God.

It released her arm. She fell to the ground gasping, clutching her discolored limb. Again, a skeletal finger tapped the edge of the pool.

Shylah rolled over, holding her damaged arm, gasping and biting her lip. The tapping continued until she passed a shaky hand over the pool.

Visions of both young women appeared. The one entwined in a lover's embrace with a black-clad figure. The other wept softly within the walls of a building.

The golden orbs blazing within the hood resembled an artist's concept of the Grim Reaper. Shylah turned her face to the ground, sobbing and pleading, as she cradled her throbbing arm. No longer could she bear to look into its eyes. Her entire body trembled until her heart nearly failed. Suddenly, the hooded figure turned and swiftly melted into the night.

CHAPTER ONE

Present Day Paris, France

"*Studio Duchenois, named for its founder Ranier Duchenois, brings to life the very essence of old France in both stage and film.*"

Emma paused in her reading and looked up from the brochure. Something flickered in and around the shadows of the statues on the Studio's roof. She rubbed her eyes for a moment and looked again, but it had disappeared.

"Go on," Doone urged as he playfully yanked on the brochure.

"Hey, stop that." Emma began again. "*Little known to most of the world in comparison to other popular Paris landmarks, the Studio, originally known as le Théâtre Ranier and built in 1870, always housed a rousing play, a passionate reading, or a little-known opera.*"

She paused again. It seemed surreal; she had been waiting to see this building for a long time, or rather, what this building contained.

Twanda, Doone, and Emma all stared up at the exquisite statues that adorned the roof of the majestic building. Emma imagined how it would feel to walk among all the splendor of its Baroque architecture in bygone days.

Emma couldn't believe she was finally here. She had been dreaming of this moment for a long time. Twanda's parents had agreed, as had Emma's, to allow them this little trip before college. Doone...well, Doone was a different story.

She looked back down at the brochure and finished its description. "*Today, Studio Duchenois presents plays both past and present, as well as allowing filmmakers the privilege of using its sets and newly added soundstages.*"

Eighteen-year-old Twanda Evans donned shades as she stepped a little farther back with her camera, trying to capture a shot of the roof.

For an instant, a shadow appeared and flickered through the statues. It remained on the dark side of the roof, as if watching the three friends. Twanda looked up from the camera. Her light brown complexion glistened with tiny pearls of perspiration from the sun's heat.

"Did anybody see that shadow moving on the roof?" Twanda asked, looking up from behind her dark glasses.

"I saw it. Could be a tour up there," answered Emma, visually searching for the flickering shadow.

"Mmm, maybe." Twanda tried to focus her lens.

Emma King wore her short brown hair in layers that met her shoulders and shone almost red in the light of day. With excitement, she turned to Doone, falling into a sword fighting position. "*En garde!*"

"Show off. Just because you took fencing lessons and Shotokan doesn't mean I can't beat you," Doone said as he wielded an imaginary sword.

Emma laughed. "I can beat you no matter what."

Even though twenty-five year old Doone had dropped out of high school, Twanda and Emma treated him like family. He wore his dark hair long and stringy. His thin, lanky frame made for stooped shoulders because of his height. The sun illuminated off his tie-dyed shirt and faded jeans.

Doone watched Emma furtively. He had always let on that he had wanted to come to Paris to walk the path of Ehrich de Natois from their favorite novel, *Dark Tales of le Théâtre Ranier*, and that was part of the truth, but he'd also wanted to be with Emma.

Since Doone could write his music and plays from anywhere, especially since no money came from them, his father had sent him on this trip to get him out of his way. He was tired of dealing with his son picking locks and being arrested.

Unfortunately, the young man habitually picked locks just to see if he could do it. He never stole anything or destroyed what wasn't his, but locks challenged him. However, the people owning the locks did not see lock picking as an exercise, and neither did the police.

"Are we going up to the roof?" asked Emma as she stepped next to Twanda, who was struggling to take a clear picture.

"We'd better. This haunted Duchenois-thing is making us all crazy. I wanna know what it was like for Cerise and Ralph up on the roof when Ehrich came after them. I know he must have been broken-hearted after seeing her with Ralph," Twanda finally snapped the picture.

"I would love to meet Ehrich. He must be so handsome and brave. Especially after he fought all those soldiers for killing his family," Emma said. She smiled and gave a long sigh.

"If you really met him, you'd faint."

"I would not. I would talk to him."

Twanda giggled and started making kissing noises.

"I didn't say kiss him. I said talk to him," Emma smiled shyly, as she playfully defended herself. "Well, maybe a little kiss." Thoughts of scenes from her favorite Ehrich movie filled her mind.

From the shadows of le Théâtre Ranier, Ehrich de Natois watched the lovely Cerise take her bows on stage.

A smiled crossed his lips as his eyes lit up at her beauty. But that smile soon faded as he watched her fly into the arms of Ralph Duchenois, a wealthy patron of the arts. He followed them to the rooftop.

"You were magnificent!" Ralph exclaimed as he kissed her tenderly. "My brougham awaits. We must leave tonight."

"I do love you, my darling. I can hardly wait to be your wife!" Cerise clung to him. Suddenly, a figure sprang from the darkness and overshadowed them and they were gone.

"I wanna be Ehrich. Such a great actor! Knowing all that Magick. All that lurking in shadows and secret passageways and coming in and out of trapdoors. Way cool!" Doone barked in his Valley-boy accent, as he tried to imitate twirling a cloak.

"You are so lame. Do you want to hide away in an old theater?" Twanda snapped.

"Why not? No rent, no neighbors, way cool! Then my dad wouldn't be complaining that I'm good-for-nothing." He half laughed.

Twanda rolled her eyes. Emma motioned for them to follow her inside. "Slow down, Emma," Twanda said.

The lobby and grand foyer exhibited exquisite sculptures of semi-nude females, and intricate carvings decorated the handrail of the grand staircase ascending to upper levels. Sconces reminiscent of the late 1800s illuminated the ascension.

The three friends couldn't possibly have imagined the huge columns and high ornate ceiling. A magnificent chandelier hung high, overlooking the grand foyer with various scenes painted on the ceiling above. Such scenes included angels flying, circling as if keeping watch over their charges.

Emma shuddered with delight. She was here; finally here. She had to see more.

Unfortunately, the Studio only conducted tours of the lobby, and even then only during performances, since filming went on in the soundstages most of the time. With no plays and the soundstages in use, the three milled around the lobby then the gift shop. There just had to be a way to see more of the building.

"Excuse me," began Twanda to the cashier. "We hear you only conduct tours of the lobby during stage performances. But what about the roof? We saw someone on the roof."

The cashier, a mature woman with her silver hair drawn up into a bun at the back of head, frowned a bit. Hesitantly, she replied in a French accent, "You are mistaken. No tours of the roof today."

The girls exchanged puzzled looks. "But we saw someone moving up there," Emma added.

"You are mistaken. No tours of the roof today," came the sharp reply. Puzzled, the girls turned to rejoin Doone.

"I don't get it," mumbled Twanda, checking her digital camera. "Bet I got a picture of whoever was up there." She flipped out the viewer but somehow, her photo was gone. "Shoot! Nothing!" she cried in disgust as she slapped the viewer shut. They left the gift shop and pretended to be interested in the lobby again. They looked down halls and wondered what doors led where.

All of the dressing rooms and seats seemed to be closed to tourists, especially Ehrich's balcony seat at the east end. But they had come all this way. The three had to get inside.

The staircase leading to the balcony seats lay before them in the center of the room a little ways from the guest relations and gift shops. A thick, golden-colored rope blocked anyone from ascending.

A sign in several languages read: *Do not enter. This area currently off limits.*

As their eyes followed the winding staircase, they could see the entrances to some of the balcony seats.

After all, what did "off limits" mean to a guy like Doone?

Emma and Twanda watched him pick the lock. They had to be quick and quiet. No one wanted to get caught. From time to time, one or both of the girls would peek around the corner to make sure no one was approaching.

Carefully, Doone jiggled the pick inside the lock. A shuffling noise caught their ears. For a brief moment, they all held their breath, afraid to look. It seemed Twanda couldn't stand the suspense and tiptoed to peek around the corner, again. A cleaning lady stood on the stairs dusting the banisters and one of the statues.

Taking a deep breath, Twanda quietly went back to the others and whispered, "It's only a cleaning lady. She's not coming up here yet. Hurry!"

Finally, after Doone fumbled for a few minutes, the lock clicked and the door opened. Rich crimson velvet walls caught their eyes first, and clothes hooks lined the wall to their right as they entered the room. A small lamp mounted on the ceiling lit the way. Four seats lay before them, just past the red velvet curtain.

They only spoke in whispers, but mainly gestured to keep from being discovered. Doone immediately went to a column behind the seat to his left. "I feel strange, like I've been there before. When I touched the pillar, its surface seemed so familiar, like I had walked right through it at some point. But no, that could not be."

Emma and Twanda tried out the seats. Emma was giddy with excitement. "Oh, Ralph, come to me, my darling. Take me away from here and from Ehrich," teased Emma in a high-pitched voice.

Twanda looked to her with exaggerated gestures, reaching out and making kissing noises.

"My carriage awaits, my sweet Cerise. Come away with me now." The two playfully faked an embrace.

Doone took the opportunity and raised both hands, comically pretending to hypnotize them. "I am Ehrich, the Master of Arts. Look into my eyes. Look, look!" Then he mimed twirling a cloak he didn't have.

However, a solemn moment occurred during their pretense. As if in a trance, Emma arose from the seat and locked eyes with Doone. Twanda sat motionless, her eyes focused between them, not sure what was happening.

Doone seemed to become very serious, drawing himself up to his full height. He extended his hand, and she walked to him.

When their hands touched, it was electric; he drew her close and leaned down to taste her lips. She leaned upward to meet his. The sweet scent of sandalwood swirled around the lovers. Twanda, exasperated, jumped up and separated them. "No, no, no. None of that!" The scent of sandalwood vanished.

Trying to dismiss what nearly happened, they headed for the exit.

As the door closed behind them, a flickering shape with blazing orbs hovered in the shadows. In a moment, a quiet rustle stirred near the column.

"Now, that was lame!" exclaimed Twanda nervously as they wandered around the lobby. "Just a bunch of seats."

"It was Ehrich's balcony. I liked it." Both girls turned to Doone and frowned. "Way cool!" he finished.

"We saw an empty balcony. What's cool about that?" Twanda retorted.

Once again, curiosity got the better of the girls, so they began searching for the dressing room of Cerise St. Clair where Ehrich had allegedly recited words of love from the mirror.

Doone sat this one out, distracting an employee by arguing about what the tour covered while Emma and Twanda sneaked up the gorgeous, winding staircase.

Both girls had wanted to see Cerise's dressing room. *Dark Tales of le Théâtre Ranier* described a full-length antique gold mirror that Ehrich used to enter and exit. This was a must see.

On the first level, they found all the dressing rooms and storage areas locked.

They wandered aimlessly through the corridor for a few minutes. Emma stopped short when she heard the faint voice of someone reciting the soliloquy from Hamlet.

"You hear that?" asked Emma. Twanda froze in her tracks to listen. The voice stopped.

"Don't hear anything. Let's go." Twanda started for the lobby; Emma froze. She heard it again. Wrapping itself around her, the mesmerizing sound of a male voice pulled her on.

Entranced, Emma moved toward the door a little ways down.

"Where are you going? Come back," whispered Twanda.

No answer.

Emma proceeded to turn the door's handle.

Surprisingly enough, the door swung open at Emma's touch. A dim wall lamp in the back of the room provided the only light. A few scattered stuffed chairs filled the room, as well as a table near the door. Deep inside the chamber stood a beautiful full-length mirror, with a gilded frame and gold leafing, beckoning to her.

Twanda timidly moved inside with Emma.

"Is this Cerise's room?" Twanda wondered aloud.

No answer.

The mirror seemed to summon Emma. Carefully, she examined it, running her fingertips along the sides and bottom.

"We'd better go. We've been gone too long." Twanda moved into the corridor.

Emma ignored her. The voice began again. It filled her soul and engulfed her mortal body. When she closed her eyes, the world as she knew it vanished while her mind and soul soared to the ethereal realm of the gods.

As the voice continued, Emma opened her eyes, and for an instant, she stared at her reflection. But as she did so, the mirror grew dense with roiling clouds, creating a vortex.

The soft, sweet voice floated up through the vents and again filled the air with strains of a recitation that thrilled her to the very bone. The scent of sandalwood waltzed all around her. A spark of light crackled and flashed as she walked into the mirror and the watery entrance to another dimension.

Gone.

The mirror now stood clear and alone.

CHAPTER TWO

Within the walls of le Theater Ranier, Paris, France, 1879

Emma felt the tingle of a small current surge through her body. Everything seemed surreal, almost dream-like.

The tall, majestic figure of a man, dressed in black with a cloak draped around his shoulders, led her by the hand. He wore the hood of his cloak pulled up around his face, so only vague features were visible in the dimness of torchlight. As they moved, he continued speaking directly to her, this time reciting Edgar Allen Poe's poem "Annabel Lee." His voice was hypnotic, and she didn't want to resist. Her face flushed warm and her heart raced. Her eyes were transfixed. Who was this man dressed as a gentleman of late nineteenth century France?

The tall, hooded man led her deeper and deeper into the recesses of a vast building, following a path to a deserted wing.

At last, he paused by the entrance and a door opened. Before them, an immense room overflowed with stray props from various performances. A musty stuffiness hung heavy in the air. The hooded man continued his recitation: "And the stars never rise but I feel the bright eyes, of the beautiful Annabel Lee; and so, all the night-tide, I lie down by the side, of my darling – my darling – my life and my bride, in the sepulcher there by the sea, in her tomb by the sounding sea."

Fay E. Simon

Emma's eyes widened with amazement and awe. His eyes burned through her, but at the same time, held her captive. She recognized the words. Deep emotion came not only from the poem, but also from the man who recited it.

Their gazes locked. He extended his hand and led her to him. She looked up into the vague features of his face as shadowed by the hood.

He pulled her closer so she could smell the sweet scent of his warm flesh, mingled with a light odor of sandalwood. Then he leaned down to brush his lips against hers. She tried to speak, but words never came.

Emma pushed him away gently, but only so she could better see his face. Pulling her back to him, he held her so tightly she nearly fainted.

"Please, *monsieur*. I cannot breathe."

"I apologize," he said as he loosened his hold.

For a moment, the young woman blinked rapidly and shook her head as if to shake away the clouds in her mind. Nothing around her seemed familiar, yet a tiny spark of déjà vù drifted. All memories of a previous life seemed vague. Whoever she was, she could not recall.

The shrouded man before her felt familiar. Somehow she remembered hearing stories about the theater being haunted. Something told her the man was dangerous. Could death be courting her?

"Please, may I ask your name?" Emma tried to divert the moment to conversation.

"Emma," he said in a smooth calm tone. "My dearest Emma..." Now she remembered

Her own name.

"You may call me Ehrich."

"Ehrich. Where are we—" but before she could finish, he silenced her with a long, passionate kiss, pressing his lips against hers warm and hard. It was like a poison, a lustful drink that Emma had never experienced.

This time, Ehrich broke away. "I've never felt like this before. Until now, this moment seemed but a dream," he said, his voice soft and hypnotic. "Please, I am forgetting my manners. Permit me to show you my home," he

13

continued, as he took her hand and led her from room to room. His hand gripped hers, strongly yet tenderly. Her fingers shifted as she felt his warmth.

"The wing was originally planned as an expansion to the theater, but in 1875 I sealed it off after stagehands discovered the body of my father, founder Ranier Duchenois, lying in a pool of blood in the midst of the construction. When the construction ceased, I divided the area into something like an apartment."

Finally, Ehrich brought the young girl to the second bedroom. Closets overflowed with dresses for all occasions, and a wedding dress of the most beautiful lace and pearls hung on the outside of one of the closet doors.

Emma's eyes widened and her mouth flew open in astonishment. "This is the most beautiful thing I've ever seen!" she exclaimed as she gently caressed the silky white lace. Everything she saw made her reel.

"You are mistaken, my dear Emma, the most beautiful thing is you," Ehrich's blazing eyes reflected nothing but love for her.

A little ways from them stood a full-length mirror reflecting their image. Emma saw herself clothed in a Victorian dressing gown of the late nineteenth century. Her hair, no longer layered to her shoulders, appeared as luscious, brown curls cascading down her back.

A slight panic seized her.

"You will belong to me, forever!" His voice still mesmerized.

She said nothing but stared into those blazing, cat-like eyes. He leaned even closer and half whispered, "You may remove the hood."

Her hands trembled. Slowly, deliberately, she lifted both hands and pushed it back.

The face staring back filled her heart with even more love as she gingerly touched the smooth skin and gently caressed the auburn-colored hair that framed his visage. He wore his hair a little long, just to his collar, and his eyes reflected a lifetime of unhappiness.

Sadness.

The grief in his eyes quelled the fear in her. Looking into his face, she read each line for a desperate attempt to mask his sorrow and pain.

Tenderly, she touched his cheek then threw her arms around his neck and pulled his mouth to hers. This caught him off guard, but he didn't resist.

The heat of his body increased. Then he caught himself and stopped abruptly, breaking the kiss.

This time he was the one who became breathless. "I…apologize, my dear Emma. I…I acted most ungentlemanly. Please, forgive me." He pulled back and looked away. "I feel ashamed for my boldness."

"I'm sorry. I didn't mean to make you uncomfortable," she apologized and looked for a chair to sit upon.

Quickly, Ehrich grabbed a chair and placed it before her.

"Please, sit down. I have forgotten my manners." He held the chair for her while she sat. Then he perched on the floor by her feet.

"Do I make you uncomfortable?" Emma asked, as she gently touched his back.

"You stir foreign feelings within me. I could literally lose myself to you." He looked away.

"I'm confused, like I don't recall things clearly. All this seems familiar, but not. You call me Emma. It feels like my name, but…I feel like I don't belong…"

"YOU BELONG TO ME!" Ehrich roared as he leapt to his feet. Grabbing her by the shoulders , he brought his face ever so close to hers, "You belong to me." His voice softened.

"I've lost so much in my life. I cannot lose you. Not after seeing you in a vision, or perhaps it was a dream." Ehrich gave a long sigh.

Emma began to feel a little more at ease, but hesitated to speak again. She reeled with his sudden outburst. After releasing her, he stormed out of the room and slammed the door so hard the light fixtures rattled.

The confusion washed over her, and she buried her tearful face into trembling hands.

CHAPTER THREE

Ehrich stood stage, right behind the curtain, talking to a refined Englishman who climbed up the steps and onto the stage. The man spoke with a British accent and stood very near the curtain.

"Is she not as I had described?"

"Oh, yes and more, Latimer," Ehrich sighed and looked away.

"What's wrong?"

"She threw her arms around my neck and begged for my lips. The feelings she stirs frighten me. Since my wife…" Ehrich's voice broke and a tear rolled down his cheek. The Englishman slowly moved to the curtain.

"Please stop hiding away from the world. Everyone knows you didn't kill your father."

"Latimer, don't come any closer to the curtain. I don't want you to see me."

"That's absurd!" Latimer jerked back the curtain.

There, in the dimness of the gaslight, he saw the lonely, broken man who had taught him the essence of true acting. Ehrich turned away and tried to pull up the hood to cover his face, but Latimer touched his arm gently to stop him.

The two men had met in Aire years ago, when the glow of youth still sparkled in their eyes; but now the only glint in Ehrich's came in the dark like a cat, evidence of the nocturnal creature he had become. Latimer had aged gracefully, with a hint of gray at the temples, and like his old friend, had retained his slender build.

"Talk to me, good man. What troubles you?" Latimer questioned.

"She stirs feelings in me which I never knew existed." The old recluse paused and shivered a bit as he spoke. "When I hear her voice, a strange peace washes over me, as though I had died and gone to heaven."

"Ehrich, I believe this young woman is the one. She truly loves you."

"But what manner of sorcery has brought her here? I thought I was the only magician in *le Théâtre Ranier*."

"Balderdash! You haven't performed a magic trick in years."

"Oh, but I have. It's very easy when everyone thinks you're dead." A lopsided smile crossed Ehrich's face. It made him feel good to see his old friend.

"Indeed, a clever trick." Latimer paused. "In time Emma may remember all. Do you love her?" he asked.

"More than life itself. It's like I've known her forever."

"Then marry her now, as planned. No more questions. Follow your heart, my friend."

"Give us time. I don't want to frighten her…any further." Ehrich brought himself to his full height.

The Englishman bowed and smiled. "As you wish, *mon ami*."

"Latimer, you must answer Emma's questions."

His friend only smiled, and for a long moment, the two stared at each other in silence.

Ehrich recalled the time when Latimer and he first practiced the craft of acting, traveling from town to town with many a broken-down theater troupe, hoping and praying they'd earn enough money to make it through the week.

Latimer, a jovial gent, had befriended Ehrich and played upon his interest in acting. Soon, other talents emerged, turning him into a true "Master of Arts." Ehrich found it easy to play any role: husband, lover, hero, villain, magician, and even butler. As a magician, he used his skill in sleight of hand, illusions, and tricks with mirrors. At the time, he had not needed magick, the use of spells and potions. Ehrich had also designed all of his own costumes and later some for the cast.

During their travels, Ehrich fell in love with Serena, a beautiful young gypsy, who used to watch him perform scenes from a Greek tragedy when he and Latimer traveled with her clan. Upon deciding to move on to another troupe, Ehrich brought Serena with them, and the couple eventually married.

Years passed. Upon reaching Paris, Ehrich found his father, Ranier, and brought his wife and child to help establish *le Théâtre Ranier*.

Sadly, in 1871, only a year after *le Théâtre Ranier* had opened, Ehrich was mistaken for a Communard sympathizer, and he had to leave the theater briefly with his father before soldiers from Versailles came to arrest him. When Ehrich couldn't be found, the soldiers murdered his beautiful wife and his seventeen-year-old son, Pinchot. His heart was broken. Afterwards, Ehrich seemed to care about nothing. He forgot the theater and shunned his friends. Without his family, life meant nothing.

Finally, Latimer broke the silence. "In time, all of Emma's questions will be answered." Then he turned and smiled knowingly to himself as he vanished from the theater and into the lobby.

Ehrich returned to his deserted wing. Emma had been standing so dangerously close to the entrance, when he opened the door, she literally fell into his arms.

She looked so beautiful and petite; he wanted to hold her to him again. At the sight of her, he caught his breath.

"*Mon Dieu, ma petite*! You must be careful." A faint smile crossed his lips.

"I apologize. I did not mean to frighten you." Emma looked up into his face to search those blazing eyes.

Part of him wanted to tell her about the prophecy from Shylah, but he felt he'd be pushing her. Too much, too soon.

~ * ~

In the following month, the two spent time taking evening walks in le Bois de Boulogne, a nearby park, with Ehrich trying to answer Emma's questions and help her to remember her past. Talking helped. After a few days, they started holding hands, and soon they discovered they both shared the love of the theater, the same types of music and above all, the time spent together.

Le Bois de Boulogne, a well-known park in Paris, looked absolutely gorgeous with its leaves changing colors to gold, red, and brown. The air grew crisp as the sun hid its face behind some passing clouds. Ehrich walked quietly beside Emma as they spoke.

"I do appreciate your patience with me, but knowing who I am is important. The last thing I recall is a flash of white light then seeing you," Emma said as she pulled the cloak around her and pulled up the hood.

"Sometimes not knowing is good," Ehrich replied quietly. "There are times I'd like to forget who I am and start my life over."

"That's absurd! Is your life so bad that you would want to start over?' Emma pursed her lips together and made a face. Ehrich forced a smile.

"I feel it is. For me, going far away from here, with a new name, where I can make new memories would be my whole-hearted desire."

"Surely you don't expect me to feel like that. I think my life before meeting you was a happy one." Emma tried to keep up with Ehrich's long strides using her short legs. "What did you see before I appeared to you?"

Silence.

Ehrich stopped abruptly and stared at the trees surrounding them.

"Are you listening to me?" Emma tugged at his cloak.

Still looking at the trees, he replied, "Yes, my sweet, I hear you. I was reaching out for you. Reciting my favorite works of literature. Then I, too, witnessed the flash of white light, and there you were."

"What was the white light?"

"Do you like music? I love music. Chopin, Mozart, Beethoven, and—" Ehrich changed the subject and Emma cut him off.

"—Debussy. I like Debussy. Strange, I remember that, but I can't—"

Ehrich turned to her, "Excellent! When we return to the Dark Wing, I shall play something for you."

"I'd like that. There is something else I seem to recall: you. I've read something about you. You were famous…"

This time Ehrich laughed out loud. "Famous? Hardly. Known, perhaps, but famous, no."

Emma didn't say anything at first. For a moment, she searched his face with her eyes. Then she placed a cold hand to his warm cheek.

"Yes, you are famous and…" Emma tried to finish, but Ehrich took her hands in his.

"My dear, your hands are like ice. Allow me to warm them," he rubbed her hands with his and blew his warm breath on them.

Then he wrapped his cloak around her as they walked back to the carriage.

~ * ~

On another occasion, Ehrich took Emma to see a puppet show in the same park. It was the famous Punch and Judy puppets getting into trouble, but then…

"Too bad this isn't a play," Emma remarked. "Not that I don't love puppet shows."

"A play? Do you really like plays?" Ehrich's eyes lit up.

"From what I can remember, I do like plays and other forms of acting," Emma stated as she chewed on her bottom lip, trying to remember what she was trying to convey. Vague images moving across the wall came to mind. Then she looked at Ehrich sitting next to her.

"What?" Ehrich seemed puzzled at the way she looked at him, as if he were a creature to be studied. "Is something wrong?

"You were moving within some flickering shadows on a wall," Emma said slowly, trying hard to make sense of what she described.

"I love plays," Ehrich said. "Next time, I will take you to a real play, at the theater."

"Oh, would you? That would be wonderful!" Emma replied as she threw her arms around his neck. Ehrich blushed a little when some people around him turned to stare. Gently, he patted her arms and pulled them from his neck.

"The show is beginning. This is not proper." He smiled and nodded to a few elderly ladies who glared with disgust.

When the puppet show was over, Ehrich arose from his seat and held a hand out to Emma. She accepted it. The two walked to the carriage hand in hand.

~ * ~

The dark wing had an extra room where Cerise had stayed when she'd visited Ehrich. Here, Emma lived during this time.

"If you saw or possessed something from your past, that might help bring back your memory," commented Ehrich as they ate dinner one night.

"I know you are right, but I've had nothing physical from my previous life."

"Come, I have something for you." He took her hand and led her into another room.

A beautiful, ornate desk stood in the corner of the study. Ehrich pulled her to him, opened one of the drawers, drew out a small ring box, and opened it. A plain gold band glinted in the candlelight.

"Will you marry me, Emma? I love you. My heart and my soul are yours." His eyes searched hers, hoping she would not turn away, and refuse.

Such a precious look on her face! Squealing with delight, she snatched the ring from its bed. Ehrich set the box down, took the ring from her, and placed it on her finger.

"I assume the squeal means yes." He gazed at her lovingly. Her gaze left the ring as she reached for him.

His mouth covered hers in an instant. She tasted sweeter than any wine he'd ever drunk. He trailed butterfly kisses across her cheeks and down her neck.

"Go! Dress for the wedding," he said, turning away from her.

~ * ~

Emma felt happy and confused. Everything happened so quickly! She turned to leave, but a strong thin hand gently grabbed hers, and she paused without looking back.

"I just want us to be together forever. I've loved you all of my life."

Still, she didn't look back but nodded her understanding. Ehrich released her hand.

Emma found her way to her bedroom where the wedding dress hung. Silently, she removed the dress she was wearing and let it drop to the floor. So many things flooded her mind. Something didn't feel connected. In the back of her mind she felt like she knew Ehrich—his life, loves, and loss. Her cold hands trembled a little.

As she pulled up the dress, a light tap came to the door. "Do you need assistance, my beloved?" Ehrich's voice floated through the door. Ah, that voice, whose golden tones filled her with ecstasy!

After pausing a moment, she moved to the door and opened it. She appeared like a vision of all one might deem beautiful and holy. The pure white of the satin brocade made her look angelic.

"May I ask a question?" she asked.

"That was a question," Ehrich said, smiling.

Emma smiled back. "Why do you love me?"

He moved to the closet and pulled out a heavy, warm cloak and extended it to her.

"Come! We must go!" he commanded, ignoring the question. Emma turned her back to him that he might place the cloak around her shoulders. As he did so, he wrapped his arms around her, and whispered, oh so ominously in her ear, "Do you fear me?"

She felt the warmth of his breath on her neck. Everything about him aroused her.

Again, he whispered in her ear, "Do you fear me?"

"Yes," came the breathy reply. Her throat felt dry and her body trembled. "Yes, I do," she gasped.

"Do you think I would harm a delicate little creature like you?" His words trailed off as his lips teased her face and neck. She closed her eyes, savoring the sensation.

He seemed ageless, with his soft, smooth face that never knew a wrinkle. Emma wondered if she was dreaming, or if this could be true. No spirit ever felt so real, so solid.

CHAPTER FOUR

Ehrich held Emma's hand tightly as he hailed a cab in the cold, damp twilight of Paris, the City of Lights. Once again he dressed in black, with his cloak draped around his shoulders, but this time he wore a fedora pulled down tight to cover most of his features.

A cab promptly responded. Ehrich opened the carriage door and helped his future bride inside. Then he drew his cape around himself, climbed into the seat next to her, and slammed the door.

"To the Madeline Chapel near *Le Rue Etoile, s'il vous plaît*," commanded the recluse. At this, the carriage began to move.

"Please answer the question," Emma said. "Why do love me?"

"Why do *you* love *me*? How can you love a broken old man like this? You don't know what I am," Ehrich retorted, yet he held her hand next to his heart.

"I know in Aire you lived with a band of earth-worshipping Celts. I know you traveled with gypsies. And I've always known you have good in you."

"How do you know about Aire and the gypsies?" he turned his full attention to her.

"I know about the trapdoors and secret passages in *le Théâtre Ranier* and the accidents which happen now and again."

"You pique my curiosity, *ma petite*. Tell me how you know of this?"

"I…I don't know. I feel like I've known you forever, yet it seems I've lived far away before coming here. Like something is in the back of my mind, but I can't put my finger on it."

"Many people have such sensations from time to time. A little too much wine makes me feel like that," he retorted.

"No, seriously, who am I? When you brought me home, you took me to each room as if for the first time. Yet, you won't explain why I feel like this. You know me, don't you?" She looked up into his handsome face. No answer.

"Those things I recalled about you, they are real, aren't they?" Her mind kept mulling over the strange vagueness, but Ehrich still said nothing.

"Should I tell her about the seer," he said half out loud.

"What?"

"Oh, nothing!"

"It's vague, but I recall something about a hidden room in your home. And why do you live within the walls?" By now, her head was beginning to ache with so many questions. Especially from trying to remember something and not being able to.

"The hidden room? No one knows about the hidden room." Ehrich gripped her hand so tightly he made her wince in pain.

"Please, Ehrich, you're hurting me."

At this, he puzzled and pulled Emma onto his lap. "So, you know about the hidden room, huh?"

"Are you angry with me?"

"Why would anyone write a book about me? What sorcery brought you here, *ma petite*?" His warm breath sent chills up her spine, mixed with fear and desire.

Even through the mixed feelings, Emma sensed this strange man loved her, and most surely stirred feelings that had lain dormant until now.

"Book?" she puzzled. "I never mentioned a book."

"Latimer mentioned the book, saying it coincided with the prophecy," Ehrich mumbled to himself.

"Don't be upset, okay?" She buried her face in his chest. He liked the feel of her next to him. Then, he realized she had used a word he didn't understand.

"Okay? What does this mean, 'okay'?"

"It means, agreed, like *bon d'accord*." This seemed familiar as well. "Why do I know this?" Emma whispered to herself.

"Your French is good. What a fascinating woman! You know so much about me and still can say you love me? Amazing!"

"Why do you love me?" Emma asked again.

"Oh, I see. I must share." Ehrich hugged her to his chest. "It's been so long since I've had a conversation with a woman…"

For a moment, he fell silent. The clip-clop of the horses' hooves tapped out a rhythm on the cobblestones. He didn't answer for a moment but then a hint of the snow-white brocade of the wedding dress gently shimmered in the dimness of lamplight. Emma's pretty little face, so soft and smooth to the touch glowed. Tenderly, he caressed her cheek with his hand.

"We shall discuss this later," he said. Then he leaned down, putting his face ever so close to hers. "You may remove my hat."

Emma smiled, "I know you want a kiss."

Eagerly, she removed his hat, and immediately his mouth covered hers. Both flushed with flames of passion.

At last, they arrived at the chapel. Ehrich replaced his hat before getting out of the carriage. Then he turned to help Emma down.

Inside the chapel, pews lay before them, with stained glass windows on either side. A life-size crucifix sat dead center. Latimer was waiting at the altar to meet them. Emma yet reeled from this dream-like world of Ehrich de Natois. Latimer stood before her, nearly as tall as her intended, straight black hair combed back from his ruddy complexion. He smiled and when he kissed her hand, his moustache tickled a bit.

"A pleasure, *mademoiselle*, and my congratulations."

Emma smiled, unsure how to respond. "Thank you. Have we met?" Emma appeared shocked when he seemed to know her.

Latimer replied, "Ehrich speaks of you so lovingly and so often, I feel I know you."

"Did I mention I'm not Catholic? A lot of things are fuzzy, but this is not one of them." Emma felt herself shrink in the presence of Latimer.

At the altar, the priest hailed them as the bell tolled the sixth hour.

Latimer took Emma's cloak and placed a garland of flowers on her head. Attached to the garland was a flowing, white, lacy veil.

"She is very beautiful, Ehrich. May the gods bless you and your bride," Latimer motioned to the heavens then bowed to Ehrich.

Again the priest hailed them. This time, Ehrich offered an arm to his beloved. Emma accepted. Her icy hands trembled and butterflies tangled the knots in her stomach.

"Ehrich," Emma whispered as they walked down the aisle toward the priest. "I'm really not Catholic. Does that make a difference?"

"Do not worry. Latimer has created your church records."

"How comforting! Forged church records!" Emma mumbled sarcastically to herself.

An hour later, the priest pronounced them man and wife. Ehrich gathered his young bride into his arms and whispered seductively, "You may remove my fedora."

The priest and Latimer smiled. With trembling hands, the bride removed the hat. Ehrich pressed his lips to hers, kissing her long and hard. His breathing grew heavy and ragged. Emma responded hungrily. After a moment, Ehrich broke the kiss and his wife replaced the fedora.

"You are mine forever! No one shall ever take you from me!" he growled. Then he bowed to the priest and slipped him some money for his services. With a smile, the priest accepted.

After a few minutes, Latimer and Ehrich swept Emma away to a nearby restaurant, where the Englishman had arranged for a light supper in celebration of the marriage.

Victorian furniture filled the tiny restaurant, and white brocade cloths were draped over the tables; only a handful of customers dined that evening.

As they sat, Latimer said, "Emma, are you not well? You look so pale."

"I...I guess it's the excitement. A girl doesn't get married every day." Emma tried to smile. Ehrich caressed her hair lovingly. "I've never been so happy."

Emma looked from one to the other and posed her question again. "How did I get here? For some reason, I can't remember things clearly. Was I in an accident?"

Latimer frowned.

"She's been complaining of this for some time," her husband explained.

Quietly, the Englishman cleared his throat. "Take Ralph to the mirror."

Emma glared at him in confusion. "What does that mean?"

"You will meet a young man named Ralph Duchenois. Take him to the mirror in Cerise St. Clair's dressing room."

Though they hadn't met, the name Ralph Duchenois felt familiar.

"If I take him there, then what?" she asked.

"What will happen will happen."

"I thought my husband was cryptic, but you're worse than he is."

"You have become very bold. Before the wedding you did not seem like this," Ehrich kissed his wife's hand.

"I thought you'd hurt me then. Are you angry with me?" she squeezed his arm.

"I am not angry."

At that moment, the waiter brought their soup, and the question dropped by the wayside.

Later that evening, after dinner had ended and Latimer had said goodnight, the couple returned to the theater. Ehrich carried his bride across the threshold of his dark wing and into the bedroom.

The groom roughly pulled his bride to him as she stared into his face glassy-eyed. The loud pounding of her heart nearly deafened her. Tenderly, he kissed her face and neck. Pulling her dress off her shoulders, he buried his face in her neck and kissed his way up to her ear.

"Do you still fear me?" he growled.

"Sometimes," she said, closing her eyes.

Tenderly came his kiss and touch, making her melt into his arms.

Things seemed like a blur after that. Everything looked surreal. Their bodies felt warm, as they lay entwined beneath the blankets. No man could have ever made her feel so sensual, so vulnerable, and yet so fulfilled!

"I do love you, Ehrich," she whispered softly. Without a word, he tightened his hold, and she knew he felt the same.

"What else do you remember?" he asked, caressing her face gently, lovingly.

"Huh?"

"About me, what do you recall?"

"It seems you had a great loss. Family, I think. And…and…" she stammered, trying to remember what she'd read. The more they talked, the more memories returned.

"Answer the question, my sweet."

"Cerise and Ralph vanished during the last performance of 'Lovers Embark,' never to be seen or heard from again; and you...you disappeared as well. Only traces of blood appeared near the old boarded-up entrance of the dark wing."

"Mmm. Did I die?"

"Everyone assumed suicide."

"My end was sad."

"Ehrich, these are just vague memories. It may not be you. I keep remembering young people dressed in clothes unlike ones here." Emma made him look at her in the candlelight. "You will not die, especially not alone. I will never leave you!

"If what is coming back to me is true, your end has not happened. Cerise is not here. I am," she reassured him with another kiss.

When the kiss broke, Ehrich said nothing. All the sadness of the world reflected in his golden eyes. But when his wife threw her arms around his neck, he surrendered to her.

CHAPTER FIVE

The next day, Emma made her way down the long corridor of *le Théâtre Ranier*, checking her surroundings so as not to get lost. Finally, she found herself in Cerise's dressing room. Before she could close the door behind her, a tall, handsome young man in Victorian dress slipped into the doorway and touched her arm.

"My apologies, *mademoiselle*. For a moment I thought you were Mlle. St. Claire," the young man said, quickly withdrawing his arm and staring at Emma in surprise.

"Cerise is not here. Who are you?" Emma inquired.

"Again, my apologies. Permit me to introduce myself. I am Ralph Duchenois, patron of this theater." He removed his hat and bowed.

This name she knew. "Ralph Duchenois, truly?" Things began to fall into place.

"Yes, *mademoiselle*—" but before he could say another word, Emma grabbed his arm, yanked him into the room, and closed the door. She placed a finger to her lips. Ralph reeled a moment but caught himself before losing his balance.

"What are you doing, *mademoiselle*?" he whispered.

Again, Emma placed a finger to her lips. Then she put an ear to the door.

Silence.

"Where is Cerise, and who are you?" Ralph demanded.

Pulling Ralph closer to the mirror, she stood next to him. Again, he asked, "Who are you?"

Before Emma could answer, roiling clouds appeared in the mirror. In awe, the two gazed as the clouds finally dispersed, and there stood a young, American black girl staring back at them from the other side of the looking glass.

"Oh, Emma! Emma!" Twanda jumped up and down with excitement. "Emma! Are you okay?"

Again, someone knew her name. After eyeing her carefully, some hazy memories returned to Emma.

"Do I know you?" Emma puzzled. She felt she knew her but couldn't put her finger on it.

"What's wrong with you? You hit your head? You know me. We're best friends," Twanda said, scratching her head. "We've been looking for you for hours. If we don't leave soon, we may get locked in."

Seeing Twanda brought back more memories. She had been on the other side of the mirror with her friend. That much she knew.

"I am Ralph," interrupted the suitor. "I am looking for Cerise St. Claire. Have you seen her?"

Twanda looked from Emma to Ralph. "She's here. Acting like she got kicked in the head too. She showed up when you disappeared. What's up with that?" Twanda worried about her friend. "She was wearing your clothes and talking all funny. You know, all proper and that." Twanda tried to mimic the way a proper lady would speak as she stood straight and stiff and made a curtsy. "It's almost like you and Cerise swapped places. Where did you get that ring?"

"I was just married." Emma held up her left hand to show off the gold band.

"What? Where the heck are you? How…who did you marry? Huh?"

"Ehrich de Natois."

"You married the man whose voice can vamp any woman? Oooh!" Twanda squealed with delight. "You rock, Emma!"

"Chill. Someone might hear you!" Emma caught herself. The words coming from her mouth surprised even her. She asked, "How do I know you?"

"What? Don't start that again," Twanda made a face. "I lost Doone and Cerise trying to get here."

"Doone?" Emma felt as though she recognized the name then a tall, lanky man came to mind. His hair looked shaggy and unruly.

Twanda groaned. "We've got to get you back. Stop acting like you got amnesia. We need to trade you for Cerise. She keeps babbling about a flash of light as she stood by a mirror. I'm guessing the same light put you wherever you are."

"Where are you?"

"Oh my God! You really don't remember. Ahh!" Twanda said in exasperation.

Twanda looked Ralph up and down. "So you're Ralph. Like in the book, *Dark Tales of le Théâtre Ranier*? Wow!"

"The book! That's right. Maybe that's why all this seems familiar but not…" Emma's voice trailed as she racked her brain to remember.

But before anyone could say another word, Twanda's image began to fade. A faint cry arose from the mirror before she vanished altogether, leaving Emma and Ralph baffled.

In a moment, a strange, sweet voice inundated the room with a recitation of a poem of love and eternal happiness, floating, filling the air like an intoxicating fragrance of sandalwood. Speechless, Ralph could only point to the glass as a face loomed up before them.

Emma was thrilled as she recognized the voice, but remembering they had company, she broke the moment. "Ehrich, we are not alone," she called out.

The voice stopped. The mirror rotated on its pivot, and Ehrich reached out for his wife. Grabbing his hand, she unexpectedly pulled him toward her, throwing him off balance a bit, but he caught himself.

"My dear, Ehrich, we have company!" Emma repeated.

The renowned actor drew himself up to his full height. "Were you trying to leave me, my sweet?" Ehrich kissed his wife's hand and held it close to his heart then he glared at Ralph.

After a moment, Emma introduced the two men. "Ehrich, this is Ralph Duchenois. Ralph, this is my husband, Ehrich." Emma looked from one to the other, hoping the two wouldn't get into a tangle.

At this, Ehrich said nothing, but glared.

"A pleasure, *monsieur*." Ralph bowed, staring at the man in black. Ehrich still said nothing.

"Do you know who I am?" Ehrich narrowed his eyes at the young man. "Does he know who I am?" He turned to his wife.

"Ralph, my husband is also known as the Master of Arts."

"The Master of Arts? He doesn't exist," retorted Ralph as he brushed a lock of dark blonde hair from his face. "That story results from the prattling of young upstarts who have nothing better to do than gossip. Master of Arts, indeed! I heard he had died and haunted the walls."

"Oh, really. I do not exist? Then who do you think the stagehands see in the shadows? Who is behind the occasional accidents?" Ehrich's face turned red, his voice low and menacing as his temper grew intense, and Ralph took several steps back.

"Stop it! Both of you!" Emma looked to her husband. "I need to know the reason Latimer told me to bring Ralph to this mirror. If you hadn't interrupted, I might have found out!'

"I missed you," he said simply and kissed his wife's hand again.

"Absurd! You both prattle as though demented or possessed," Ralph frowned.

When Ralph looked away, Ehrich slowly reached out for his throat.

"No!" Emma cried, as she tried to pull Ehrich away.

"You know? But how?" Ehrich withdrew his hands.

She didn't explain but caressed his chest and patted him lovingly. Ehrich smiled at the contact and leaned down for a kiss.

"Are you two quite finished? I am sorry to intrude, but I am concerned for Cerise. The theater manager will be looking for her as well," Ralph interrupted, but he stepped back when Ehrich shot him a murderous look.

"My dear Ehrich, let me go with Ralph for a moment. After all, Latimer did tell me to bring him to the mirror. Since you interrupted the vision, please let me see what I can do to return Cerise." Emma looked up at the man she loved.

Ralph cleared his throat. This time, both Ehrich and his wife shot him an annoyed look.

"Again, my apologies, but I need to speak to you, Madame—"

"Call me Emma."

"Emma, please, we must speak with the theater manager before the play tonight."

"My beloved Ehrich, I shall return to you in little while." She grabbed the lapels of her husband's coat and pulled him down to her. He gathered his wife into his arms and pressed his lips to hers.

"How long have you two been married?" Ralph asked.

"Hardly a day," huffed Ehrich, and with that, he released his wife and disappeared into secret passageway behind the mirror, which fell back into place.

"Emma, how did you come to marry such a man?"

"How did you come to love an actress? Isn't that beneath a noble like you?" Emma retorted. Ralph didn't answer but opened the door for her.

Unbeknownst to both, two blazing orbs glared at them through the mirror as they left the room.

CHAPTER SIX

As Emma and Ralph hurried down the stairs of *le Théâtre Ranier*, Ralph asked, "Madame Emma, please tell me how you came to meet and marry your husband?"

"You are a curious one," Emma said, her voice returned to the cadence of a nineteenth-century lady. "He captivated me with his voice and his love, and so we married."

"But how did you meet him?"

"He called out to me," Emma said, trying to avoid a direct answer.

"That doesn't make sense, *madame*." But before Ralph could continue, a short, balding man met them as he hurried up the stairs.

"At last, Mlle. St. Claire…oh, but you are not Mlle. St. Claire." The man fidgeted with worry.

"No. Mlle. Emma Verlain, this is M. Toussaint, the manager of *le Théâtre Ranier*. M. Toussaint, this is the visiting cousin of Mlle. St. Claire," the patron lied.

The manager bowed and kissed Emma's hand. "A pleasure, *mademoiselle*, but where is Mlle. St. Claire? She performs this evening."

"Mlle. Verlain will perform in her place. Mlle. St. Claire has decided to take a short leave of absence," smiled Ralph. Emma frowned and shot him a look.

"Does she know all the lines? After all, she plays the lead," M. Toussaint worried.

"She will learn them. Please excuse us, or we'll miss rehearsal." Ralph and Emma made haste to the theater, leaving the manager.

As they made it to the doors of the theater, Emma stopped short and turned on Ralph.

"'She will learn them?' I can't learn an entire play in a few hours. A lot of things I don't remember, but two things I do know for sure: I'm not Catholic, and I'm not an actress," grumbled Emma.

"I know, *madame*, but you can reply to what is said as you would in everyday life." Ralph looked her up and down.

This handsome young man has such a sparkle in his blue eyes when he smiles. Then Emma shook herself and returned to the topic at hand. "Of course I can, but—"

"Just react and reply to what others say and do. The audience won't mind. They come to be entertained. So, entertain them." He gave Emma a light kiss on the cheek then pushed the doors open for her. She realized he meant for her to improvise, something she seemed to recall in another life.

She blushed from the kiss, but then a wave of fear and nausea passed over her. What if her husband had seen that quick little kiss? He could be in any shadow or beneath any trapdoor. Nervously, she looked around before entering the theater, imagining those blazing eyes boring a hole through her.

"If Cerise is not here, isn't there an understudy?" asked Emma.

"She was the understudy. Just answer and react to whatever is said and done as if it actually happened to you," smiled Ralph.

As she and Ralph entered the theater, making their way to the director near the stage, Emma glanced toward the balconies. For a fleeting moment, she thought she saw something shadowy move in one of them. A small rustle stirred in the seats. Ralph's head jerked up toward the balcony nearest the stage.

"Your husband, *madame*?"

"I think so. He's very possessive."

"And dangerous, I hear…" Ralph muttered under his breath.

Emma grew cold, and her voice quavered a bit as Ralph introduced her to M. Benoit, the director. Briefly, he explained the situation.

"Explain the premise of the play?" the director frowned.

"Then Mlle. Verlain will simply react and respond to whatever goes on. She will create her own lines."

"What? Well…yes…I suppose so," the director stammered as he cast a glance or two at the rest of the cast behind him.

Ralph bowed to Emma and kissed her hand. "*Mademoiselle*, you command the rehearsal. I will be at your performance later this evening."

After Ralph left, Emma tried to smile. She felt like making several sarcastic remarks, but thought better of it and again looked up at the balcony where the silhouette lurked. Knowing how much Ehrich loved plays, she had to slip into the role left behind by Cerise. She could not disappoint him.

Emma felt Ehrich watching with his burning cat-eyes. They glinted down at her. Smiling, she mouthed the words, "I love you." This tamed the glare, and she felt him settle in his seat.

Emma straightened her dress and turned to the director, who gave a brief synopsis of the play. Murmurings from cast members rumbled throughout the room, but M. Benoit brought them back to order and rehearsals began.

The cast quickly picked up their lines and rolled with Emma's adlib and improvisation. Even though this practice seemed strange, the director and cast fell into step and the play began to move.

In one scene, Emma's character, a poor girl, tried to sell tiny, pitiful bouquets of flowers in front of a bakery. She shivered as if cold, pulling the ragged shawl around her and her filthy looking clothes.

"Get away from here, wench! Selling flowers will do you no good. You'll die on the streets," came the hurtful words of a large female merchant wielding a broom.

"Then I shall offer my flowers to God," replied Emma. The actress/merchant quickly strode offstage.

"Then I will go to a better place and will offer my flowers to the gods," should have been the line. The director, M. Benoit, shook his head and mopped a damp brow with his handkerchief.

In the next scene, Emma moved across the stage set up like the center of the village as people milled around. A man in shabby clothes pushed a cart filled with hot chestnuts. Emma walked closer and held up her hands to feel the warmth of the cart.

"Chestnuts, miss?" asked the chestnut peddler.

"I've got no money," replied Emma, casting her eyes to the ground as she put her hands down and stepped back.

"Why, you're shivering. Please, take a few, as a gift from an ol' peddler," said the man as he scooped up a few chestnuts. "Hold out your apron, please."

Emma obeyed. The peddler then poured a scoop of chestnuts into her apron. Quickly, she folded the apron and held it close to her, reacting to the imaginary heat as if it warmed her freezing bones.

"Oh, thank you, sir. God bless you for having pity on a poor flower child." Emma didn't even think about the term "flower child." The audience thought it odd, and a few whispers rippled through the crowd, as poor M. Benoit again shook his head and mopped his damp brow.

The line should have been, "God bless you for having pity on a poor flower girl," but somewhere in her subconscious "flower child" came to mind and Emma said it. However, the slip of the tongue didn't seem to matter. Ladies in the audience wept for the poor, pitiful flower girl, and men actually wanted to throw her money.

Emma lost herself in the performance, feeling her husband's smile upon her.

CHAPTER SEVEN

The evening performance at *le Théâtre Ranier* dubbed Emma the new starlet. Ralph spoke truly: the audience came for entertainment, and entertain she did.

Emma's last line, "All the earth may pass away, but our love is eternal," made the audience weep. For this, she received a standing ovation. Finally, her stomach settled within. Her trembling ceased.

Taking her bows, she glanced up at the balcony, where she spied a shadow with eyes glowing ember-like. Smiling, she threw a kiss and again mouthed the words, "I love you." Emma didn't pity or condemn him, the true attribute of a soul mate. Without a doubt, she loved him for all that he was, regardless of his past.

"I love you too, my beloved," whispered Ehrich, as he joined in the standing ovation.

Later that evening, while Emma made her way through the crowd of adoring fans, Ralph stopped her at the foot of the stairs.

"You were magnificent, *madame*. My congratulations!" He bowed and kissed her hand.

"You were right, they only wanted to be entertained. If you'll excuse me, I must go to my husband."

"May I take you to supper? I'd like to talk to you about Cerise," he said, looking hopeful.

"We do need to talk. Perhaps tomorrow." Emma's gazed upstairs.

"*Madame*, please. I love Cerise as you love your husband." Ralph's eyes pleaded with her.

"Tomorrow. I promise. Come to Cerise's dressing room at noon." The young man agreed, bowed, and once again kissed Emma's hand. Quickly, she took leave of him and ran upstairs to the dressing room. The entire idea of trading places with another woman in another time sounded insane. However, it seemed the only possible reason for her mixed emotions and vague memories. *Didn't Twanda say something about this?*

As she suspected, her husband called out to her as soon as she entered the dressing room. His voice filled the air with sweet tones of love.

"Before the world, there was a light that brightened the darkest night. A flower so dear, I must have her near, to hold close in my heart so tight."

When he reached for her, the mirror pivoted open, leaving an opening, and she took his hand, following him down through the narrow passage within the walls, with only a small torch for light.

As they reached the dark wing, Ehrich concluded his recitation of the love poem he had written for her.

"Gentle is my flower that brought me back to life. So exquisite is my darling, I've thrown away the knife. No longer do I seek for that eternal sleep. Beloved Emma, I tenderly kiss thy delicate hand. For only thee, I am at thy command."

Then he took her hand and brought it to his lips. When he drew himself up to his full height, they stood silent for a moment, gazing into each other's eyes.

"You may remove my fedora," he said, as he leaned down very close to her face. Gently, she removed the hat. Ehrich lovingly pressed his lips to hers. They held each other like they'd never let go.

When the kiss finally broke, Ehrich remarked, "No one ever played Hélène like you did. Brava!"

"I performed for you and only you. My apologies for not learning the lines. I had to improvise."

"Improvise? Interesting," Ehrich smiled then laughed when he seemed to realize what she meant.

"It's good to see you laugh." Emma held him tight as she thought about what she had said. Strange words and phrases always seemed to slip from her lips, as if she had lived in another world.

"I haven't had a reason to laugh in a long time. Where did you learn to act?"

She shrugged. "I just made up stuff."

"Made up stuff?" Ehrich smiled at her strange words.

"If I really do come from another time, would you go back with me?"

"The question is, why won't you stay here?"

He squeezed her tight.

"Sometimes I feel like I don't belong. At times I see a different world around me, where people wear clothes different to those here. Women wear short trousers and strange blouses that show a lot of skin. Men wear trousers that close without buttons and wear shirts with short sleeves."

"This saddens me. Why do you feel like you don't belong here? I am here. You will want for nothing. I promise to keep you safe. How can you feel like you do not belong?"

"It's not you. I am yours eternally, but even you do not belong. I can't explain it, but after seeing Twanda, the dark-skinned girl in the mirror, flashes of this other world come before me. I think I am remembering something." Emma hugged her husband. She didn't want to hurt his feelings, but she had to tell him what she felt and saw.

Am I losing my mind?

"This is why I asked, if I were able to return to wherever this other world is, would you go with me? I will not leave without you." Emma laid her head on his chest. The thump, thump of his heart pounded softly and rhythmically.

"Do you realize the evil I've done?" He pushed her away.

"It's a little late for details. Yet, I do need to know some things…"

"Please don't ask if you can ask a question. Just ask it!"

"Did you kill Ranier?"

After a long pause followed by an exasperated sigh, he snapped, "An audience of five hundred people cleared me of all allegations! I had a performance that evening."

"That's not an answer. You've become a scary legend in this theater."

"Ranier was my father. He fell from the scaffold by accident."

"I recall a rumor…in the book that said you were deeply in love with Cerise. Would you have killed Ralph and Cerise if they had planned to elope? I mean…"

Ehrich bit his lip. Suddenly, he grabbed his bride and gathered her up into his arms once again, startling her. "No more questions! Of all things, this you choose to remember."

He brought his face inches away from hers. She could feel his warm breath. For now, she had to leave her thoughts and questions aside. No matter where she came from, she now lived here, with her quick-tempered husband.

"I'm good." Emma tried to smile. Again she trembled at his roughness.

"'I'm good'? Is that like 'okay'?"

"It means, 'No more questions.'"

"At least for now," he growled. He leaned in, caressed her lips with his tongue, then crushed his lips to hers. Emma melted into his arms and again surrendered to her husband.

CHAPTER EIGHT

Three minutes before noon Emma found herself waiting for Ralph in Cerise's dressing room. Frayed nerves made her pace the floor, stopping every now and again to stare at the mirror in hopes she'd see the young woman who claimed to be her friend again and perhaps finally get some real answers.

As soon as Emma saw Ralph burst through the doorway, she closed the door softly behind him.

"No one saw me enter *le Théâtre*," Ralph panted.

"Good," Emma turned to the mirror. "I don't know how to make it work. It seems to act on its own."

Ralph said nothing but studied the young woman closely.

"*Madame*, you gave a rousing performance as Hélène," he smiled as his lips met her hand. Quickly, instinctively, she jerked away from him.

"Ralph, we're not here to talk about me—" she started to say, but the patron cut her off with an unexpected kiss on the lips. He held her close and tight.

Quickly, Emma pushed him away and looked around nervously.

"Don't do that. I love my husband."

"What a very fortunate man! Loving you would be easy."

"Ralph, snap out of it!" Emma snapped her fingers. "What is wrong with you?"

"Ever since I saw your performance, it's like…"

"No, no don't say it. You love Cerise. Remember Cerise?" Emma shook him hard. He pulled away.

"Why are you shaking me?"

"You love Cerise. Not me. My husband will kill us both!"

"I'm concerned for your safety. He doesn't deserve you."

"Ralph, have you been drinking? Remember Cerise?"

At this, Ralph fell silent.

Desperate to get on with what she'd come for, Emma turned to the mirror. "Mirror, mirror on the wall, who's the fairest of us all?" No response.

"What should happen? Is something supposed to happen?" Ralph regarded her as if she had lost her mind.

"One can hope. Maybe I need to find different words. Let's see. Mirror, mirror, tell me true. Tell me what I need to do."

In a moment, roiling clouds appeared in the mirror and a voice boomed, "Who calls forth the magick of mirrors?"

Emma jumped backwards into Ralph's arms. The two trembled before the mirror.

"I said, who calls forth the magick of mirrors?" The voice again roared.

The young bride swallowed hard, and replied, "I...I did."

"Speak up. You have a question?"

"I think a white light brought me here, trading places with a woman from this century. How do I return home?"

"Click your heels together three times while saying, 'there's no place like home, there's no place like home,'" said the mirror and then roared with maniacal laughter.

Fear drained away as Emma grew angry. "Wise guy, huh?" Again from somewhere deep in her memory she recalled the timeless classic, *The Wizard of Oz*, and her speech changed. Slowly she was beginning to remember her life in another place and time.

"I've always wanted to say that. You people have no sense of humor."

44

"I need answers and you make jokes. If I don't belong here, how do I get home?"

"Wonderful! Another one who's lost their memory. You dare ask me that?" the guide spat with sharp sarcasm.

"I don't know who else to ask."

"Look for the spellcaster. The magick of mirrors has no involvement."

"What does that mean?"

"Look, honey, I talk to dozens of people from different centuries and dimensions. I don't control portals or doorways. I'm only a guide.

"Look for the spellcaster. They control the portals. Not me." At this, the clouds churned, then dispersed and the voice fell silent.

"Mirror!" Emma tapped the glass. "Mirror! Voice! Where are you? Great! Just great. Even the mirror's cryptic."

"Who is the spellcaster?" Ralph wondered aloud.

"Don't I wish I knew the answer to that question," Emma sighed.

She and the patron waited a few minutes. Emma fidgeted with the lace on her dress as they waited for the mirror to do something. Ralph tried to touch her, but she moved away quickly.

"Emma, we need to talk. Your husband has gone mad," he started.

"Ralph, please. If you don't want to die, you'll let it go." With that, Emma headed for the door.

The clouds reappeared in the mirror, roiling and churning. "Emma, if you want to talk to your friends, return here at noon tomorrow," the voice boomed from the looking glass.

"And bring Ralph."

Emma and Ralph turned back to the mirror. "You know our names?" Emma asked in surprise.

"I know the names of everybody who looks in a mirror or a reflective surface. Trying to help, here. So come back at noon tomorrow."

"Thank you, mirror. Tomorrow at noon." In a moment, the clouds disappeared and the mirror fell quiet again.

"Then we must return tomorrow. Perhaps Cerise will be here." The young patron sounded hopeful.

"That's right. Think of Cerise. She'll be here tomorrow." Emma smiled and opened the door. As they left the room, they didn't see the two blazing eyes watching them from the shadows.

CHAPTER NINE

Emma and Ralph were making their way down the corridor, away from the dressing room, when the quiet click of a door sounded. They froze. It seemed to come from the floor. They looked behind them.

Nothing.

But just as they turned around, something caught Ralph by the throat. He couldn't breathe, nor could he loosen the grip of the hands.

"No! Please! Don't kill him. I beg you," Emma pleaded, laying a hand on his arm. Ehrich would have snapped Ralph's neck, but his wife's touch distracted him. He loosened his hold. Ralph dropped to his knees, rubbing his throat and gasping for air.

Emma pushed her husband back.

"Ralph was not himself. Don't hold him responsible." Emma pressed her lips hard against her husband's. Ehrich responded like a starving man but pulled back long enough to speak.

"I saw his lips touch yours. I won't let him take you from me!" Ehrich hissed, half crazed. His wife soothed him with another kiss and held him tight in her arms.

"I love only you, my husband. Ralph is just a friend. Please." She kissed Ehrich again, until his anger subsided and he offered Ralph his hand.

Ralph coughed and sputtered as he continued to rub his throat. He glared up at the crazed actor and the extended hand.

"Take his hand." Reluctantly, he obeyed, and Ehrich pulled him up to his feet.

"My wife assures me the kiss was harmless and that you have not been yourself."

"Truly. I have not been myself. I beg forgiveness from you and your beautiful wife. The incident shall not be repeated."

Ehrich dusted off his clothes and straightened his vest. "See that it doesn't," he muttered.

"Ralph, please go. I will see you tomorrow." Emma smiled and waved him on.

"Tomorrow at noon. *Madame*. *Monsieur*." Ralph quickly disappeared down the corridor. Emma glared up into her husband's face. "You could have killed him."

"But you stopped me."

"Don't you ever ask what happened before you strike?"

"Ask what? I saw him kiss you. I became enraged," Ehrich hissed again.

"You can't kill everybody that makes you angry."

"Why not?"

"It's not right. You need to talk to the person and let them know how they upset you and work things out."

"Why? They will do it again."

"Depends on the sitch."

"Sitch?"

"Ooops! I mean, situation. Ralph doesn't deserve to die because he kissed me. If you eavesdropped, then you know I shook him hard and assured him I love only you." Emma embraced her husband.

CHAPTER TEN

Brianna, sorceress and high priestess of the order of Dylon, stood in her elegantly decorated bedchamber, admiring herself in the mirror. Humming softly, she made sure to give her raven hair the number of brush strokes it deserved. She pursed her ruby lips, enjoying the way they brought out the color in her clear, pale cheeks.

Smoke made vain attempts to fill the mirror, as though something tried to manifest itself.

What hindered the communication? With years of practicing magick, she knew when something wanted to speak through a looking glass.

"Manifest yourself," she called out. "Who are you?" As she spun around, the shimmering, satin nightgown gently clung to every sensual curve of her body.

A distinct feeling of being watched made her move about the room, calling for the visitor to identify itself. Possessing the level of magick she did, she felt no fear, only annoyance that the visitor refused to speak. *Friend or foe?* Should it be the latter, she wouldn't hesitate to blast it with fireballs.

Suddenly, the chamber door burst open and two extremely handsome young men rushed into the room. The ash-blond model-type was called Landru, and the dark-haired pinup-boy was called Etienne.

"May we be of service, my love?" asked Landru. His open, ruffled shirt exposed the luscious ripples of a well-defined chest.

"Someone or something is trying to communicate with me." Brianna moved about the room, searching each corner.

Etienne looked to his friend and they both shrugged.

"Bring me a large crystal, quickly!" ordered Brianna, as she grabbed a silky robe and wrapped it around herself.

Quickly, the men left and returned with a large crystal sphere that they placed on the dresser a few meters away. With her men, Brianna situated herself on a bench in front of it. Calling to the entity, she passed her hand over it several times before it darkened then grew light enough for the handsome, chiseled features of a man's face to appear.

As the face became clear, she recognized the creature she worshiped and bowed in reverence to Dyonacalus, ruler of the *"in between."*

"You honor me, my lord. What can I do to please you?" Brianna asked. Etienne and Landru stood with bowed heads.

Dyonacalus explained in a loud, distorted voice. "At noon tomorrow, take a ride outside of Paris until you see where the road divides. Take the road on your right. Drive for precisely half an hour and then feign some reason you need help to move on. Maurice D'Auberge will ride along in moments. Seduce him and persuade him to help you bring about a coup d'état in France. This will implement the offering of young maidens with pure hearts to me."

Brianna agreed to Dyonacalus' every demand. She even offered to destroy Ehrich, but the demon said he wanted such pleasure for himself.

Etienne and Landru absorbed every demonic word that issued from the creature's mouth and shuddered.

Before this evening, none of them had ever seen or heard Dyonacalus—not even Brianna. The only verification that he was the demon they worshiped were the red glowing eyes and the way he was constantly morphing into various monsters, back to a man then finally a leathery-skinned beast with two horns. An evil grimace spread across Brianna's face. She could never pass up a chance for power. Several well-known ancient books said that anyone who helped free the demon would be rewarded handsomely; no one, not even Brianna, knew that anyone or anything ruling the *"in between"* would never be able to return to our time unless someone took their place. A few scattered verses from some rare religious writings had given accurate accounts of the *"in between,"* but nothing that most churches would accept as doctrine.

"For the moment, I can only appear as a shadow or spirit," said the demon. "My powers of projection grow weak. Do my bidding and make me corporeal, that I may take vengeance on the man who dared resist my command!" he demanded in a loud, distorted voice. "Do as I command and you shall have untold power. You could rule the *"in between"* and walk through dimensions."

The promise sounded enticing. Brianna imagined herself ruling the world as all paid homage to her and the dark master. No one could stop her.

She had no idea what lay within the *"in between,"* but the idea of ruling anywhere lit up her eyes and gave her heart palpitations.

Delighted with the demonic promise, Brianna quickly sought out Maurice D'Auberge.

CHAPTER ELEVEN

The Le Havre shipyards seemed eerily quiet in the cold dampness of twilight. A rough looking, stocky nobleman of fifty-something barked out orders to the crew of the ship.

Known as *The Sea Witch*, the vessel belonged to Ehrich de Natois. Maurice D'Auberge, infamous for smuggling illegal goods in and out of France, commanded the ship and oversaw the imports. The seaport town of Le Havre nestled on the northern coast of France some hundred and twenty-five miles from Paris, making it convenient for illegal trade.

Tonight's cargo would bring a higher price than the usual collection of spices from the Orient or natives of various lands. Eight young Caucasian girls thirteen to eighteen years old, kidnapped from their families for sale to the highest bidder, would bring much more profit.

The ship would also be carrying opium straight from the Orient: an item sure to profit the seller more than rugs and silk.

A wicked smile crossed D'Auberge's face as he listened to the soft cries of the girls from the cargo hold.

His nephew Alain, in his thirties, stood tall and muscular and wore his dark hair shaggy and unruly. He often worked for his uncle in hopes that someday he'd save enough to have a ship of his own. Alain's heart raced with excitement as his eyes searched for the girl who made him flush with passion. He opened the door of the cargo hold and peered into the dank depths of the ship. Burlap sacks scattered about the cramped quarters served as beds for the girls, who were still in their bedclothes, pulling their cloaks around them to keep warm. Several large, wooden crates lined the walls, causing even less room for comfort. The stench of urine rose up from the hold.

Alain eyed one in particular, a pretty little brunette named Laurette. Barely fifteen, she would make a delicious treat for any man. Already she showed womanly curves and plump, full bosoms. Alain eyed her lovingly. He hated to see her imprisoned and sent to market like cattle. Trembling, the child looked up to see the sharp-nosed, shaggy-maned man staring down at her. Cold engulfed her from fear of what he might be thinking.

She jerked her head back to the other girls, desperately trying to hold back the tears.

He wanted to take her into his arms and taste her lips, to crush her against his chest. When he could endure no longer, he closed the hatch and went straight to D'Auberge.

"Uncle, I have a request," Alain panted. His body glistened with perspiration.

"What now, Alain? Do the cries of the girls excite you?" D'Auberge smirked knowingly.

"Only one. Laurette. The little dark-haired angel with the beautiful, sad eyes. I beg you, uncle, give her to me. I love her," Alain said, looking back now and again to the cargo hold.

"She will fetch a handsome price. Why should I give her to you?"

"Please. Keep the money you would pay me for this journey and give me the girl."

"You would buy her? Intriguing. Why? You at thirty-eight and she barely fifteen? She will fight you. You will wish I had sold her." D'Auberge laughed wickedly, taunting his nephew.

"Have pity on me. We've been at sea for over a year. I can't eat. I can't sleep. She's all I think about," Alain said. His uncle laughed again.

"Not tonight, my nephew. I shall consider your request, but tonight, we must wait. My partner will come in a day or so, and all of the cargo must be here and untouched." D'Auberge handed him a few coins. "Amuse yourself in town. There must be some wench who can satisfy you for the night." The nobleman dismissed his nephew and motioned for the other men to watch the girls.

"No one goes in or out. Food will be lowered into the hatch as usual. Understood?" D'Auberge ordered two rogues, Jacques and Arnou, who guarded the hatch. Each man bowed his head in acknowledgement and tightened the grip on his rifle.

D'Auberge shot his nephew a look. "This means you. Stay away from the girls. My men will kill you, regardless of our kinship."

Alain cursed under his breath and stormed off the ship, passing a courier, a young lad of fifteen or so, who walked briskly to Alain's uncle. "M. D'Auberge?" the boy looked to the nobleman. The courier's drab colored clothes pegged him for a child from the lower class trying to eke out a living. His dark blond, disheveled hair and smudgy face looked as though they had never seen soap or water.

"I am D'Auberge. What have you got there?" came the gruff reply.

The boy handed him an envelope. The nobleman dug into his pockets and tossed him a few coins. He could appear grateful to a chosen few, should he need to use their services again.

"Thank you, *monsieur*!" the lad smiled at the generous tip. D'Auberge took a moment to read the letter. Then he shook his head. "No reply." The lad took off with a smile on his face.

The nobleman walked to his cabin on the other side of the hatch. Turning to the men guarding the girls, he then shouted for all hands on deck.

He ordered the cargo's preparation for a trip overland to Paris, since the plans had changed. Because of such a perilous journey, it became necessary to conceal the young girls with the opium. Any sign of his illegal merchandise could cost him and his men their lives.

D'Auberge had broken most of the men out of prison or given them sanctuary, protected by his noble standing in Paris. All the magistrates owed him. D'Auberge knew this motley crew found it difficult to stay away from the girls, but fear of death at his hands held them back.

Transporting opium and young girls for sale didn't give D'Auberge a second thought. He knew his men, like him, appreciated the opportunity to have more money, regardless of who suffered for it.

D'Auberge had acquired three rather large wagons, which looked much like the kind of caravans the gypsies used. Quickly and quietly, his men loaded one with opium and the other two with the frightened girls.

Derrell, D'Auberge's most faithful employee, stood at the nobleman's left, making sure the wagons looked inconspicuous. Each caravan concealed a false bottom with an area large enough to cram four of the petite maidens inside. Bolts of silk and rolls of rugs from the Orient filled the visible parts of the caravans.

Derrell stood about as tall as Alain. D'Auberge grinned, "I'm glad you have no thought of females. I can always be sure your only desire is money and power."

Derrell nodded.

"Are we ready to leave?" asked his employer.

"*Oui, monsieur*, but what about your nephew?"

"We must pass through town. Fetch him then." D'Auberge mounted his steed and rode off alongside the wagons.

CHAPTER TWELVE

In the study of the Dark Wing, the day after Emma's successful theater debut, Ehrich wrestled with his play, *One Last Tomorrow*, the one he'd been working on for years.

Meanwhile, Emma explored the remainder of the house. She stumbled across the library, where she marveled at the luxurious furnishings, along with the tapestries and sword collection adorning the walls. Everything looked dusty, moldy and decaying.

The locked door in the corner piqued her curiosity, but for now, she spent her time admiring the weapons, especially the small broadsword that seemed to call her name. Gently, she ran her fingertips along the blade, as if to seduce it.

Ehrich appeared in the doorway and watched his wife with interest. She seemed so out of place in front of a weapon display. Lately, he had begun to feel more comfortable with her, and a smile came to his sober face.

He walked to the broadsword, removed it from the wall and handed it to Emma. In much delight, she grabbed it with both hands and sliced the air with expert precision.

"You surprise me. Where did you obtain such skill?" Ehrich asked with curiosity.

"I don't know. Although, it feels right," she smiled, as she again went through the katas for swordplay.

"I take my life in my hands, should I upset you," he said with a faint smile.

"A joke? First my husband laughs and now he jokes?" Emma gave an impish grin.

For a few silent moments, Emma whirled around, slicing the air, splitting open an imaginary foe.

"Brava, my sweet! Brava! I am amazed! You could truly do damage with this sword. Have you drawn blood?"

"I don't think so."

"Then, you have not killed…"

"I really don't think so. It just feels right in my hands." Emma held the broadsword at her side, as her husband leaned down and kissed her.

"I recall memories of learning such skills for discipline coming back," she said.

"We make a fine pair, you with the broadsword and me with my skillful touch," Ehrich smiled as he flexed his hands, but the smile faded when he saw the look on his wife's face.

"You worry me. I had no idea you had such a temper. You nearly killed poor Ralph."

"We've discussed this. I allowed him to live, didn't I?"

"Yes, and I thank you."

Moving to a screen, Ehrich pulled out a mannequin; pushing it to Emma, he motioned for her to practice. She bowed and proceeded with the swordplay, eventually running the dummy through.

Ehrich applauded her. "I'm impressed. You compare to no woman I've ever seen." He paused a moment before changing the subject. "Since I use no weapon, why do I upset you so?" When he saw the look on his wife's face, he dropped his eyes and added, "I do what is necessary. Some people must be removed."

"Removed? Ehrich, do you realize what you just said? You can't just *remove* people. How many…?" Appalled, Emma backed away.

"Do not ask. Let's just say they will never kill any of my loved ones again." His wife caught his arm.

"I'm sorry. I didn't mean to hurt you." She leaned the sword against the wall and reached up to him. He leaned down, collected her in his arms and held her close.

"Forgive me, my husband," she whispered softly in his ear.

Ehrich said nothing. Softly, gently, he buried his face into her neck and kissed her tenderly.

Then she whispered, "Do I frighten you?"

"With a broadsword in hand, yes," he smiled.

Emma pushed him back playfully and grinned. "You've made another joke."

He gave a faint smile. "No joke. You are frightening with that sword."

Emma nodded toward the locked door. "Why is the door locked?"

"This room is forbidden. No one goes in there. No one!" A mix of anger and sadness made any trace of a smile disappear.

"What secret are you hiding? Why would anyone keep a room locked up?" Emma persisted.

Only a glare came from her husband.

Once again, she pushed for an answer. "One look. That's all. What are you hiding, gold?" she tried to smile.

Ehrich narrowed his eyes at her. His demeanor changed, and he flew into a rage and began shouting like a madman. "Do you want to see it?"

He broke away from her and disappeared into the study for a moment, leaving his wife reeling in the wake of his rage.

In a few minutes, he returned with a small key.

"You must never touch this key!" he screamed as he grabbed her arm and shook her. "Do you understand?" Emma nodded, afraid to utter a word.

He opened the door and dragged her inside the forbidden room.

Emma shuddered at the cold of the chamber and in fear of her husband's anger. A few lit candles revealed two portraits hanging side by side on the wall. One was of a beautiful, raven-haired woman with dark, flashing eyes, dressed as a fine lady, and the other was of a young lad with a handsome, thin face like his father. All around the room lay furniture and mementos of the deceased. One in particular caught Emma's eye. A beautiful piece of powder-blue ribbon marred with a red stain lay next to a dark gray vest, also bearing dark stains and several holes. She moved toward it, and Ehrich drew closer with the candle as she gingerly touched the ribbon.

"Is this what you wanted to see? You kept asking about it." His eyes blazed and his face flushed with anger.

"Ehrich, please, I meant no harm…" Emma dropped the ribbon.

"No one knows about this room. After the murder of my family, I put all their belongings in here," he explained, a slight tremor of grief in his voice. "They wore that ribbon and that vest the day they died." He nodded for her to look closer. "See the blood stains on the ribbon? And the bloody vest with holes?"

Emma cowered at her husband's anger.

For a moment, Emma looked away and gasped for air.

"My son bled to death in that vest," he hissed with a wicked tone, putting his face next to hers. Emma shook her head. She tried to turn away, but he grabbed her arm and forced her to look.

"Make sure to take note of the ribbon. My wife wore it every day after I gave it to her. Note the bloodstains!" His eyes blazed and his face twisted in an evil grimace.

"Ehrich, please stop! I meant no harm. You're hurting me. Please stop!" Emma pleaded. Her arm throbbed with the vice-like grip of his hand.

"But this is what you wanted to see. Look around. Look!" he forced her to look at each and every article in the room, making sure she'd remember the pain and horror of his loss.

After snuffing out the candles, he and Emma left the room and quickly locked the door. Then he seemed to realize she was sobbing. He gathered her up into his arms.

"I'm sorry," he whispered into her ear. "I…I'm sorry. Your tears are breaking my heart."

She buried her face into his chest and continued to sob.

"I didn't want to talk about the room." Ehrich hugged her to him, cursing himself for his weakness.

Continuing to weep, Emma said nothing, spilling tears all over his loose-fitting white shirt. Those tears tore him apart.

"It hurt so much," he whispered, trying to compose himself as he held her to his chest. "Now you know what kind of monster I am. Do you still see something good in me?" He felt like dying for the pain he had caused her.

"Yes," came the reply between sobs.

Ehrich made his wife look at him and saw her beautiful, tear-stained face. He wiped the lingering drops from her cheeks.

"I'm sorry I asked about the door. I didn't know. Forgive me."

"Some questions I don't wish to answer for they stir bad memories. And it is I who must ask forgiveness of you." He leaned down and gently kissed her sweet, quivering lips. She responded lovingly, surrendering to him. Even as his kisses began to calm her, she yet trembled from the ordeal.

Ehrich could feel her heart pounding like a trip-hammer within her breast. He felt her body quiver at his touch. So he pulled away from her lips and began reciting a poem he had written for her. One he hadn't had a chance to share yet. "Thy sweet face fills me with joy and drives away all specters from my past. The taste of thy ruby lips like honey, brings peace and comfort at last."

Now his voice softly, gently told of never-ending love and eternal happiness. Those angelic tones enveloped and hypnotized Emma as she closed her eyes. The sweet words carried her far away from the hidden room and its pain. When Ehrich spoke, her soul soared to the lofty ether of the Divine One in heaven. Truly he had earned the title, Master of Arts.

CHAPTER THIRTEEN

Maurice D'Auberge and his men escorted the caravans carrying the strange cargo along the road that led straight into the town of Le Havre. It would take at least six days to reach Paris, so they had to move quickly in order to keep their appointment with D'Auberge's partner.

They pulled up outside a tavern that gleamed with candlelight and roared with bawdy, rowdy laughter. Derrell dismounted his horse and entered in search of Alain, D'Auberge's nephew. Tonight looked like a full house, with the roughest of men filling tables all around the room, drinking, laughing, and teasing the barmaids who served them. But no Alain.

Derrell pushed his way to the bar and questioned the bartender. Alain had been there. No one knew where he went.

"What do you mean, he left? Alain could drink any one of those men under the table. Drinking's his passion!" exclaimed D'Auberge. The young man had never left a tavern without being dragged out.

"Should I search the town for him?" Derrell asked

"No time. We'll be late for the rendezvous. He'll have to find his way. If the ship is empty, he'll know we're in route to Paris. Go!" commanded D'Auberge.

The caravans pulled out with their escorts. D'Auberge's men threatened the life of each girl if she uttered a sound. Spices from the Orient covered the floor of the third caravan, concealing the opium. The aroma of the spices overpowered the scent of the drug should the authorities stop them.

One uneventful day of travel melted into the next, until the eve of the fifth day.

The night grew damp and cold. The full moon shone over the land like a dim lamp in a pitch-black room. Shadows darting in and out from among the trees stalked the caravans as they rolled along, oblivious to their environs. An occasional rustle of leaves broke the silence, as well as muffled footsteps.

Hours passed, and the drivers changed. They continued moving nonstop except for eating and personal care. When they stopped, whatever lurked in the shadows could pounce on its prey if it chose, but everything remained still.

After some time, the caravans made a temporary camp along the roadside. Derrell released the young girls from their cramped prison. The men seemed to eye the sweet, tender maidens like hungry wolves in the midst of a herd of lambs.

Two of the men who sought Laurette had stood guard over the hatch on the ship. Both were in their late thirties, just like the missing Alain. The first, called Jacques, wore his hair in a tangled dark mane, and his unshaven face bore a deep, hideous scar. He stood at a medium height and build and smelled like a mix of rotten meat and body odor.

The other man, called Arnou, had no visible scars. He reeked with the stench of his filthy, yellowing clothes and vile body.

For some reason, Arnou and Jacques both hungered for the smallest, the most timid of the girls, Laurette. She tried to cover herself with her cloak.

D'Auberge watched the men closely. He knew what they wanted, so he motioned for Derrell.

"*Oui*, M. D'Auberge."

"Remind Arnou and Jacques not to touch the merchandise. Just because they stood guard does not mean they have privileges," the nobleman said solemnly. "Tell them I would sooner lose *them* in the woods then have my goods spoiled. The guards are expendable!" His words rang with finality.

Derrell made a brief bow and delivered the message to the men. Arnou growled and cursed. Jacques advised him to be silent. Another chance would come before reaching Paris.

The shadow crept through the darkness, taking in all it had heard from D'Auberge and his men. What stalked the wagons moved gracefully, like a lion tracking a zebra. It came very close to Laurette.

The girls sat around the fire eating what Derrell had given them. They were given dried meat and biscuits and fresh water. Some bowed their heads and clasped their hands before their faces, while others silently mouthed prayers for deliverance.

Now came the task of letting the girls relieve themselves. Knowing that only Derrell had self-control, D'Auberge had him escort each girl to a point of privacy and then to return her to camp.

Jacques and Arnou watched in silence as Derrell escorted each girl to and from the woods. They calculated the time spent. It looked like Laurette would have the last turn. When they saw their chance, the two took off into the woods.

When it came her turn, Derrell escorted Laurette to a tree a little ways into the woods but still in eyeshot of the camp. He turned his back to her, like a gentleman. Derrell never made conversation with any of the maidens.

Five minutes passed. Laurette should have finished by now. Derrell called out to her.

No answer.

He turned, only to meet a rather hefty thump on the head.

Jacques and Arnou turned back to the terrified, trembling girl. Arnou held her wrist tight. Both men grinned wickedly, but something caught their ears. A twig snapped. As they turned toward the noise, something came at them quickly, snapping the neck of each man. In moments, the two men lay dead at Laurette's feet.

A black mass wrapped the child in her cloak and spirited her away from the camp and the dead men.

Farther and farther into the woods melted the shadow, with the sobbing, whimpering girl in its arms.

But what held her so tightly as they moved swiftly and gracefully through the night? What indescribable torture lay ahead of her? What held her, man or devil? Tears flowed freely from her eyes.

At last, they reached a tiny cottage in a clearing, so far out of the way only some nocturnal creature could have found it in the darkness. As they reached the door, Laurette heard the neigh of a horse somewhere behind the house.

Inside, a small fire blazed in the fireplace and warmed the chill in her bones. The strong arms released her and bolted the door behind them. When she turned, Laurette saw that no devil or demon had brought her here. The familiar face of a young man with long, disheveled hair met her gaze. Nervously, he gave her a lopsided smile.

"Please, Laurette, sit down by the fire. Warm yourself," Alain bade her kindly. She obeyed. At least he had a friendly, familiar face. He had never tried to harm or disrespect her.

"You know who I am, don't you?" He brought out a blanket and wrapped it around her shoulders as he sat next to her.

"Yes. Alain. M. D'Auberge's nephew," came the sad reply as she stared into the fire. She trembled even as she drew the blanket around her. "Are you going to hurt me?" Tears rolled down her delicate cheeks.

"I mean you no harm. See, over there is a bed for you. Only you. I swear I won't touch you. Laurette, I love you. Please marry me. I swear I will protect you." He reached for her, but she flinched.

"Marry me. I will take care of you, and we can visit your parents," he promised.

"Visit my parents?" She turned her tear-stained face toward him. "You promise?"

"I promise. And I will never let any man lay hands on you. Please, say you'll marry me?" Alain drew a small box from his pocket and handed it to her. At first, she stared at it then her eyes met his.

He motioned for her to take it. Inside gleamed a beautiful gold band. Alain had bought it for her in town; that was where he had been when Derrell came looking for him. Taking the ring from the box, Alain put it on her finger and smiled. Then he took both of her hands in his, kissing first the back of each and then the palms.

"Yes, Alain. I will marry you," she replied softly, partially in fear and half by choice. Out here, she had no one to protect her. It would be better to stay with one man than to go out on her own to possibly be ravished and killed.

"May I kiss you?" He quivered with anticipation.

"Yes," she gave a faint smile and reached for him. Their lips met as Alain gathered her into his arms. Then he gently broke the kiss.

After digging around in a box, he pulled out a pot and placed it on the fire so he could start preparing food.

Laurette moved to the bed in the corner, which Alain pointed out was hers.

Alone.

Alain turned to her as the food cooked, "I assume you know nothing about being alone. You must be frightened, but believe me, I will not harm you, I swear it."

When Derrell regained consciousness in the woods, he stood and looked about in the dark, blinking and squinting, trying to get his bearings. Moonlight filtered through the trees, allowing only a small ray of light to tease the weary traveler. With the campfire still within eyeshot, he could make out the silhouette of Maurice D'Auberge headed straight for him, carrying a lit torch. Derrell suddenly remembered Laurette and spun around behind the tree.

No one.

Where could she have gone? Did she knock me out?

"What's taking so long?" came D'Auberge's gruff voice.

Derrell rubbed his sore head. "Someone hit me from behind."

"Where's the girl?"

"I…I don't know. When I came to, she was gone."

"Come. Jacques and Arnou are also missing." The nobleman led the way into the woods, holding the torch a little ahead of him.

The cry of a nightbird filled the air. In the distance, a wolf howled while the night grew increasingly cold. D'Auberge halted a moment.

"What's wrong?" Derrell tried to see around him.

"Look! Jacques and Arnou." The nobleman bent down and cast the light over the dead bodies. He examined them, trying hard not to show his fear.

"Broken necks, both of them. The girl didn't do this." D'Auberge cast his eyes about nervously.

"Do you think he…?" Derrell started and swallowed hard.

D'Auberge stood up and glared at his right-hand man. "Who? My partner, Ehrich de Natois?" He laughed out loud. "In the woods? I believe he's more suited to *le Théâtre Ranier*."

"So he's never been known to linger in the woods or kill outside of…"

"Silence!" D'Auberge cut off Derrell before he could finish. Then he again looked about nervously. "Let us return to camp."

"What about them?" Derrell nodded toward the bodies.

"Leave them for the wolves." D'Auberge sounded cold and brave, when he actually wanted to run and hide.

D'Auberge headed back to camp. Derrell took one last look at the bodies and shivered before following him.

"M. D'Auberge, should we look for the girl?" Derrell caught up with him.

"No. We don't have time. We must be in Paris tomorrow night."

"Do you think the girl is dead?"

"Doesn't matter. For now, we move on before anything else happens."

Upon reaching camp, D'Auberge barked orders to his men. "Get the girls loaded and move out, now!"

"Where's Jacques and Arnou?" shouted out one of the filthy looking men.

D'Auberge hesitated a moment, shot a look to Derrell then back to the crew. "Dead. No more questions. Just load the girls and mount up. Go quickly!"

At first, no one wanted to move. Fear seized their hearts.

As the men murmured, D'Auberge heard bits and pieces of their complaints: "Two of the cruelest men we've ever known lay dead, and the assassin roams free. Any one of us could be next."

D'Auberge pulled out a gun, "I said we go now. Do as I say, or I will blow a few holes in you and make sure you die a slow, painful death. Any idea how long it takes for a man to die if he's shot in the gut? Can't dig out the bullet unless you kill him first. Either way, it's slow and painful."

The men still muttered their dislike. "As far as I can see, death faces us no matter what. If we keep moving toward Paris, we'll have a chance to earn our money. After all, power is the ultimate prize," slurred out one of the men. The others agreed.

As they ushered the girls into the false bottoms of the caravans, a howling wolf in the distance unnerved even the bravest of men. Quietly, they continued their murmuring amongst themselves, careful not to let their employer hear.

CHAPTER FOURTEEN

Once again, Emma graced the stage of *le Théâtre Ranier* in a stirring performance of the same play. This time, she closed the evening with a recitation of a love poem that she dedicated to Ehrich.

"No painting could ever convey your handsome face. No words could utter what's felt in my heart. Only the seraphim from heaven would know, the ecstasy my beloved can impart."

The audience gave her a standing ovation once again. Looking up toward the balcony closest to the stage, Emma threw a kiss to the shadow.

Ehrich stood to join the crowd's standing ovation.

Amidst the theatergoers, Ralph met Emma in the theater lobby and congratulated her, as before.

"He's here, isn't he?" Ralph looked around, nervously toying with his hat.

"Yes, so do not attempt to touch me. Last time I only stopped him by the grace of God." Emma smiled as people passed.

"Indeed, *madame*. And for this I thank God and you that I am still alive," he responded, rubbing his neck. "When did you wish to meet at Cerise's dressing room? I am concerned for my beloved Cerise."

"I don't know," shrugged Emma.

"Is my darling lost forever?" he asked sadly.

"No. Don't worry. We'll get her back. I promise we'll talk soon. Excuse me, I must go to my beloved."

Emma turned to leave, but Ralph caught her arm, "Ehrich is most fortunate to have you." Then he slipped a small, folded paper into her hand. "If you should need, please feel free to call upon me," and with this, he bowed and brought her hand to his lips.

The slip of paper had directions to his *château.*

~ * ~

Ehrich and Emma entered the Dark Wing. "I know," he smiled, realizing the hat annoyed her. You may remove my hat." Happily, she obeyed.

"You performed beautifully. Cerise never had emotions like you." He kissed her again.

"Thank you," she smiled.

"Acting comes naturally to you. My sweet, tonight I must leave you for a short time. There is some business to which I must attend."

"Can I go with?" Emma looked up into his face.

"I beg your pardon? You want to go with me?"

"Yes. Sorry."

"Interesting. Can I go with? Mmm, no. You may not go with." Even though he smiled, his words rang with finality. "Where I must go, a lady should not. I must attend to a man's business."

"You're not going to…you know…?" She made choking motions.

"I hope not. I will be in the city, and I will return by one or two in the morning. If you wish, you may wait for me."

"Well, if you had a television, I could entertain myself easily."

"What are you talking about? Never mind. Explain later." He kissed her once more then he left her at the doorway of their bedroom. "This time, I must truly blend into the night. The great Ehrich de Natois must merge into the depths of darkness for his next performance." He bowed to his true love as he pulled the fedora down about his face.

"Be careful, sweetheart. Come back to me safely. I'll wait up for you."

"Wait up for me? Yes, interesting phrase. Do that. Wait up for me." Ehrich smiled and moved to the entrance of the wing, which opened at the touch of the counterweight.

She sighed and watched him disappear into the dark of the winding passageway hidden deep within the walls of the theater. Never before had he left her alone at night, and the deathly quiet echoed within the walls. The dampness and cold chilled her to the bone as she turned back into the chamber and the door closed automatically.

What could she do until her love returned? The clock chimed the tenth hour. She had four hours to kill. For a while, she tinkered with the piano, picking out a few melodies that came to her.

Bored, she looked around for books to read.

She made her way into the library, where she reviewed the books in a case at the far corner of the room. Loneliness and fear crept over her. How could her husband stand to live in such solitude for so long? One could truly go mad in the deathly stillness.

At the very top of the bookcase, setting side by side, were what looked like a series of personal journals, identified by year. They were dated 1840 to 1878. Emma knew if Ehrich found her snooping, she would suffer his wrath. Still, she decided to take a peek then carefully replace the book. No harm done.

At first she pulled some books off the shelf at random and thumbed through them. Finally, she removed the one labeled 1849, which began with the seer's prophecy. This intrigued her. Upon taking the book into the sitting room, she lit a few more candles, settled into the sofa and commenced reading. As she did so, the prophecy seemed to explain her mix of feelings. There were times she felt strongly attracted to Ralph, yet she loved Ehrich more than anything in the world. This had to be the same thing Cerise had felt, having both Ralph and Ehrich vying for her affections.

Emma gasped audibly. The girl from another time in the seer's vision was her! She turned page after page, looking for clues. The other woman had to be Cerise. No more misunderstandings. But the last part of the prophecy she didn't comprehend: "Two separate, yet intertwining destinies." What did this mean?

~ * ~

Before attending to business, Ehrich requested that his cab stop at Latimer's apartment. A chilly fog encircled the carriage as he stepped out. He hurried to the door and rang the bell. After a moment or two, Latimer's manservant, James, peered out through the peephole in the front door then opened it.

James hailed from London like his master. He wore his jet-black hair straight and combed back from his ruddy, rugged face and stood just an inch shy of his master's height. He had worked for Latimer for a number of years, and he knew Ehrich from his less than frequent visits.

Ehrich rarely came to visit Latimer. He did so only when the spirit moved him.

"M. Ehrich, please come in," smiled James. The old Master nodded a greeting.

"Who is it, James?" called Latimer from another room.

"M. Ehrich, master."

In a moment, Latimer appeared. "Ehrich! Good to see you. Come, sit down." Latimer attempted an embrace, but Ehrich backed away. Understanding, the Englishman bowed instead.

Giving a faint smile, Ehrich followed his host to the sitting room where a rather large fire blazed in the fireplace. The room seemed cramped but cozy. Some rugs from the Orient lay on the floor and dressed the walls away from the fireplace. The old furniture had some scars but still showed its Victorian elegance.

Ehrich sat on the sofa opposite Latimer, who sat in a large overstuffed chair. James brought a tray of tea and sweets and set it on the small table before them. He poured two cups of steaming tea and added cream and sugar to the taste of each man. James had a remarkable memory for such things.

When James left the room, Latimer turned to his guest. "What brings you here at this late hour? Not getting along with your bride?"

"Nothing like that. I must attend to business." Ehrich sipped his tea.

"Trouble?"

"Perhaps. I fear all you have prophesied and what I may have to do."

"I prophesied nothing. Shylah, the seer, showed you many things in the mystic pool." Latimer drank his tea and took some sweets to his lips.

"Nevertheless, the prophecies came because of you. You sent me to her." Ehrich set the cup and saucer down so hard they broke in two. Then he arose, moved to the fireplace, grabbed a poker and began moving the wood about amidst the flames.

"Remember, we cannot change history."

"Shylah said that! Whose history? Ours or Emma's?" Ehrich stopped prodding the fire long enough to jerk his head around and glare at his friend. Latimer ignored the question.

"She also said I have two separate yet intertwining destinies running parallel to each other. Do you know the meaning? Explain!" Ehrich continued to stare at Latimer. Since the fedora covered most of his face, the glint of his cat-like eyes flickered back at Latimer.

"Has Emma returned with Ralph to the mirror in Cerise's dressing room?" asked Latimer.

"No." Ehrich lied as he grew more irritated when he received no answers.

"She really must."

"What does that *mean*?" His voice rang with irritation. Then he let out a long sigh of aggravation and stood up, replaced the poker, and straightened his clothes.

"I just think it's time for her and Ralph to return to the mirror." Latimer looked thoughtful.

"Latimer, you drive me to madness. What is the purpose in Emma taking Ralph to the mirror?" It seemed Ehrich's agitated voice grated on Latimer's nerves.

Latimer remained silent as he continued to sip tea and eat sweets. Again, Ehrich gave a long, drawn out sigh.

At last, he broke the silence. "I must go. My visit with you has been wasted." He took off in a huff, but Latimer set down his cup and saucer, rose quickly, and grabbed him by the arm.

"Wait! I can only say she must return to the mirror with Ralph. Something should happen. I cannot tell you any more. Please. Trust me," Latimer pleaded. Ehrich pulled away from him in haste.

"All right. I shall tell her. Thank you for your kindness and refreshments, but I must meet with someone. Should I need your assistance, may I call upon you?" Ehrich stared him in the eye.

"Of course. I am at your service." Latimer bowed as Ehrich swept out of the room.

James opened the front door and Ehrich flew past him and vanished into the cab, which melted into the night almost instantly. As James closed the door, Latimer bade him to lock it.

"Make sure to secure the lock. I feel evil in the air." He shuddered and returned to the safety of the blazing fireplace.

CHAPTER FIFTEEN

Maurice D'Auberge and his men brought the three caravans to the back alley on the dark side of a huge, empty building that had once been used as a porcelain factory. Quietly they unloaded the cargo and ushered them in.

In the alley where the caravans stood, a dark figure lurked unnoticed in the shadows and followed the girls into the edifice. He stood motionless as Derrell passed within inches of touching him.

Only a lone, scarred desk with a single chair behind it and two others in front decorated D'Auberge's office. Here, he lit a few candles and made himself comfortable with a glass of wine and some bread and cheese he had brought in a large basket. Meanwhile, Derrell oversaw the men pushing the girls into a room deep inside the factory, which they generally used for storage. The opium they placed in a far corner.

Derrell reported back to D'Auberge, who then checked his pocket watch.

Half past midnight. His partner was running late. He pulled another glass from the basket and poured some wine for Derrell, who happily accepted and sat in a chair opposite the desk.

As Derrell helped himself to some cheese and bread, a shadow blocked the light. Both Derrell and D'Auberge looked up and gasped. Ehrich hovered over them, dressed in black, with his cloak draped around his shoulders and the fedora pulled down tight about his face. Between the hat and the shadows dancing across his striking visage, the eerie glint of his eyes stood out, like those of a nocturnal feline.

D'Auberge shook his head and caught his breath. "*Mon Dieu*! You never enter a room like a normal man. You always scare us to death."

"To death. Ah, yes. I apologize for my tardiness." Ehrich swept by and found a seat next to him.

"Where is Alain? I don't see him." Ehrich accepted the glass of wine and sniffed it before tasting.

"He's not here at the moment."

Ehrich took another sip. "Good vintage. I see he's not here. Where is he?"

"He chose not to come this journey. Please have some cheese and bread."

Ehrich refused. Something didn't ring right. Alain would never miss an opportunity to earn money.

"I haven't much time tonight. May we get on with business?" Ehrich set down his empty wine glass.

"Of course." D'Auberge arose from his chair and led the way into the factory, carrying one of the candles.

The old building still had some dusty tables and overturned chairs scattered about in the darkness. The high ceilings made it feel much colder than normal. A wisp of cold air struck them and snuffed out the candle as they passed a window with a small broken corner. D'Auberge had to strike a match to relight it.

The young girls drew back in fear as D'Auberge entered with the candle, followed by Ehrich and Derrell. They cringed when he inspected them carefully.

"These girls, how did you get them? I don't recall this as part of the bargain." Ehrich glared in disgust. Blazing eyes conveyed his anger.

"Business is business. What does it matter? They will fetch a high price. Virgins always do. I've made sure that none of my men have touched them," D'Auberge reassured.

"Have you no respect for womanhood?" Ehrich turned to the smallest girl, a pretty little one with soft green eyes and fluffy red hair who was trying to keep herself covered with her cape.

"What's your name, little girl?" Ehrich questioned.

"Margaret, sir," she replied with a distinct English accent.

"She's English?" Ehrich shot a look to D'Auberge, who only shrugged, trying not to show fear.

"Margaret, have you been hurt?"

"No, sir."

"How old are you?"

"I am thirteen years old."

"Thirteen years old? She's but a child!" bellowed Ehrich. "Have you gone mad? How could you do this?" he snarled at his partner.

"Please. You frighten the girls."

"*I* frighten them? *You* have kidnapped them. Ripped them from their parents for what? So you can fetch a high price? Fools call me a monster, when the monster is YOU!" Ehrich turned on D'Auberge, but Derrell and several men trained their pistols on him.

Feeling more confident, D'Auberge seized the opportunity to needle his partner.

"Well, my dear Ehrich, looks like we will have to settle our business in the other room. I see your displeasure. Perhaps I shouldn't even mention the opium." One of the men cast the candlelight over the crate in the far corner.

"Opium? What happened to the silk, rugs, and spices?" growled Ehrich.

"They don't bring as much money as virgins and opium," laughed Maurice, as he handed Ehrich the list of merchandise for him to sign.

Ehrich stared at the paper before him, itching to get his hands around his partner's neck. He'd had a feeling a night like this would come.

The paper listed the name of each girl, her age, and her state of health, as well as the weight and quality of the opium. Ehrich looked up from the paper then glanced back at the girls.

"There's a girl missing. The list says eight. Where is the other one?" demanded Ehrich. D'Auberge cowered in spite of the pistols.

"She got lost," came the lame excuse. Ehrich suspected Alain must have her, since both were absent at the same time, and so said nothing more.

"I will buy all of the girls from you. Name your price." The golden eyes blazed from beneath the fedora.

"Don't be ridiculous! You could never afford to pay what they would bring on the black market. Sign the papers and you'll get your share of the profits when the merchandise sells." D'Auberge tried to laugh through his fear. Crossing his partner would sign his death warrant, but he couldn't pass up the money or the power it would bring.

Ehrich eyed each pistol pointed at him. Fury only made him think of snapping the neck of each man, but would he be quick enough before a bullet caught him? The thought of never seeing his precious wife again became unbearable, so he gave in and signed the papers.

Before they left the room, Ehrich looked back one last time at the poor, frightened girls. The oldest didn't look much younger than his own dear wife. He prayed for the gods to give him strength to endure.

Before knowing how it felt to love again, the sight of such suffering might have been enough to make him despair of humanity. Many a dark, lonely night he had tried to seduce the Grim Mistress into taking him with her, to allow him that sweet rest and eternal peace. But tonight, he didn't want to go with her; he needed her as an ally.

D'Auberge led the way back to his office through the factory. This time, Derrell and three other men each held a lit candle with pistols trained on Ehrich. They stood too close to miss. But just like before, a puff of icy air snuffed out the candles. In the sudden darkness, three pistols fired. One sickening thud after another echoed in the dark, empty room. Fumbling with the matchbox, D'Auberge finally lit his candle. His partner had vanished, but three of his men lay dead at his feet. He gingerly examined them; their necks were broken, guns still in hand. Pulling back quickly, he gasped in fear.

From the depths of the factory where the crew and girls stayed, ten men rushed to his aid brandishing pistols, swords and lit candles after hearing the gunshots. D'Auberge assured them he had no injuries, but they stared in horror at their dead comrades.

Derrell lay on the floor with his arms over his head. Both he and D'Auberge shuddered in the wake of Ehrich's vengeance. D'Auberge motioned for the others to follow him as they raced back to those guarding the girls.

Ehrich made his escape from the factory, melting into the empty void of night. He crept through the shadows until he saw a cab.

Inside the carriage, Ehrich closed his eyes against the horrors of the night. His breathing grew heavy and laborious, while a sharp pain stabbed his right side. He examined himself. Blood! A bullet from one of the pistols had grazed his hip, leaving a bloody gash. Sinking back in his seat, he closed his eyes.

His mind wandered to the factory, the girls, and D'Auberge's betrayal. Most of all, he dwelt on the faces of the men he'd killed. Once again, society had forced him to take lives. In the dimness of the street lamps, he stared at his hands with disgust. How easy breaking a man's neck had become! Like second nature. How could he ever face his sweet wife with the smell of death encompassing him?

Certain D'Auberge could not keep the girls in the factory now. Ehrich figured he'd have no choice but to hide them at his *château*, a nearby estate that spread out over about a mile of land. The rescue would be no easy task. Ehrich could dispose of just so many men before they'd overpower him.

He knew he had to act quickly, or his partner would sell the girls, making their retrieval even more difficult. First, he'd have to find the missing child then he'd decide how to accomplish the rest.

At the stroke of two o'clock, the carriage rolled up near the theater. Ehrich got out and paid the driver. After glancing about in the dark to make sure no one followed, he hurried to the rear of the building. Here, he engaged a counterweight, which opened the entrance leading down into the storage areas then to a secret passage that wound its way to the dark wing. He winced only once from the pain.

~ * ~

As Emma read the journals, she came across the prophecy of Shylah, the Celtic seer. *What did she mean Ehrich had intertwining destinies? Was this magick?*

The poor wretch described in the journal sounded more like Death or a specter of sorts than the man Emma knew as her husband. A chill ran through her at the thought.

The journals detailed her husband's deepest emotions; the grief of losing his first wife and his son. He still mourned his father's death and the pain of living alone.

Emma shuddered at how he'd found his family dead, lying in their own blood, but her stomach turned and she nearly threw up at the details of how Ehrich had slaughtered the soldiers of Versailles.

After a while, Emma grew weary reading prophecies, physically and emotionally. Finally, she replaced them in the bookshelf, shaking her head in confusion.

She bathed and lay in bed, half asleep, trying to wait up for her husband. All night, she had been praying for God to keep him safe.

Wrapping her husband's ruffled shirt around her, she savored the lingering essence of sandalwood, the oil he liked to use after bathing and shaving. Enough scent remained to create a cloud of heaven to which his wife could cling.

Emma turned over to face the door when suddenly her lover appeared. She hadn't heard him enter.

"Did I awaken you, my sweet?" Ehrich tossed his cloak on the chair in the corner. Then he sat on the bed and reached for her, leaning over for a kiss. As he pulled her to him, he kissed and held her tight.

He removed his hat and continued kissing her.

Emma enjoyed his touch and the sweet taste of his lips. But he reeked with the smell of death. In folklore, people referred to the scent of decaying flesh as the smell of death, especially in a mystical way, when no actual corpse was close by.

She broke the kiss gently and whispered, "Are you hurt?"

"No. I am well," he lied. His side pained him and still bled, making him feel weaker by the minute.

"What happened tonight? Something went wrong, didn't it?"

"I kiss you and something went wrong? How can this be?" He tried to smile, but his wife saw right through him.

Humanity dubbed him a murderer and a ghost that clung to the darkness of the innermost evil of the human mind, due the deaths and disappearances that occurred in the theater. Regardless of the audience verifying he was onstage at the time of his father's death, many rumors still blamed him for the accident. Eventually, he had lost interest in acting and people. Alienating himself from everyone and from the theater in general felt more secure, so he had sold the theater to the current manager, M. Toussaint.

"Ehrich, what happened? There's a sadness about you, and you reek of death."

Her words hit him like a ton of bricks. He did reek of death. Would this incident destroy his marriage? If he lost Emma, he would surely die. How could he tell her? What would he tell her?

"Nothing happened," he lied again. "I only attended a business meeting with my partner. We import and export."

"Import and export what?"

"A beautiful woman should not worry about man's business." He tried to kiss her again, but she gently held him at bay and insisted he tell her the truth.

"You don't lie very well. Did you 'do the deed' tonight?" She made him look at her and he knew he couldn't lie anymore. He wanted to be angry with her for meddling in a man's business, and perhaps yell at her as he had done before.

Life was good with this woman, but also complicated. Now, he wanted to live and be like a normal man, in love with his wife. He wished he didn't have to plot the rescue of eight helpless girls from a ruthless, power-hungry nobleman. The thought made him shudder. He'd have to kill again.

Emma noticed the dark wet spot on his vest. When she touched it, he winced.

Blood!

"My God, Ehrich, you are hurt!" Quickly she crawled out of bed. He tried to stop her, but she pulled away to get something to clean and dress the wound.

"Where are the bandages and medicine?" Emma asked from the other room.

"Cabinet, in the kitchen."

Ehrich could hear his beloved rummaging in the kitchen. Finally, she ran back to him with bandages, medicine, and a bowl of water with a towel floating in it.

Carefully, Emma unbuttoned and removed his vest. Then she did the same for his shirt, gently peeling the blood-soaked fabric away from the skin.

"If I wasn't bleeding, this would be most pleasurable." Ehrich tried to smile.

Emma returned the smile. "Looks like it's just a graze, but we need to stop the bleeding," she said while cleaning and examining the wound.

"In the kitchen. Lower shelf of the cupboard. I have some special powder in a very small bottle that I picked up in Asia," came the reply.

After making him press the towel against the wound, Emma ran back to the kitchen and opened the cupboard. A small bottle marked with Chinese characters met her eyes. She grabbed it and quickly returned to her bleeding husband.

"Is this it?" she held up the bottle.

"Yes."

"Do I pour the powder into the wound?"

"Yes. Then bandage."

Emma obeyed. After she made him comfortable in bed, she went back to the kitchen to get him something to drink and eat. The blood loss had left him weak.

When she came back, his breathing had returned to normal. He actually ate and drank without an argument.

"I can't believe you are really here," he admired his loving wife.

"I love you, Ehrich. You don't think I'd let you die?" She reached over and hugged him. He winced a little.

"Sorry," she released him.

"Don't stop. Just don't squeeze too hard. Be gentle with me." They both laughed. In many ways, Emma reminded Ehrich of his first wife. Serena had loved unconditionally and never questioned his decisions. Emma loved in the same way, even if she questioned everything.

"Do you want to tell me what happened? Who shot you?" His wife nestled to his left, pulling the blankets over them. Then she wrapped her arms around him and laid her head on his chest.

"I'm not going to get out of this, am I?"

"No. Not when you're grazed by a bullet. The ones who shot you, did you…kill them?"

"Yes."

For a moment no one spoke. Emma listened to her husband's heart beating and the rhythm of his breathing. Normal.

"Are you going to explain?" she persisted, as she tenderly caressed his bare chest. He grabbed her hand, brought it to his lips, and kissed it lovingly.

After much prodding from Emma, Ehrich explained the details of the night's events.

"You think Alain has the little girl?"

"I think I know him well enough, but we'll see. I must find the child for sure then I must devise a way to rescue the other seven, but how? D'Auberge employs around a hundred men, not counting servants. Besides the crew, the others do things for him not fit for a lady to hear." Tears glistened in his eyes. "The youngest is thirteen years old. A baby. The eldest is only a little younger than you."

"Ehrich, that's horrible! We've got to help them."

"Not 'we.' Me only. I will not put you in danger."

"You can't do this alone. I know you're the 'big scary' around here, but you can be out numbered."

"The 'big scary?' What does that mean?"

"Means you are the chief of making people afraid."

"More phrases from home? We must discover where your home is."

"Yes, yes, we must."

"Mmm. The 'big scary.' Interesting! You are correct. I am outnumbered."

"But I can help. We can think of something together."

"Together? What a delightful thought, but no. I will not lose you."

"Ehrich—"

"No! Listen to me. You have no idea what Maurice D'Auberge can do. He lived as a pirate before he became part of society. He has killed as many as I. But I have never killed a woman, and I have never been a part of anything like selling women.

"Fear keeps him at bay. On one of our voyages, I killed six of his men who, on his orders, tried to seize the ship. Six of his best men lay dead at his feet, and he fainted at the sight of their bodies." Ehrich paused to take a swallow of water.

"Rest a while then we can go after Alain."

"You insist on going with me, don't you?"

"Yes."

"Do you want to take the broadsword?"

"Oh, yes."

"If you have to draw blood, will you?"

"In defense of myself and someone I love, yes."

"If you have to take a life, will you?"

"Same answer. In defense of myself and someone I love, yes."

Ehrich released a long and weary sigh. He closed his eyes and hugged his wife with one arm. Sleep overcame him. After a few minutes of silence, Emma checked his breathing. The bleeding had stopped. Tenderly, she kissed him and nestled in his arms.

CHAPTER SIXTEEN

At the *château* of Maurice D'Auberge, he and the sorceress Brianna intertwined their arms and drank a toast from each other's champagne glass. She sat on the edge of the bed in her exquisite nightgown, and he sank down next to her. Bubbles tickled her nose and made her giggle.

Not only did he speak of love, but also of the wealth they would obtain with a coup in place.

"You are the most beautiful woman I've ever seen. With you at my side, no magistrate in France would ever refuse our offer," D'Auberge whispered in her ear as he nuzzled her face and neck.

"Tell me you love me, Maurice. I just want to hear it from your lips," Brianna demanded.

"I love you," came the reply.

"That's it. Even if you don't mean it, I just love to hear it." Then she pushed him back. "Now, a bit of business. We must approach the magistrate in each province. They must agree to protect our cargo of opium and young girls so that we will not have trouble with the local *gendarmes*."

"Why don't you just use your magick, my dear Brianna? Why go to all the trouble?" D'Auberge gently pressed her hand to his lips.

"Magick must follow the order of nature. A spell is needed from time to time. Potions are used for special reasons, but taking over an entire country has to come with an agreement from the magistrates. You have to understand,

my dear Maurice, power must be obtained by physically conquering France."
Brianna sipped her champagne.

D'Auberge complained endlessly about his stubborn business partner. The problem with Ehrich didn't interest her, even though Dyonacalus wanted his soul.

She cuddled and cooed with D'Auberge for a while, and when he was sufficiently intoxicated with her charms, she left him in bed sleeping.

In his study, she rummaged through the documents they would present to one of the reigning magistrates in hopes of swaying him to their side.

The smuggling of opium and young girls came about at her suggestion. The fall of many countries came by defiling the women and poisoning the population. Degradation always brought royalty and politicians to their knees. She smiled to herself.

After reviewing a few more documents, she came across a file filled with newspaper clippings about Ehrich and his theater beginnings and end. Still unconcerned, she tossed the file aside with hardly a glance, remembering Dyonacalus said he would take care of Ehrich himself.

~ * ~

Etienne stretched out on the sofa in the parlor while Landru read from a book he had found in the library. Etienne could still feel the intense presence of Dyonacalus but didn't want to mention it. Worshipping something unseen gave him security. Nothing was demanded, so he didn't have to do anything. Even the hand-carved figures of the beast with the leathery skin and horns didn't affect him as much as actually looking at the thing in the crystal and hearing its distorted voice.

Etienne knew that once Brianna overthrew France, the human sacrifices needed to bring Dyonacalus into the human world would be easy to attain.

Landru felt the same, but talking about it only depressed him more. For centuries, he and Etienne had followed Brianna throughout France.

CHAPTER SEVENTEEN

When Emma awoke in Ehrich's arms, she found him awake and clutching her like he'd never let go. She rubbed her hand across his muscular chest and leaned up toward his face for a kiss. He graciously obliged. Waking up to each other brought a sweet pleasure.

"We must go," Ehrich whispered as he broke the kiss. "It will take most of the day to reach the woods. Dress quickly, my sweet."

"What about your wound?" his wife moved his arm to examine his side.

"I have no pain. The bleeding has stopped. You have excellent nursing skills. One of your many talents." He tenderly kissed her.

Gently, Emma broke the kiss. "Thank you, my husband." Reluctantly, they separated to dress.

Before leaving, Ehrich packed some provisions, since they'd be gone at least overnight. Emma snatched the broadsword from the wall, along with its sheath. Her husband looked up when he saw her dragging the sword into the kitchen and gave a lopsided smile, breaking into laughter.

"What?" she puzzled.

"You dress like a man and with that sword! What a sight," he exclaimed as he roared with laughter. She looked down at the sword. It felt good to hear him laugh. And she agreed, she did look amusing. Now they both laughed. Indeed, she brought out the best in him. Listening to his laughter, Emma couldn't believe this was the same man who had written the journals.

In a distant corner of the theater grounds, hidden by bushes, behind yet another secret panel, lay a corral and barn. Ehrich built it to keep horses stolen from the stables of *le Théâtre Ranier*.

Ehrich and Emma packed the provisions on the stallions and walked them along a narrow path leading up to the main street. However, they didn't notice the figures lurking in the shadows, watching their every move.

"I never knew this path existed," Emma remarked as they mounted the horses.

"I know," smiled her husband.

They rode the back streets of Paris while some shadow riders slowly brought up the rear. In the stillness of the early morning, the soft stir of merchants preparing to open their shops hummed through the sleepy, frosty town. The unpolluted air filled their lungs. It smelled clear and clean, except for the occasional stench from various alleys.

Soon they found themselves on the road leading out of Paris. Emma had no idea where they were headed, but since Ehrich knew, that was all that mattered. As they rode, he pointed out choice sections, which had significant meaning to him.

"Over there," Ehrich pointed to his left, "is the place I bought my first fedora. I recall it, because I walked out wearing it with pride of how fine I looked, but then a poof of wind snatched it from me," he finished with a laugh.

"That didn't make you angry?" asked Emma, surprised he would laugh.

"At first, yes, but then," he pointed to the left, "there is where I found it. Some vendor with a horse and carriage had it and placed it on the head of the horse," Ehrich finished.

Emma tried to keep a straight face and not laugh.

"I decided the hat looked better on the horse than me," Ehrich laughed again and shot a look to his beloved wife. Not being able to keep holding back, Emma laughed with him.

At the moment, he seemed happy and in a particularly good mood in spite of what he'd been through a few hours ago.

Still smiling, Emma took in all her surroundings. She'd always wanted to see Paris, but not quite like this. It still felt surreal, dream-like.

"Do you still have questions of me?" asked Ehrich, who was again dressed in his signature black cloak with the black fedora pulled down tightly around his face.

"You won't get mad?"

"Get mad? Mad meaning insane?"

"No. Mad meaning angry."

"More speech from home?"

"Yes. Sorry! Things like that just seem to pop out."

"No, no, I won't be angry. Ask your questions. I am prepared to answer them."

Emma puzzled at her husband's change in mood. Carefully she thought, as she surely wanted to take advantage of this rare opportunity. "Where did you learn to act so perfectly and recite with such emotion?" she finally asked.

"The gods bestowed the gift upon me," came the answer.

"No formal training?"

"None whatsoever."

"How did you learn ventriloquism?" she asked, thinking of what she'd read in his journal.

"From here and there. Actually, when I lived in Scotland, I traveled with a band of gypsies who had the most amazing skills in magick, illusions and throwing one's voice.

"While in London, quite a distinguished gentleman helped me perfect the art, enabling me to completely confuse the very best of Versailles's soldiers. It caused quite a commotion, since I had chosen a particularly small band, and I was able to convince them they had been seized by thousands." Ehrich chuckled.

He probably wondered how she knew about his acting and ventriloquism, but said nothing. He might have even suspected she had snooped in his journals, but it didn't matter.

"You're so smart. You know a lot of stuff. I wish I knew as much as you."

"You know a lot of…'stuff' as well. You've mastered the broadsword and the art of entertaining a theater of wealthy mongrels hungry to end their boredom."

"Wealthy mongrels? Is that what you think of people who attend plays?"

"Yes. They are beneath me."

"But you love the theater, don't you?"

"I love the plays, the genius of the writers, the art mastered by the actors, not the mongrels who come to watch."

"Okay, moving on. What kind of automatons did you make?" she asked absentmindedly.

"You know about the automatons? Mmm. I made several in the likeness of a theater manager in London."

"He delighted in fooling his friends, but better to fool his enemies. Do you know what an automaton is? Of course you do, or you would have asked what they were," Ehrich chuckled. "Mmm. Ask me something else."

"Such a good mood! How come you're so happy to answer my questions?"

"Because you love me, I shall happily answer your questions. All I've ever wanted was to love and be loved. All creatures want that, don't they? You've nursed me back to health, and this puts Ehrich in a good mood. A good mood to answer any and all questions."

"Ramble much?" his wife mumbled under her breath with a smile.

"Huh?"

"Tell me about Alain. DeBarge's nephew."

"DeBarge? You mean D'Auberge, don't you?"

"Oh, yeah, D'Auberge. DeBarge…was a singer, I think. Sorry!"

"Singer?"

"I think. Anyway, tell me about Alain. Have you known him long?"

"We met when he turned eighteen. He had just begun to work for his uncle," Ehrich explained. "He wanted to learn everything and did so very quickly; quite easy to mold. He enjoyed my company, and I taught him how to survive in the woods, especially at night. Neither his father nor uncle cared to spend such time with him.

"I'll never forget the day I showed him how to blend into the forest and move as swiftly as a deer. He loved trying to fool me by hiding, hoping I'd never find him. Even at that age, he seemed child-like, immature. Poor thing…" Ehrich paused and turned to his wife as they continued to ride at a quick and steady pace.

"Why so quiet? Have I bored you to tears, my sweet?" he asked.

"No, not at all. I've never heard you talk so much. It's…it's nice." Emma looked him in the eye. His hat prohibited her from seeing most of his facial expressions, but his eyes told her everything.

Some of the old Ehrich still existed, the one who had written all of the journals, experienced all the traveling and acquired all the skills, even the deadly kind. But then the sweet, loving Ehrich whom she adored also surfaced. How strange to see the two together! Like nothing she could have ever imagined.

"Please continue. I love to hear your voice." She smiled shyly and looked away.

"You love me, don't you? Yes, I can see it. I knew it when I first saw the vision of you in the Mystic Pool."

Huh? she wondered to herself. Then it dawned on her. He'd mentioned something she'd read in one of his journals.

"I do love you. Please continue. What Mystic Pool?"

This he ignored and went on. "Ah, yes, Alain. He's in his late thirties by now. He still loves the house we found in the woods some years ago.

Someone had abandoned it. Why? We never knew, but we cleaned it and often spent time there, talking, eating, and hunting. I taught him magic, just sleight of hand tricks and illusions, and how to find food…"

"I see. Boy Scout stuff."

"Boy Scout stuff? What does this mean, 'Boy Scout stuff?'"

"What you taught Alain. Survival in nature." She again smiled, remembering more of her past. Ehrich gave her an odd look

"You'd make a good father." Emma smiled shyly and looked away.

"A good father? My Serena and Pinchot would attest to that," he said sadly. "I had abandoned the idea of having another family, until…until now. Do you really think I could be a good father again?"

"I know you would. Ehrich, are you smiling? With that hat pulled down so, I can't tell."

"I am smiling. I'm in a rather good mood."

"Do you think Alain will give us any trouble when we find him?"

"No. He can't give me any trouble I can't handle. So, it won't be any trouble at all."

"You know you ramble, don't you? I love you, but you ramble, ramble, ramble!" Emma gave a lopsided smile and waited to see his reactions.

"Ramble? Me? I hadn't noticed. Depending on the mood and the circumstance, I suppose I can ramble. Does it trouble you, my sweet?" He pulled his horse toward her so he could catch her hand and put it to his lips.

"How could anything you do trouble me?" she smiled, but turned in time to notice something out of the corner of her eye.

Her husband sensed it, too, and they both looked behind them to see four horsemen riding hard to catch up.

"Friends of yours?"

"Perhaps. I can think of only one greeting for such." He made a one handed choking motion.

"Shouldn't we ask what they want first?"

As he ducked a bullet fired by one of the riders, Ehrich calmly replied, "Ask if you wish."

While their pursuers increased speed, Ehrich and Emma kicked their horses to go faster, ducking the occasional shot. A vast, open space lay before them, with no trees or shrubbery to provide cover. At this point, they could only stay ahead of the shooters and sway from side to side, making themselves more difficult to hit.

The chase went on until a patch of trees loomed up ahead. If they could get there first, they'd have a chance to turn and retaliate.

As they drew closer, they slowed the horses. They could almost feel the hot fetid breath of their would-be-assassins at their backs.

Ehrich signaled his wife to grab a tree branch and let the horses go. She obeyed, and they each grabbed a branch and swung a leg over it to sit upright for a better hold. The horses continued without riders.

The shooters halted a little distance from the foliage and dismounted with weapons ready. Slowly, cautiously, they crept toward the tree into which they had seen Ehrich and Emma disappear.

"Try to keep one alive for questioning," Ehrich whispered to his wife. She nodded in agreement.

Actually, Emma shook with terror. Had she let her husband go alone, she would have worried to death, but now, coming face to face with the devil's disciples came near to gut-wrenching horror. She knew she'd have to draw blood and even take a life. The thought sickened her.

Little by little, the steps of her training in swordplay crept back into her mind as she readied the broadsword. First, disarm if they have weapons. Second, disable by taking out an arm, a leg, or anything to weaken them. Third, go in for the kill. Aim for a vital spot and give it all you've got.

Ehrich cast a glance toward his beloved. He worried she might hesitate and get them both killed. But they couldn't change the plan now. The four assassins separated to encircle the tree. Ehrich focused on the two he'd targeted.

As soon as one strode directly below him, he jumped down on the man, disarmed him, grabbed him by the neck and with one swift, deadly jerk, the neck cracked and the dead man hit the ground. Ehrich then dodged another bullet and knocked the shooter to the ground, kicking away his gun. With lightning speed, he snapped the neck of the second man.

At the same time, Emma brought down her sword on the gun hand of her first target, sending the pistol flying as the man screamed and cursed. Quickly, she swung the sword at the other man, splitting his head open. As the dead man hit the ground with a gruesome thud, she tried not to look or think about it.

Then she jumped down from the tree, kicking out at the one she had disarmed, sending him sprawling into the dirt. Without hesitation, she rolled over and leapt to her feet, slicing his thigh open with one graceful movement. Grabbing his leg, he let out a curse. Ehrich moved to support his wife, marveling at her skill. She stood shaking with the sword poised over her head, ready to strike again.

"Are you hurt, my sweet?" He moved to his wife's side. He could see tears in her eyes, but she held the sword tightly, ready to kill again, if necessary. At first she didn't answer, but nodded slowly.

"Do you wish to question him?" Ehrich grinned as he rubbed his hands together. The bleeding man trembled and grimaced in pain.

"You ask him," she muttered.

Ehrich turned to the man. "What is your name? Who sent you?"

"I'm bleeding to death!" he screamed. His tangled, chocolate-colored mane looked greasy while his eyes showed anguish, the pupils blown so wide that Emma and Ehrich couldn't make out the color.

"I asked you two questions. Answer them!"

"They call me Michel…Michel Yvon Didier...M. D'Auberge hired me to kill the demon actor," came the reply. Again the man wailed as he gripped his bleeding leg.

"Ah, so you're Maurice's brother-in-law?"

"*Oui, monsieur*. Please help me. I'm dying!"

"How much did he promise you?"

"Please, I need a doctor."

"Answer the question."

"20,000 francs."

"20,000 francs? That's all? Hardly worth the effort."

"Please, help me. I cannot go back. D'Auberge will kill me. Let me join you, and I'll help you fight him. Please, please help me stop the bleeding. I am dying," moaned Michel.

Ehrich moved to one of the dead men and picked up a gun. Quickly he checked the chamber without being noticed.

Empty.

"Here." He tossed the pistol to Michel. "Join us, then."

Emma lowered her sword. As she turned her back, the click of the gun sounded. Upon whipping around, she found Michel pointing it right at her. Without a second to lose, Ehrich snapped his neck like a brittle bone, and he dropped like a sack of coal.

Quickly, Ehrich moved to his terrified wife and embraced her. The sword dropped and she buried her face into his chest. "Your sobs break my heart. What can I say or do to comfort you?"

"Ehrich, Ehrich, I feel horrible. I killed a man! And this one almost killed me!" she sobbed and hugged him so tightly he winced. "I'm sorry." She loosened her grip. "I forgot your wound."

"No, no. Think nothing of it. Come. We must go if we expect to reach the woods by nightfall." He pushed up the hat a bit so he could brush his lips across hers.

"What about them?" She nodded toward the dead men.

"Leave them. We have no shovel to dig graves, and we cannot waste any more time." He whistled for the horses. Not far away, the animals heard it and trotted back. Quickly, he checked to make sure none of the men lived, and soon he and his wife returned to the road.

"The first time is the most difficult. I remember my first, a rather complicated one I must add. I stood unarmed with no knowledge of—" but before he could finish, Emma cut him off.

"Comfort me another time. I get the picture. How did you know he'd try to kill us?"

"An assassin's loyalty lies with money. We didn't offer to pay him. Therefore, his loyalty still lay with D'Auberge. I recognized the one you killed. He has attended each of your performances. He probably knew you. That means D'Auberge does as well."

"I've never been through anything so horrible." Emma sighed and looked away.

"Do you regret coming with me?"

"I'm glad we're together but sorry terrible things have to happen." Tears rolled down her cheeks. "I saw you check to make sure they were dead. I couldn't. I saw what I did to the first man. My God! How awful!" Her tears flowed like a river. Ehrich drew a handkerchief from his coat pocket and offered it to her; she tearfully accepted.

"They would have killed us without a second thought; you know that, don't you? Of course you do, that's why you weep. I understand."

"Did you know they would come? You tried to tell me about D'Auberge."

"I knew, but I didn't think he'd try so soon. We must reach Alain before he does. Maurice will want the girl as soon as possible. I am proud of you, Emma. You were not only skillful but brave. I had concerns that you would hesitate."

"How could I hesitate when they came to kill you? I love you so much, Ehrich. I don't know how or why things happened like they did, but we are together and I won't let anyone take you from me."

"I'm sorry you had to...but it was self-defense."

"I know. I can deal."

"Deal? I can deal? What does this mean?"

"It means I can cope with the situation," she corrected herself.

"Ah, yes. I understand. I can deal. Okay."

Finally, she smiled. "You're getting the hang of it. I mean..."

"I know. The hang of it. I am understanding. I can deal," he smiled.

CHAPTER EIGHTEEN

Twilight settled over the French countryside, spreading its shadows from heaven to earth, through the trees and into the woods.

Emma and her husband rode cautiously. Their earlier encounter with assassins still unnerved and made them more alert. Ehrich explained that very few knew the woods as well as he and Alain.

At first they stayed on the main path, following the signs left by D'Auberge and his crew. Ehrich stopped in the center of the trees and found the ashes of their campfire. His expertise as a tracker showed as he explained to his wife what to look for, even in the dark—especially in the dark.

Ehrich took a piece of wood, wrapped it in foliage, and lit it with a match from his pocket. By the light of this makeshift torch, they led their horses down a path where tracks in the dirt looked like something had been dragged. After a bit, Ehrich could see dark forms on the ground ahead of them.

Dead bodies.

He broke off a tree branch from overhead and moved on.

"Stay back here with the horses and keep the light. I can see quiet well in the dark. Looks like some bodies up ahead," he whispered to his wife.

"No. I'm going with you. I can deal."

"It's not a sight for a lady."

"If I can kill them, I can look at them."

"Okay. Was that right? Okay?"

"Yes, my husband. That's right. Okay." They moved ahead.

The bodies showed teeth marks where the flesh had been torn away. Emma turned her head and stepped back. Everything she had eaten felt like coming up as she covered her mouth with her hand. Flies had gathered for the morbid feast, sending chills up her spine to shake hands with the nausea in her stomach.

Her husband examined the remains, using the stick to move them around.

"Necks are broken and wolves came later," he concluded.

"Thank you. Like I needed to know that," Emma tried to be brave with a little sarcasm and not puke. "Can we go?"

"I know these men. Arnou and Jacques, two of Maurice's men. Someone killed them."

"Alain?"

"I am certain of it. Come. We must go."

"Thank you. Where to?"

Ehrich put out the light and whispered for her to mount the horse and follow him. Emma couldn't understand how they'd find their way in the dark, but then, she had married a man who had spent a large portion of his life in darkness, lurking in shadows and blending into the void of night.

Ehrich and his horse moved through the forest with such speed that Emma and her poor mare could barely keep up.

They galloped past what looked like an endless number of trees. Then they came to an abrupt stop. Ehrich held his hand up as a signal for Emma to be silent and follow him. Now, they would have to lead their horses and use stealth to proceed.

The little cottage had a small light behind its dreary curtains. Everything seemed quite still. Not even the cry of the night bird sounded. Nothing stirred.

They led their horses behind the cottage and found a little barn which housed a single horse. Here, they tied up their animals and crept toward the house.

Emma slipped the sword from the sheath strapped to her back and poised it to her left, ready to strike. Ehrich tried the doorknob.

Locked.

He motioned for her to move back. With one firm kick, the door gave way and Ehrich and his wife charged inside.

Alain was cooking food in a kettle over a blazing fire in the fireplace. Laurette sat on the bed with a blanket wrapped around her. She screamed at the sight of a man in black crashing through the door. Alain turned and jumped up, but before he could say a word, strong hands had him by the throat. He grabbed and clawed at the hands, which brought him to his knees.

Laurette leapt from the bed and tried to pull Ehrich away while frantically screaming, "No, *monsieur*! Please, no!"

Emma realized the girl remained with Alain willingly, and immediately dropped the sword and pushed her way between Ehrich and his victim.

"Ehrich, no! Stop! She's here by choice!" Emma pushed her husband back hard. He caught his balance, causing him to release Alain.

"Don't do that, woman! You distract me," he gently scolded. Alain, still on his knees, gasped for breath as he rubbed his throat. Laurette gathered him into her arms and held the gasping, sputtering man to her breast. Tears rolled down her cheeks.

"She is not a victim. Can't you see she's here by choice?" Emma whispered.

Ehrich clung to his wife but turned to study the child and man who clung to each other.

"Ehrich, why?" Alain gasped.

"I thought you had kidnapped the girl and...and..." Ehrich stammered.

"You thought I had hurt her. Is that it?"

"He loves me, *monsieur*. We are to be married," the girl cried.

Ehrich released Emma and moved to the door. The lock hung by one nail. From his inside coat pocket, Ehrich drew out a knife and repaired it. The lock would not hold forever, but it would do for now. Then he closed the door and placed the wooden slat across it.

Emma picked up her sword and replaced it in its sheath. "Sorry. We made a mistake. The girl disappeared and we just assumed…"

"He saved my life, *madame*. Alain cares for me, and I for him," said Laurette. The young man looked at her lovingly.

Ehrich truly felt like a heel. Seldom did he make mistakes in judgment. And now he saw how much Alain reminded him of himself. At one time, he had felt the same for Cerise, giving his all to a woman who didn't feel the same.

"Laurette, that is your name, isn't it?" Emma addressed the child.

"*Oui, madame*. I am Laurette."

"Did he hurt you?" Emma examined her limbs.

"*Mais non, madame*. He has been a perfect gentleman. Alain loves me. He will marry me. See?" The child put forth her hand to show off the ring.

"Laurette, do you love Alain? Do you want to marry him?"

"*Oui*, I love him. I want to marry him. He will take care of me and allow me to visit my parents. This is good, *non*?"

Emma said nothing but smiled and nodded an approval. Ehrich felt sorry he had misjudged his protégé. His bride had changed his life so much. In the old days he would have killed Alain—and Ralph, for that matter—as quickly as he had the would-be assassins, with no remorse or second thoughts.

"Have you hurt her?"

"No, Ehrich. I didn't hurt her. I killed Arnou and Jacques because *they* tried to. I love Laurette as you do your wife. I see the way you act around her. I see it in your eyes—in fact, your eyes are all I can see." said Alain, who sat on a stool by the fireplace. After brushing back his shaggy mane, he peered under the black fedora. A golden glint assured him Ehrich looked back.

"Are you trying to be witty? Does my misjudgment amuse you? I would have killed you if she had not stopped me." He glanced at his wife.

"I know this. But you should know me by now. I would never hurt or mistreat a woman. I love Laurette. I wanted her so much. I couldn't eat or sleep. Do you understand? I would go mad without her!" The young man began to cry and buried his face in his hands.

How well Ehrich knew the feelings. "Stop crying, Alain. It's not becoming of a man."

The young man dried his eyes and sniffled. Ehrich looked into the fire and continued. "Tell me your plans."

"We will marry, and I will love and care for her," came the reply.

"Your uncle will look for you. He's already sent men to kill my bride and me."

"Then we must leave at once." Alain arose. Ehrich pushed him back.

"Where will you go? Do you have money?"

"No, I haven't thought of anything. At first, I had considering remaining at the cottage, here in the woods. I have a little money but would fare better if I had the salary D'Auberge owes me for this last journey," said Alain.

"Just as I'd thought. You have no plan." Ehrich reached into his inside coat pocket and drew out a pouch. Opening it, he pulled out several bills and handed them to the young man. "Here. This is not a loan but a wedding gift. I will take care of your uncle. You must come with us in the morning. This place is no longer safe."

"You have given me too much money. I couldn't..." Alain seemed at a loss for words.

"Just take it. Remember, I nearly killed you. It's the least I can do." Ehrich turned away.

"You are not safe here. Maurice's men attacked us earlier. We must take you to safety in the morning. You can hide at *le Théâtre Ranier* until you find something better. I must deal with Maurice, and I must do it quickly before he sends assassins for you and to reclaim the little girl." Ehrich seemed thoughtful. Like Alain, Emma had to peer beneath the fedora to spot a glint of gold from his eyes.

For now, they sat and broke bread with the couple. Alain cooked quite well. Ehrich had taught him how to sweeten wild game, so the venison tasted delicious and the biscuits savory.

Ehrich and Emma took note of how well he attended to Laurette's needs. He dished out food for her, saw to her comfort, and made sure she had enough to eat. If the blanket slipped from her shoulders, he'd pull it up and adjust it. He couldn't do enough for her. Every bite of food he took with his eyes glued to his delicate, petite love.

Laurette appeared contented enough, but they couldn't be sure if she loved the man or just needed him. She hardly looked his way as she ate and tried to make small talk with their new friends.

"Come, come, you can tell me the truth. You cannot insult me. Do I frighten you?" asked Ehrich as he ate.

"*Oui*, you frighten me. You look like the one in the tales of death that comes for us at one time or another. I do not wish to die, nor do I wish for you to take my fiancé. We love each other." Sadness filled her voice as she continued to eat.

"But I sit and eat with you. What makes you think I would kill you and Alain now?"

"Ehrich, apologize," Emma nudged him.

"What? Apologize?" he stopped eating and glared at his wife.

"Ehrich…"

"I will not. I have nothing to apologize for. I made a natural mistake. You had the same misjudgment."

"I didn't try to strangle Alain. Apologize, please."

"No!"

Emma gave a long sigh and went back to her food. Still, her husband glared at her. For some reason the scenario made Alain and Laurette laugh out loud.

"What? Waiting for me to apologize amuses you?"

No one dared to answer. Instead, they tried in vain to stifle their laughter. Alain had known him far too long. If Ehrich made a mistake, he never apologized.

"It is all right, *madame*. He does not have to," Alain smiled.

"There, I don't have to," replied a stubborn Ehrich.

"Apologize." Then she leaned over and whispered softly into his ear, "If you don't, I will have a headache tonight, do you understand?"

After a brief pause, Ehrich said a rather quick, "I apologize." Then he immediately returned to his food.

This time they all laughed in unison.

CHAPTER NINETEEN

Alain offered Ehrich and Emma the bed, saying that he and Laurette could sleep on the floor, but Ehrich refused and insisted upon the barn. The hay would warm them enough with the blankets they had brought, and they could have privacy.

Moonlight filtered in from the loft high above. Dancing moonbeams skipped across the hay, past the horses, nestling on the dirt floor just outside the stalls.

Ehrich laid out some blankets on the hay while Emma removed her boots.

"How's your wound?" she whispered with concern.

No answer.

Ehrich removed his boots and settled back on the blankets, pulling Emma to him and pressing his lips to hers.

The creak of the barn door sounded in the background of their kissing.

"Ehrich! Ehrich, do you or your wife need anything?" Alain called out. Emma groaned.

"Not now," Ehrich mumbled. Quickly, he rolled over and stood up.

"Stay there, Alain. I will come to you," he called, tucking in his shirt then searched for his cloak.

In a few moments, Ehrich emerged from the far corner wrapped in his black cloak.

"We need nothing. Thank you for asking." He slowly moved to Alain.

"You are human," Alain replied.

"That's an odd remark."

"All these years you seemed like a spirit. I'd never touched you or even seen you eat. Tonight, I saw how you looked at your woman. I watched you eat. You apologized to me, and we laughed together." The poor lighting of the barn shadowed Alain's face.

"I knew that apology would cause me trouble," Ehrich mumbled as he drew closer.

"I beg your pardon. What did you say?"

"Your point, Alain?"

"Thank you for sparing my life. When my uncle saw you kill his men, he swore you were 'Death' itself. Many times he's told me to keep on the good side of 'Death' and it won't take me.

"Tonight, I knew for sure you had come for me. Then I heard your wife's gentle voice pleading for my life.

"You are my friend, Ehrich." He bowed in respect and gratitude.

Ehrich backed away. "I have no friends," his voice rang cold and harsh. "Go back to your woman. Treat her well. Should you mistreat her, she will learn to hate you."

"She doesn't love me, does she?" he asked sadly.

"How can she? Taken from her mother and now you. Handle her with care. This delicate child can learn to love you. Let her know her feelings come first, not yours," came Ehrich's fatherly advice.

"Thank you, Ehrich. I will be good to her. I promise I will care for her..."

"You babble. Go to her. I must have peace." In spite of Ehrich's cold, harsh manner, Alain gave a faint smile then turned and walked out, closing the barn door behind him.

As Ehrich returned to his wife, he tossed his cloak aside.

"Why were you so mean to him?" asked Emma, shivering beneath the blankets.

"Mean? I spoke the truth. I have no friends," he said coldly. Then he lay down on the blanket next to Emma.

"You have Latimer and…me." She leaned over and kissed his shoulder. He grabbed her roughly and kissed her hard.

"This is a man's business. It doesn't concern you," he growled, pulling the blanket over both of them.

"I think I held my own like a man when we were attacked. What is man's business? If I'm here, then it concerns me."

"I was just advising Alain to take care of Laurette. That's all," Ehrich replied wearily.

His wife whispered, "Are you still in the mood for questions?"

"What now?"

"If I had refused to marry you, what would you have done?"

He let out a long deep sigh and buried his face in her neck and whispered, "I would have had no other choice…but to let you go. I could not bear to be under the same roof with you if I could not touch you, and I would never, never hurt you. I love you with all my heart and soul."

Emma smiled, caressing him tenderly. "You are a good man."

Morning's icy breath spread frost over the sleepy land, only to fade when seduced by the sun's warm rays. Alain packed and made sure Laurette wrapped up warm and comfortable on the horse before mounting behind her with an arm wrapped around her waist.

Ehrich helped Emma repack the blankets on their horses, and soon everyone was mounted and headed for Paris. Instead of the well-traveled road they had taken earlier, Ehrich suggested an alternate route, off the beaten path, that would get to Paris faster. The terrain seemed a bit more rugged and treacherous, but the likelihood of meeting highwaymen or assassins was slim to none.

The trail carried them and the horses to a path high above the main road and to a spectacular view of Paris, which lay dead ahead.

From this vantage point, they could see that several riders roamed the main highway, as Ehrich had predicted. D'Auberge had sent more assassins.

They seemed confused as they searched for their prey. Not many knew the path Ehrich and Alain followed with their women.

Hours went by with few words passing between them. Silence as well as stealth and vigilance became their companions.

Ehrich abruptly halted the group and motioned for silence. The crackle of branches and underbrush sounded in the distance behind them.

"I can see the majority of the riders below," commented Alain.

The men took the women and horses to higher ground. Ehrich knew Emma would want to go with him to track the riders, but someone had to protect the child.

Reluctantly, she agreed, pulling her sword from the hilt. Ehrich and Alain camouflaged Laurette with tree branches and fallen leaves alongside the horses.

A few moments later, two rugged horsemen dismounted their horses and walked them along the treacherous trail. The one in the lead, who kept nervously twisting his moustache, had keen eyes that looked from side to side, searching for movement or clues to their bounty.

The second man was clean-shaven and could have passed for an aristocrat or nobleman as he drew his gun and started poking around in the brush. He even looked as though he would enjoy the kill.

"I've seen them before," Alain whispered, but Ehrich hushed him. It didn't matter.

As soon as they drew close enough, Ehrich came out from where he was hiding and snapped their necks in a blink of an eye.

"You...you could have killed me instantly last night." Alain's voice faltered.

"But I didn't. My wife distracted me. Take one of the horses and the guns. If they have provisions, take those too, and release the last horse."

"And the bodies?"

"Leave them. You know that. Go quickly!"

Alain scurried about, honoring Ehrich's words.

While Ehrich and Alain were both occupied, a third man climbed to higher ground, overlooking the women.

Emma stood guard. Within her chest, her heart pounded wildly. Something crept up behind her. The soft sound of a twig snapping and leaves crunching gave away the stalker.

The click of a gun cocked.

Silently, she whirled around and ducked at the same time. The gun went off, the bullet missing her by a hair's breadth, and her sword sliced open the man's stomach. Then she brought the blade back and hacked into his skull.

Blood and entrails spewed everywhere as the man hit the ground. She focused on the sword dripping with blood.

Ehrich and Alain barreled up the hill. Ehrich ran to his shaken wife. No longer able to cry, she buried her face in his chest. Again, her breathing grew heavy and labored as the horrible truth stared her in the face. Another man was dead because of her.

Laurette remained crouched in the bushes beneath the camouflage, shaking.

When Alain found her, she was cowering with eyes shut tight. Enveloping her in his muscular arms, he kissed her head tenderly as she muffled her mournful sobs in the folds of his shirt.

Emma and Ehrich tried to comfort her, but she pulled away, muttering something only Alain could hear.

"She's not hurt, only afraid. Especially of Emma. My angel calls her Lady Death, because she's never seen anything like this before,"

"But Emma just saved her life," Ehrich puzzled.

"I had to kill him," Emma tried to explain, but Laurette would neither answer nor look at her.

"Come. Let us go. She'll understand one day," Ehrich said, leading the horses down to the trail below while the others followed.

Alain placed his little angel upon the horse he had secured. Then he mounted his own and followed the others as he led her horse behind him.

No longer would Laurette look at anyone but Alain.

Ehrich and his wife seemed very much alike. Ehrich didn't have to worry about Emma taking care of herself. She could watch his back, whereas Laurette was totally helpless.

"Ehrich, she called me Lady Death," she whispered.

"This troubles you? After all, you married Death." Ehrich snickered under the fedora.

"You are not Death."

"The child will forget."

"But I don't think I'm much older than she is."

"You were raised differently. You belong to me!" her husband grabbed her hand and kissed it tenderly. "Very soon this path will lead us into Paris. This time, we will have to take to the main road to get directly into to town." He released her hand and kicked his horse to go faster. The others followed suit.

CHAPTER TWENTY

Nightfall arrived softly as they returned to Paris. Ehrich and Emma helped Alain and Laurette hide their horses with their own in the corral at the other end of the theater in the underground passageway.

Ehrich led Alain and Laurette deep into the theater to Marmie, the box attendant he could always rely on. Of course, a few francs always insured her loyalty. After her daughter had married and left, Marmie still retained the same dormitory, which had two bedrooms. Here Alain took the sofa and Laurette took the spare bedroom.

Ehrich didn't have much time to plan and execute the rescue, so he locked himself in his study while Emma took a bath and changed her clothes.

Strange things, automatons! The spring had to be placed just right or the key would do nothing.

Ehrich needed just the right automaton to cause a distraction, but he needed to make it light enough to carry on the horse and not weigh it down. Assembly would occur when he reached his destination.

Ehrich tinkered, tapped, and knocked about for several hours. Emma rapped on the door. "Darling, how is your wound? May I bring you something to eat?"

"Not hungry. Forget the wound. Busy!" came the reply.

The clock was striking ten when her husband emerged from the study with a fairly large bag thrown over his shoulder. It looked like Santa's bag of toys.

"What is that?" Emma wondered, circling her husband and the bag he placed in the middle of the front room.

"Part of my plan," came the answer.

"Plan A or Plan B?" Again, the words felt familiar and fell carelessly from her lips.

"What does that mean? Plan A? Plan B?" Ehrich frowned.

"Plan A means your initial plan. The main one. If that doesn't work, you need to have a backup plan. Plan B." Emma smiled as she inspected the bag. "Laundry?"

"No. Plan A," he smiled.

"Plan A? Explain, please."

"No! Here." He drew two crumpled envelopes from his pocket and handed them to her. "If I have not returned by one o'clock this coming morning, read the one with your name on it and take the other one to Latimer. The envelope bears his address." Ehrich kissed her.

"You will not go without me!" she protested.

"Listen very carefully! If Plan A doesn't work, I need Plan B. You are Plan B. Understand?" He looked down into her pretty little face. "I love you. I intend to return."

"Don't die! I want babies. You'd better come back." She pulled him down to her. They kissed like they'd never let go. Neither one wanted to separate, but each understood the parts that needed to be played.

"Mmm, so you want babies, huh?" Ehrich murmured after a moment.

"Yes, I do. We should attend to that," she mused and hugged him. He winced.

"Oh, your wound!"

"Not bleeding. Just be…"

"…gentle. I know," Emma smiled, and they both laughed.

Quickly, Ehrich gathered his cape around him and engaged the counterweight. The door opened, and he walked out into the passageway carrying the bulky bag over his shoulders.

After the door closed, Emma retreated deeper into the dark wing. One o'clock seemed too long to wait, so she ripped open the envelope addressed to her and read:

My beloved Emma,

Please obey my words to the letter. If you are reading this, it's because I have not returned at one o'clock or you have become impatient and are reading this just after I've left.

In any event, I know you will come to my aid with your broadsword. Make sure Latimer reads my letter, and stay with him until he has done so. Then you and he must decide what to do next, as I may be trapped within the château of Maurice D'Auberge.

Come to me, my beloved. And DON'T DIE! I love you more than life itself.

Your obedient servant and husband,
Ehrich

Emma reread the letter, lingering on the part that said, "And DON'T DIE!" Precisely the words she had said to him. Their bond seemed to grow stronger by the minute, as though they had become as one.

Tears glistened in her eyes as she pressed the letter to her heart. Memories of the two men she'd had to kill popped into her mind. It might become necessary to repeat this action. Emma did not look forward to it, but she would not lose the man she loved, whatever the cost.

Emma folded the letter and tucked it into her dress pocket. Latimer's letter…should she read it? Was that ethical? She took the letter to the stove, lit a fire in it, and placed a kettle of water on to heat. As soon as the steam drifted from the kettle, she carefully held Latimer's letter over it, gently melted the wax seal, and opened it.

Latimer,

If you read this, know I am trapped in the château of Maurice D'Auberge. You know its location. I need your assistance. I have taken some magic and an automaton with me. I can keep the enemy at bay for just so long.

Discuss with my wife the next plan of action. If I know her, she has already read this letter before giving it to you. She fights like a man, especially with a broadsword.

Your obedient servant,

Ehrich

How well he knew his wife, especially for the short period of time they had lived together. Emma folded the letter and replaced it in the envelope. Again, she held it over the steam, just long enough to slightly melt the wax to reseal it.

She ran into Cerise's old bedroom and rummaged around in the closet where she found a fresh pair of pants and a shirt to fit. Quickly, she dressed herself. What would she need to bring? Something made her think about the novel and the cellar it described existing beneath the hidden room, storing barrels of gunpowder for use against invading armies.

Once in the cellar, she found the barrels. Grabbing a few empty bags from a pile in the corner, she proceeded to fill them with gunpowder. A plan formed in her mind.

Lugging the bags behind her, she retreated upstairs, replaced the trapdoor and secured it. After leaving the hidden room, she made sure to lock the door and replace the key on top of the desk.

She set the bags of gunpowder near the front door for easy pick-up upon her return. Now, she had to acquire allies.

Ehrich had shown her only one way in and out of the dark wing, so she followed the winding passage to the right.

After many twists and turns, praying she hadn't forgotten her way, she finally came to the corridor leading to Cerise's dressing room. Upon reaching the pivoting mirror, she ran her hand along the wall, searching for the blasted counterweight.

At last, the wall gave way and the mirror swung out on its pivots; Emma made note of the section that engaged it and proceeded into the dressing room. The mirror swung back into place.

As soon as she entered, Ralph burst through the door, coming in from the corridor.

"Emma! Where have you been? I've come here several times. What ill has befallen you?" Ralph stretched forth his hand.

"I am well, but I need your help. My husband's life is in great peril, and he needs your assistance." Her eyes pleaded as she reached for him.

"I am your servant." He bowed and kissed her hand. "You have but to command, dear lady."

"My husband has gone to the *château* of one Maurice D'Auberge. This same man tried to kill us earlier."

"Maurice D'Auberge?" The young patron looked startled. "Maurice D'Auberge has prominent status here in Paris. We suspect him of some very treacherous deeds, yet no one has ever brought charges against him. His crimes have never been proven."

"Well, I can prove it. He sent a number of men to kill my husband and me. Please, we must go, I have some other assistance to enlist." Emma tried to move past him, but he wouldn't release her hand and pulled her to him.

"I've never seen you dressed like a man. Still, you excite me." Again he kissed her hand. "I have one request. I desire a reward for my assistance."

The young woman glared at him in astonishment. "A reward? What kind of reward? A kiss? Ralph, this is not the place or time—"

"One kiss, I beg of you." His face looked so sincere, his eyes held so much desire.

Why does he act like this? Why am I drawn to him?

114

"All right, just one kiss." She drew near to him. Ralph wrapped his arms around her, tenderly brushing his lips over each ear, each temple, and finally her lips.

When the kiss finally broke, she pushed him back hard and gasped to catch her breath. "Ralph, enough!" Her face turned red in anger as she shook her fist at him.

He smiled and bowed, motioning to the door. She huffed before making her exit with the young patron in tow.

They didn't speak a word as they wound down the stairs into the lobby. This evening's performance did not require Emma, so she and the young patron slipped quietly through the crowd. As they reached the exit, they spied Latimer strolling about, chatting with various attendees.

"We've got to talk to him," she whispered to Ralph. He nodded an acknowledgement.

Latimer saw her pushing through the crowd. With a smile he reached out, took her hand and kissed it. She returned the smile.

"Dear lady. So happy to see you again. Yet, you seem so sad."

Emma said nothing but drew the envelope from her pocket and handed it to him. Latimer recognized the handwriting. They moved aside to an isolated corner as he opened the envelope and pulled out the letter.

When he finished reading, he looked up. His face had drained of color.

"He will be killed. D'Auberge has no conscience." Latimer's hands trembled.

"I have a plan, but I need you and Ralph to go with me. I'm sorry, this is Ralph Duchenois." Emma looked from one to the other.

"A pleasure, *monsieur*." He and Ralph bowed to each other. "Please, let us make haste."

"I must return to the dark wing to pick up something we'll need for my plan, and I have one other person to contact," Emma said. "Meet me at the end of the street at the rear of the theater."

"We will wait for you there, Emma. Be careful," Latimer cautioned as he and Ralph parted ways with her.

As the clock struck midnight, Emma arrived at Marme's dormitory where Alain and Laurette rested. It took a number of raps upon the door to awaken someone. Alain came to the door, bleary-eyed with sleep. "*Madame*, what's wrong at such a late hour?" He reeled a little from sleepiness.

"I need your help. May I come in, please?" Her eyes begged. He moved back to allow her entrance.

After relating all that had transpired, she asked for his assistance. He agreed without hesitation and awakened Marme, the old, widowed box attendant, to watch over Laurette.

"I don't like to do favors, but since I know you from past visits, I'll agree," said Marme after he explained the situation. Emma led the young man through the winding passage to the same path she had taken previously. They reached the dark wing at exactly one o'clock in the morning.

No Ehrich.

Just as she had thought. So Emma and Alain took up the bags of gunpowder and carried them to the corral. There they prepared the horses and loaded them up with the bags. Emma strapped on her broadsword, and Alain took a couple of guns from Ehrich's collection in the library.

They led the horses to the entrance of the underground passageway and up to the street behind the theater where Ralph and Latimer waited on horseback. Emma and Alain mounted their horses, and the four rode off together.

Alain explained how they had avoided the back streets upon their return to Paris. Assassins might lie in wait for them. Latimer asked if they could stop at his apartment before going on. There, he picked up a couple of pistols, more bullets, a few bottles of cheap wine, and some empty metal containers as well as his servant, James, who went with them.

The five valiant souls stood united to aid in the rescue. No doubt, Maurice's men outnumbered them, but Emma explained her plan as they rode to the *château*.

~ * ~

Derrell stood in the study before the desk of Maurice D'Auberge, desperately trying to explain the deaths of the assassins he'd hired.

"Two were slashed to pieces, *monsieur*. No one dares go after them," Derrell finished. His lower lip quivered with fear.

"All of them? Even Michel, my brother-in-law?" D'Auberge looked flustered and his hands shook. Little beads of perspiration broke out on his forehead. Drawing a kerchief from his inside coat pocket, he mopped his brow.

"*Oui, monsieur.* Slash marks covered the body, and his neck was broken," came the disquieting reply.

D'Auberge pushed away from his desk and stood up on shaky legs, only pausing a moment to steady himself. Then he moved to a cabinet where he kept his liquor, opened it and removed a couple of snifters and an opened bottle of cognac.

"Derrell, cognac?" D'Auberge offered a snifter which Derrell accepted with quivering hands.

D'Auberge poured each of them half a snifter. Cognac should be sipped and savored, but in view of so much death, each man threw back his glass like a shot of rotgut. They repeated this two more times to calm their frayed nerves.

As they downed the last drops, blood-curdling screams and scurrying feet sounded from the rooms beyond the closed door of the study. The two shuddered, afraid Death had made its way to them. Dropping the snifters, they reached for their weapons, Derrell for the pistol in his belt and D'Auberge for his sword from its sheath.

The last bone-chilling cry echoed throughout the *château* before the door cracked and popped open in splinters. There before them stood a figure dressed in Ehrich's signature black attire and cloak. Again he wore the black fedora pulled down tightly about his visage. In the dimness, D'Auberge could see no face, only the eerie glint of orbs like tiny embers from a dying fire. Death personified stood ready to snap the neck of its next victim.

"I have come to dissolve my partnership, Maurice. Sign the papers and pay the dissolution money," came the demand as he made ominous steps toward them.

In time, Death comes to everyone, but to actually watch it approach seemed more terrifying than the wait.

A shot rang out. Derrell trembled with the smoking gun in his hand. But if the bullet had hit its mark, no evidence showed, for the shadowy figure continued advancing, and he neither bled nor faltered.

Derrell screamed, dropped his pistol, and bolted for the door.

"Come back, Derrell. You coward!" shouted D'Auberge, trying to comfort himself by giving orders. His sword drawn, he thrust forward, striking the chest of the slowly approaching man. Only the sword did not pierce the chest. The end merely popped off. D'Auberge screamed and pled for mercy.

Upstairs in the winding corridors of the *château*, another dark figure wandered quietly in the shadows.

Small candles in every other sconce on the wall dimly lit the seemingly deserted halls.

Moving with the shadows, the figure melted into the darkest part of the corridor. Dim silhouettes guarded both sides of the door and shouldered rifles as they whispered to one another.

Darkness enveloped them, and in seconds the crumpled silhouettes lay on the floor, motionless.

With a hard twist of the doorknob and a strong, firm push, the door gave way. The dark figure half stumbled into the room full of frightened, sobbing little girls.

A soft whisper tried to calm and hush the terrified children.

"I am here to take you home. I will not harm you. Quickly, let's go."

Gathering their belongings, the girls followed the figure, side-stepping the dead guards. In silence, they made their way downstairs to the main entrance.

Suddenly, D'Auberge met the dark figure with his broken sword.

"Going somewhere, Ehrich? You were always good at building mechanical things," D'Auberge sneered and stepped aside to give a clear view inside his study. There slumped the automaton that had attacked him, now motionless and quiet.

CHAPTER TWENTY-ONE

Led by Latimer, Emma and her allies rode the moonlit path to *le Château D'Auberge*, which lay on the outskirts of Paris. It stood a few kilometers from the old porcelain factory where D'Auberge had held the little girls and opium for Ehrich to inspect.

Because Emma worried that something might go wrong, she made the men recite the plan. Alain knew the layout of the *château* and its grounds, so he would help Latimer and James set the homemade bombs of metal containers filled with gunpowder. Also, the cheap bottles would be stuffed with rags and lit as bombs, Molotov cocktails. They had plenty of matches between the five of them.

Ralph would accompany Emma in search of her husband and the girls. Obviously, they needed a means of transporting the young women once they found them; therefore, Alain would check out the stables.

They still had an hour's ride ahead of them, so the conversation turned to questions about each other.

"Latimer, how did you come to know Ehrich?" asked Ralph.

"We shared the love of acting and joined many a theater troupe some years back," Latimer answered thoughtfully.

"Truly? Then you still grace the stage?"

"I do. London adores me but France worships me."

Ralph frowned.

"How did Ehrich become the Master of Arts? I assumed he had died and haunted the walls of the theater, if he had ever existed at all," he said with a bit of sarcasm.

"He has mastered many talents, so to name one would not do justice. Let's just say he has created more characters on stage and displayed more skill than any other man could in one lifetime."

"Oh, really? He must have been quite the rage in his day. Upon our second meeting, he tried to strangle me with his bare hands." Ralph rubbed his neck.

"We have something in common, *monsieur*." Alain smiled knowingly. "I too have felt those deadly hands around my neck."

"And yet you came to rescue the man?" Ralph puzzled.

"And *you* come to rescue him as well. Why?" Alain tossed the question back to him.

"*Touché*, my friend. I am here at *madame's* request," he took Emma's hand and kissed it tenderly. Giving a faint smile, she politely reclaimed her hand.

"Latimer, how long have you known Ehrich?" Alain turned the subject.

"We've been friends for so long, I can't recall. And you, Alain?" Latimer looked to him.

"I've known him since I was eighteen. He taught me how to hunt and track. I believe he even showed me how to fire a gun," smiled Alain.

"Did you tell them about the assassins?" Alain asked Emma.

"Assassins?" Ralph and Latimer cried in unison.

"I don't recall you mentioning assassins," Ralph frowned.

"We took care of them," came Emma's retort.

"She held her own. My Laurette calls her Lady Death."

"Thank you, Alain," she huffed.

"How many assassins?" asked Latimer, as he and his servant exchanged looks.

"I saw three," Alain offered. "Ehrich killed two with his bare hands, and *madame* killed one protecting my beloved."

"You killed one?" Ralph's eyes grew large.

"Broadsword." The young bride patted the weapon strapped to her back. "Standard hack and slash or slice and dice," she grinned. Ralph swallowed hard. Latimer threw back his head in hearty laughter.

"No wonder Ehrich indicated she could fight like a man," he said, bowing his head in Emma's direction.

"I guess we'll see. Looks like company again!" Emma drew her sword as the others followed her gaze.

In the pale moonlight, five or six shadowy riders appeared on the roadway up ahead. Had Maurice D'Auberge found someone stupid enough to pick up the contract on Ehrich and his wife?

The others drew their weapons—Alain, Latimer, and James their pistols, while Ralph had both sword and pistol ready.

Drawing closer, they discovered the riders had not come for them but seemed occupied with a fine carriage. The riders trained guns on it. "Throw out all your money and jewels," they demanded.

Emma and company surrounded the thieves, taking them by surprise. Two shots fired, leaving one on the ground holding his arm and crying out in pain.

The remaining five seemed very willing to give up as they easily surrendered their pistols. One of the men dismounted and quickly wrapped the wounded man's arm in a handkerchief. After helping the man back onto his horse, he remounted. The faces of the robbers looked drawn and pale in the moonlight. Their eyes widened as they shuddered and took off without looking back.

"What was that?" Emma puzzled.

"They seemed more frightened of you and your sword than of us," Latimer smiled. "You should be flattered. I know of no other woman so revered."

"Revered, nothing. They were totally wigged."

"Wigged?" Latimer wrinkled his brow, confused.

"Speech from her time," Ralph explained with a faint smile.

Emma ignored them and turned to the carriage.

Etienne drove, looking handsome as ever in his Victorian dress. He flashed a smile at Emma, trying to look grateful.

Inside the carriage sat Brianna, dressed in the finery of a wealthy lady. Her forest green velvet dress clung to her luscious curves. She sported emeralds and diamonds whose brilliance rivaled the sun and moon together. A heavy woolen cloak with a satin lining enveloped her, and a dainty chapeau of lace and feathers covered her head.

Next to her sat Landru, dressed the same as Etienne in a handsome Victorian suit and cloak.

"Thank you, *mademoiselle et messieurs*. It is most kind of you to aid in our rescue," Brianna smiled as Landru stepped from the carriage and helped her out. Etienne climbed down to join them.

"I am Brianna, fiancée to one of Paris' greatest noblemen, Maurice D'Auberge."

At the mention of the name, Emma and the others exchanged looks and dismounted their horses. Ralph and the other men each bowed to the sorceress and kissed her hand.

Emma eyed the newcomers suspiciously. The would-be victims didn't look shaken or unnerved by the attempted robbery.

"I should like to reward you."

"A generous gesture but highly unnecessary. Are you in route to Paris?" Emma asked coyly.

"Why, no. My cousins and I make our way to my fiancé's *château*."

Latimer and Emma exchanged looks. What should they do now? They had only planned to fight D'Auberge and his men. And they were running out of time.

"Tonight may not be the night for a visit. Especially since you've just encountered highwaymen," said Latimer.

"I don't believe your cousins are armed," mentioned Ralph, straining to see beneath their cloaks.

"Not with weapons familiar to you. We will be safe. Not to worry. If you will not take a reward, please excuse us. We must hurry on our way. However, if you change your mind or should need anything, please don't hesitate to ask," Brianna curtsied to Emma.

"Anything, *mademoiselle*?" Emma asked, thinking ahead.

"Anything," came the reply.

"Grant me this: that you and your cousins will return to Paris instead of going to your fiancé. Please, I implore you," Emma requested in a rather ominous voice. It appeared to send a chill through Brianna, in spite of all her magick.

"I gave my word to grant anything you wished, so let it be. We will return to Paris immediately. Such urgency in your voice disturbs me. Is there something you'd like to share?" Brianna's eyes sparkled in the moonlight, making her even more ravishing than usual.

"Perhaps, when this night has ended." Latimer bowed and kissed Brianna's hand. The other men followed suit and remounted their horses. Emma smiled and bowed her head. "Thank you. Be safe."

"Wait. You have not told me your name. Nor have your men," said Brianna. "You killed one of the assassins Maurice sent. You are Ehrich's wife!"

Emma hefted the sword. "Go now, for I have granted your life once. I will not do it again." Emma sheathed the sword and remounted her horse.

As Emma and her men rode away, Landru helped the sorceress back into the carriage.

"Must we really return to Paris?" he asked as he sat next to her and closed the carriage door.

"Of course not. We will proceed as planned." She turned to Etienne, who looked in from outside. "Proceed to the *château*. There might be a bit of excitement. If this woman is bound there, so is her spouse. Ah, Death, how..."

"...morbid," finished Etienne as he sadly resumed his place as driver.

When the carriage began to move, the beautiful witch looked to Landru. "It appears Etienne is no longer amused with our sadistic pleasure. Can we still trust him?"

Landru brushed his lips against her delicate cheek. "He would do nothing I wouldn't do. Look at me, my beloved. Can you trust me?"

She turned, looked into his pleading eyes, and melted into his arms. In a moment, their lips met, hungry for each other.

~ * ~

Emma caught up with the others in time to hear their murmur of distrust for Brianna.

"Do you believe she will turn back?" asked Latimer as Emma caught up.

"Of course not. She didn't appear to be scared of the robbers or of my warning. She will arrive there in a bit."

"You have no concern?" Alain worried.

"No. We proceed as planned. If they get in the way, they become casualties," Emma answered coldly. Her urgency to aid her husband overtook her.

Alain kicked his horse to catch up. "You sound more and more like Ehrich by the minute. You have that…" his voice trailed off.

"I have what?" She wouldn't look at him.

"Coldness. Almost heartless," Ralph interjected.

"Thanks for the analysis, guys. If I need a shrink, I'll get one."

"Shrink?" Ralph questioned.

"Yeah, yeah, I'll send you a dictionary." More and more things came to her as she spoke. The usage of words and phrases, the essence of another period, another life seemed to slip into her mouth automatically. A few times she bit her tongue to keep from saying more. For a moment, she contemplated all that had happened. Before having Ehrich lead her to his dark wing while reciting "Annabelle Lee," she remembered nothing; not even her own name until he said it. Yet, slowly things came to her at selected moments, mainly during times of heightened emotions.

"Do you know Brianna?" asked Latimer, sensing her concern.

"I think Brianna's not what she appears," Emma replied slowly.

Alain and the others stared at her. Ralph shook his head in disbelief and muttered to himself.

"I hate secrets," Emma snapped suddenly at Latimer, the only one who didn't look surprised at her outburst. "Why won't you tell me how I got here and why my memory takes so long to come back?"

"The truth will be revealed shortly. Be patient," Latimer smiled. Emma shot him a frustrated look.

The others took in all they heard and wondered what Emma meant.

"Something seems wrong about the highwaymen. They didn't put up a fight and seemed surprised with the exchange of gunfire," Alain thought aloud.

"He's right. Do you think the robbery was for our benefit?" Ralph looked to Emma and Latimer.

"There have been rumors of a witch named Brianna in this area. She might be the one. I've heard of her in mystic circles. How very astute of you, M. Ralph—the robbery was staged," Latimer seemed thoughtful. "Tonight will give us more than what we've bargained for."

"I don't know anything about magic, but I can pray for God's help," remarked Emma. "And do the standard hack and slash or slice and dice, depending on the situation." She patted the sword.

"I know some magick, so with the help of the gods, we will defeat them," added Latimer.

All agreed, especially James, who never had much to say. In silence, he rode beside his master.

"Okay, let's go. No telling what has happened to Ehrich." Worried, Emma kicked her horse to go faster. The others followed suit.

CHAPTER TWENTY-TWO

The clock was striking two in the morning when Maurice received Brianna at his *château*. They greeted each other with passionate kisses and heated caresses.

Landru and Etienne left them and wandered to the men's quarters. They had become accustomed to Brianna using them when she wanted and then tossing them aside when another opportunity presented itself. Since they didn't want to attract unwanted attention, they communicated with each other by telepathy, a method used when they didn't want Brianna to hear them talk about her.

Murmuring and plotting to escape, they settled into the lounge. Derrell and several others greeted and passed them, without noticing a hint of treachery brewing.

Brianna was an opportunist. Maurice promised her many things, including the reign of France. His small-time smuggling didn't compare to the coup d'état he had planned with the reigning magistrate of Paris. All this fell into the scheme of her dark master, Dyonacalus. After all, the dark one had promised she'd rule the *"in between."* The idea of ruling anyone anywhere sounded very appealing. *"in between"* existed. It was close to saying she'd rule in hell. Very close.

This morning's *tête-à- tête* not only indulged the joys of the flesh but also gave the couple time to plot their coup. Dyonacalus had told Brianna of Ehrich, but after meeting his allies, he seemed insignificant and meant nothing to her. She couldn't comprehend how any of them could stand against her powers.

"Brianna, my exquisite gem, please understand. A number of my men are dead because of him. Ehrich has many deadly skills and works against us. Kill him!" D'Auberge insisted.

"Do it yourself," she retorted. "He is mortal, is he not?"

D'Auberge shuddered. As much as he wanted Ehrich dead, he feared even giving orders to his men to kill him.

Brianna muttered thoughtfully to herself, "Most of the magistrates have agreed to allow the trade. The next step is to assassinate President Jules Grévy. For some reason, he cannot be persuaded to permit the same."

"Are you listening? Ehrich will get in our way. Kill him!"

The beautiful Brianna turned on her heels and gave a look that withered D'Auberge.

"Silence! Your personal vendetta means nothing. Eventually, he will be removed."

In the meantime, four guards escorted Ehrich to the dungeon. They barely reached the staircase leading downward when he suddenly whirled around very quickly. Grabbing a sword from one, he took down all the men before they could blink.

Silently, he slipped into the night and melted into the shadows, creeping about, looking for more guards. So many. *What to do? Where was the broken automaton?*

Ehrich lurked just outside the window of the study where the nobleman entertained his lady.

One of D'Auberge's burly men burst into the study, out of breath as his entire body shook. "He's gone. The prisoner." He rubbed his head. "I barely got away."

Ehrich's escape unnerved D'Auberge.

Waving the sword in the air, D'Auberge stood, rambling to Brianna. "Now you know why I'm afraid. The man cannot be killed like a mortal. He's Death, I tell you! Kill him with your magick!"

Brianna glared at him. "Sit down and stop ranting! As long as we work together without fear, we will overthrow France. Now sit down and shut up!"

Where are my wife and Latimer? Wondered Ehrich. He worried that some ill had befallen them. He couldn't just leave. If they were here, they would need each other.

~ * ~

Alain led Emma and the others to the iron gate of the *château*.

Myriad trees and bushes lined the fence surrounding what seemed like endless land filled with more trees, the silhouette of a huge building lurking in the background.

Strangely enough, no one stood guard, and yet the gate remained locked.

Emma dismounted and drew Ehrich's letter from her pocket. Folding it into a funnel, she poked the corner into the lock and motioned for Alain, who poured a small bit of gunpowder into the paper funnel, filling the lock. After removing the paper, she took a strip of the precut fabric they carried to put into bottles of wine they would use as bombs and stuffed it into the hole then struck a match. The tiny flame illuminated the fabric like a miniature lamp. As the makeshift fuse burned, Emma motioned for the men to move back. A small 'poof' sounded with a tiny spark that popped open the lock, and the gate swung open.

Quietly, they tied their horses to some nearby trees and slipped through the gate, passing the bodies of two dead guards. Latimer stopped briefly to examine how they died. He nodded, as he turned to the others and whispered, "Ehrich has done the deed." Alain and Ralph exchanged looks, rubbed their own throats, and shivered.

Then Latimer repeated what he, James, and Alain would do. Since Alain had the most knowledge of the grounds, he would lead them to the men's quarters at the rear of the *château*. There, they would arm the small bombs of gunpowder encased in metal containers that they had fashioned on the way. Emma reminded them to make the fuses long enough to give themselves time to clear the area, or they'd be victims of shrapnel.

Emma took Ralph with her to find Ehrich.

For an instant, Emma's vision shifted, and the trees and night vanished. In their place sat Twanda and Doone, talking as they sat in the lobby of the hotel where they stayed. For some reason, Emma missed Ralph and longed to be with him. Doone turned to her and asked something she couldn't hear. All at once, Emma remembered being with him and Twanda when they first arrived at Studio Duchenois and called out, but the vision changed. The night and forest returned.

When they paused in the darkness from time to time to get their bearings, Emma looked at Ralph lovingly. Beneath his rigid, noble, military upbringing laid a kind, gentle, and loving man. A man she could depend on in times of need.

Even at this, her feelings turned to Ehrich, the man whose voice set her soul aglow. She had to find him.

This mélange of feelings must have also plagued Cerise. Can a woman equally love two men at the same time? Passages from the novel *Dark Tales of le Théâtre Ranier* slowly came back to her.

When Cerise heard Ehrich's sweet voice reciting poetry of love or romantic lines from a well-known play, her heart beat rapidly and she could have melted in his arms. However, Ralph's touch made her head spin and his kisses caused her to forget the world around her.

Alain asked Ralph and Emma to circle around the *château* and enter from the rear while the others headed for the men's quarters to plant the bombs. Since it appeared no one stood guard, they would have no trouble entering.

As Ralph and Emma crept closer to the back door, about six men swarmed the area. Ralph's pistol would be noisy.

The two separated while drawing their swords. Emma hefted her two-edged broadsword used best for making larger cuts, especially through bone. Ralph stood with his rapier poised to strike, also double-edged, but slimmer, used for thrusting.

The men attacked from both sides. In spite of her hatred for bloodshed, Emma swung with all of her might, striking a killing blow each time. Memories from her past training came back to her: how to hack into bone at an angle so she could pull it out quickly, ready for the next strike.

Skilled as a swordsman as well as a marksman, Ralph proved so as he thrust and parried the rapier against each attacker. Some cried out for assistance. Back to back, he and Emma stood wielding their weapons as the guards fell. From a distance, the scramble of feet rushed toward them.

As they quickly moved to enter the *château*, a ruckus arose from the men's quarters, way out past the gardens.

Emma shook her head. *Latimer and the others must be in trouble. What bad timing!*

The two sighed and headed toward the disruption, fading into the darkness.

Now Ehrich, too, heard the calamity past the gardens and headed toward his beloved.

Alain explained to Latimer and James where to set the charges around the building. However, to ensure no one escaped alive, the explosives had to be set at the four corners of the building, inside, while D'Auberge's men milled around and in and out.

Alain had agreed to enter the structure. Even if someone recognized him, no one would be suspicious of D'Auberge's nephew coming and going. None of the men knew of his dissention.

He walked in with the small bombs in his coat pocket. No one paid any attention to him, even when he went to each corner and set the bombs, lighting the fuses.

Latimer and James would give him exactly five minutes to do his part, and regardless of whether he came out or not, they would light their fuses.

This would set off the first explosion, igniting the trail of gunpowder and using the domino effect to set off the others, causing an explosive change reaction.

"What about Ehrich?" asked James with concern. "How can we be sure he won't get hurt or killed by these small bombs?"

Latimer looked away. "We don't. It's a chance we'll have to take. Ehrich will be looking for the kidnapped girls. More than likely he'll be in the *château* and not here."

The bombs going off inside and out would trap and kill anyone within range. The concussion and shrapnel would scatter as far as ten feet. Anyone unfortunate enough to be outside during the explosions would fall victim to the Molotov cocktails, the bombs made of strips of cloth stuffed into the bottles of wine and lit.

All seemed to go as planned, until Derrell met Alain as he attempted to leave the building. Their gazes locked and the fight began.

Derrell shouted, "Alain? Where've you been, you son of a dog?" Then he threw a punch. Alain ducked. His heart raced in panic. He only had seconds to get out of there. As he turned to run, Derrell grabbed him by the shoulders and spun him around for another jab to the jaw.

Etienne and Landru emerged from the lounge. Noticing the burning fuses, they bolted for the door.

Etienne shouted, "Get out, now! Hurry!" as he began pushing men toward the door. Landru pulled out his share of employees.

Looking back to the fuses, they saw them getting closer to the metal containers.

On the way out, they grabbed the two fighting men and dragged them outside to safety.

The first explosions went off with a bang then like clockwork, the others followed. Screams, shattering glass, and gunfire ripped through the night.

Emma and Ralph hit the ground at the first explosion. Remembering her warning of shrapnel, Ralph covered Emma with his body. A sharp, burning pain bore into his left shoulder. Fighting back the urge to scream, he bit his lip then asked Emma if she was hurt.

"No," she whispered. "I'm not hurt."

In the pale moonlight, they found themselves staring into each other's faces as Ralph remained on top of her. Even with the ruckus and chaos in the background and the burning pain in his shoulder, Ralph claimed her lips.

Emma tried to push him away, but his soft, warm lips made her mind spin. She put her arms around him, moving her hands up to his shoulders. He broke the kiss and winced as she touched the piece of metal embedded into his flesh.

Gently, she pushed him back and tried to grab hold of it, but she gasped as the sharp edge cut her hand. At that moment, a huge, winged like shadow blotted out the moon. Emma and Ralph flinched in unison.

"It is I, Ehrich. Are you hurt?" came a whisper.

"Ralph got hit by shrapnel. It's jammed in his shoulder. I can't get it out," replied his wife.

Ehrich knelt beside them and examined the wound. Since he wore gloves, he was able to grab the jagged piece of metal and yank it quickly straight from the other man's shoulder. Again, Ralph bit his lip to keep from screaming.

"It must be cleaned, or it will become infected," said Ehrich.

"Latimer brought some bottles of cheap wine for Molotov cocktails," Emma remembered.

"Molotov cocktails?" Ehrich puzzled.

"I'm bleeding here," Ralph reminded them.

Ehrich ripped off a strip of his own shirt and wadded it up. This he applied to the wound to absorb the blood. Then he used another strip to secure the wadded up piece.

Without warning, Ralph pushed him back, pulled his gun and aimed it straight at Ehrich. Totally stunned, Emma and Ehrich said nothing, even when the gun went off. A dead man hit the ground behind them.

"He crept up behind you, Ehrich." Ralph scrambled to get up, jamming the gun into his belt.

"You saved my life," Ehrich forced out. No one other than Emma and Latimer had ever done that.

"Let's go. The others may need our help," Ralph drew himself up to his full height and took a deep breath. Bleeding sapped his strength and weakened him.

"You could say thank you," said Emma, as she hugged her husband. Ehrich squeezed her tightly but said nothing.

Shouts and more explosions came from the men's quarters. Ehrich and the others pushed through the smoke. The dead and dying lay all around them. It looked like a battlefield, especially as the building lay in rubble and debris.

Stepping over mangled, lifeless bodies, they searched for Latimer and the others in the dim moonlight and burning remains of the structure. Through the smoke, they saw a faint silhouette waving and ran toward it.

James greeted them and led them into the gardens where Latimer and the others waited.

Shrapnel had also hit Alain, but the wound would quickly heal. His arm barely bled.

Derrell had been hit the worst. He lay on the ground gasping. Shrapnel was embedded deep into his back, one piece settled near his heart and yet another lodged in one lung. He gasped and struggled for breath.

Landru and Etienne had escaped unscathed; they knelt by Derrell trying to help him.

"Are you all right?" asked Latimer of the three.

"We are, but Ralph's been hit by shrapnel. Ehrich pulled it out, but the wound needs cleaning," Emma answered, as her gaze fell upon Derrell. "He's been hit."

"We know. He's done for. He was my uncle's right hand," Alain snarled with contempt.

In a moment, Derrell drew his last ragged breath and died. Emma stood horrified and turned away.

"We could do nothing. He was too far gone," Latimer explained, placing a comforting arm around her.

"We must hurry. Who are they?" Ehrich referred to Landru and Etienne.

"Allies, I hope," Latimer turned to the newcomers.

Emma and Ralph recognized them from the carriage they'd rescued.

"We want to help," began Etienne. "Landru and I could occupy Brianna so you can collect the girls easier."

"Brianna? If you're her cousins, why would you betray her?" questioned Ralph, holding his wounded shoulder.

"We're not her cousins. We're...more than that…" Landru hesitated to reveal their promiscuous lifestyle.

Ehrich puzzled then came the dawn. "Both of you are her lovers, aren't you?"

"When she chooses it. Tonight she has other opportunities."

"So I've heard. How do we know you can be trusted?"

"We could have let Alain and Derrell blow up in the building. Even now we tried to save his life. But alas, magick cannot interfere with the natural order of things." Etienne stood up.

From the pack he carried, Latimer removed a bottle of his cheap wine, and using more of poor Ehrich's shirt, he cleaned Ralph's wound. Then he redressed it the best he could without medicine.

A few men still lived at the rear of the *château*. Some worked as servants, but most acted as bodyguards to D'Auberge.

The majority of his men had died in the explosions at the men's quarters. And Ehrich had eliminated all the exterior guards.

Ehrich said, "I don't trust the newcomers." He had overheard D'Auberge and Brianna's plan for the coup. Volunteering to aid in the rescue did not convince him Landru and Etienne would betray her so easily.

Emma held him back to whisper her thoughts.

"I feel like they're telling the truth. Give them a chance." Noticing his hands twitching a little, she gently placed her hands on his. She knew his first reaction called for their deaths.

"Can they be trusted? They serve a witch. I've heard of how they stood with Brianna trying to extract magick from the gypsies." Ehrich looked into his wife's face. Then he gave a long sigh and replied, "They may come with us. But should they make a move against us…"

"I know, you'll snap their necks like twigs." She patted his hands and gave a lopsided smile.

Since Ehrich's plans had come together, with the addition of Landru and Etienne, the next phase was to get the girls. Ehrich told Latimer to take James and Landru with him to the stables to find and prepare the caravans then meet them at the main gate where they had entered.

Ehrich attempted to lead his wife to the rear entrance of the *château* along with Ralph, Alain, and Etienne, when out of the night several men jumped them.

With swift precision accuracy, Ehrich wrapped his hands around one man's neck. Ralph used his sword again, since he had not reloaded the pistol. Alain and Etienne met their attackers with hand-to-hand combat.

Several more joined the fray and tried to capture Ehrich, but before they could turn around, a sickening 'crack' of their necks rang out. Two were dead before they hit the ground.

Jerking around, Ehrich released his kill, and there stood Alain with two dead men at his feet.

"You saved my life," he hissed, not wanting to give in to gratitude.

Alain gave a nod and returned to the fray. Ehrich had taught him well.

"How many more, M. Ehrich? They swarm like ants. The more you kill, the more advance," Ralph remarked as he ran another man through with his rapier.

"Remember, D'Auberge has more than a hundred in his employ," he said.

Emma felled two. Yet, in the skirmish, no one noticed the shadows emerging from the darkness. With her attention on Ehrich and Ralph, she flinched and tried to cry out as a strong hand clamped over her mouth and an arm wrapped around her waist. Struggle as she did, the shadows still pulled her into darkness and carried her off to the *château*.

As Ehrich turned around for the next attacker, the man fell dead in his arms. Ralph pulled his rapier from the dead man's back.

"Once again, M. Duchenois, you have saved my life," he hissed.

"It's becoming a habit, I'm afraid." The young man gave a faint smile.

When all the attackers lay dead, Ehrich and Ralph realized Emma had vanished.

CHAPTER TWENTY-THREE

Maurice was escorting Brianna from the study when two ruffians burst in from the rear, dragging Ehrich's struggling wife into the hall near the main entrance and the study.

Brianna smiled wickedly. "Ah, Maurice, how delightful! A gift from you?" She circled the now motionless young woman. "I can think of so many ways to torture a sweet child like this."

"Remember what I said, Brianna, I granted your life once. I won't do it again." Emma's voice sounded direct and ominous. The enchantress fell silent.

D'Auberge eyed Emma suspiciously. Then he asked Brianna to wait for him upstairs. He collected the beautiful sorceress into his arms and crushed her lips with his.

"Oh, please, do I have to watch this?" Emma asked sarcastically while the wheels turned in her head.

D'Auberge broke the kiss and stared at the arrogant child. He puzzled at such blatant boldness and rudeness from one so young and female.

Brianna saw the look on his face, and she thought it best to let him handle things. After all, how much harm could a little girl do? She sashayed upstairs with visions of lovemaking and treachery in her mind.

D'Auberge motioned for the ruffians to bring the young woman into his study.

~ * ~

"Ralph, don't go charging in like that," Ehrich stopped him. So they hid in the shadows by the open door of the study.

Seeing his chance, Etienne whispered something to Ehrich, who grudgingly agreed. Etienne slipped off toward Brianna's chamber.

In the study, D'Auberge moved to the cabinet where he kept his liquor. After pouring two fingers of cognac into two snifters, he picked them up and turned to Emma, motioning for the captors to release her.

The ruffians obeyed but only took a couple of steps back.

"Cognac, mam'selle?" He offered her a snifter.

She refused. "I don't drink."

"Oh, yes, it's not proper for a lady to drink in public. But I won't tell," he persisted, holding the cognac in her face.

"I'll rephrase that. I only drink with my friends," she answered venomously.

"Did no one teach you politeness?"

No answer.

D'Auberge sat on the edge of his desk; he put down one of the snifters as he sipped the other. "Who are you? How did you get past my guards?"

"What guards?" She gave a cold, steely glare. He looked to the ruffian at his right. The burly man related brief details of the explosions and the causality count.

"You killed six of my men?" D'Auberge asked, surprised. After looking her up and down, he continued. "Tell me your name and what brings you here."

"I came for Ehrich."

At this, he put a hand to his stomach and shuddered. "You came for Ehrich. What would you say if I told you I had killed him?"

"I'd say you're a liar. Since I barged in, I should ask the questions."

139

The tough guy on her right stepped up and caught her wrist. Quickly twisting out of his hand, Emma grabbed his forearm, jerking him forward, simultaneously throwing a sharp kick to his groin.

When he doubled over in agony, she spun around and rammed an elbow into his ribs. He went down for the count.

The second man charged instantly. Waiting until she could smell his fetid breath, she quickly sidestepped, grabbed one of his extended arms and led him past her, crashing him into the nearby wall. In a moment, he recovered and turned on her again, growling like a wild animal.

Emma looked around for a blunt object. When he came close enough for her to see the color of his eyes, she sidestepped again, grabbed a large vase from a nearby table and slammed him in the head with it.

As the man went down, D'Auberge screamed for the loss of his priceless vase while Emma kicked her attacker in the head. He laid before her quiet and still. Scanning the room for her weapon, she noted the broadsword on the floor near the first man downed.

D'Auberge went for the pistol in his belt; by that time Emma had taken a dive, rolled to the sword, and grabbed it on the way up. Emma hefted the sword as D'Auberge aimed his pistol.

"You have quick reflexes, woman. That surprises me. I shall enjoy taming you."

"Taming me? Get real. I came for Ehrich and the girls."

"Oh, the girls. That's it. You're an opportunist, as I am."

"I came to rescue them, not sell them."

At that moment, Ehrich looked into the study, with Ralph aiming a gun at D'Auberge.

"Are you well, my beloved?" Ehrich smirked beneath his fedora.

"I'm good."

"Maurice needs to sign the contract to release me as his partner, and he owes me 30,000 francs to buy out my share. He also owes Alain 20,000 francs for the last journey before he left his employ." Ehrich moved into the room, with Ralph in tow. Alain braced himself in the doorway.

"That's it, you've brought reinforcements. Clever, very clever." D'Auberge kept the gun trained on Emma. His hands shook now, and so did his legs.

"My dear Ehrich, allow me." Emma indicated she could handle D'Auberge. Ehrich bowed and motioned for Ralph to step back.

Before D'Auberge knew what happened, Emma whipped the pistol out of his hand with the tip of the blade. Then she took a fighting stance, the sword poised a little above her left ear.

"You're both mad. Murderers!" he shouted fearfully.

"And you're not? Get real!"

"Where did you come from?" D'Auberge puzzled at the boldness and temperament of the young woman, which seemed so out of place in his society.

"Again with the questions? Don't you ever shut up? I'm holding the sword. Sign the stinking papers and pay up!" Emma frowned, itching to get rid of the coward.

In the meantime, three of D'Auberge's remaining men, armed with guns, quietly crept up from behind Ehrich, Alain and Ralph.

In the stables, Latimer and James readied the caravans for the trip. Landru helped but stopped suddenly when Etienne sent him a message by telepathy.

Etienne relayed his and Brianna's whereabouts. He had no plan but knew the witch hungered for power and would try to destroy the world if she couldn't obtain it.

Landru thought quickly. Certainly, they had no qualm with Ehrich and his band. Nor did they really want a *coup d'état*. But Brianna could not be easily deceived, nor easily persuaded, especially since she did her master's bidding. What to do?

As Landru rounded the corner to another stall, he gasped and stumbled back. Latimer and James rushed to him, only to find the man wide-eyed, pointing, and speechless. They followed his gaze.

There in the far corner of the stall, camouflaged with hay, slumped Ehrich's automaton, motionless and quiet. Latimer moved to it and brushed off the hay. He marveled at the workmanship. After careful examination, he found a small key in its breast pocket. Upon removing the key, he looked for a place of insertion. Finally, he found it in the machine's belly button. He inserted the key and twisted it until it could go no further. The mechanical creature straightened up immediately and turned to the others.

"Quite real, isn't he?" Latimer laughed. Finally, the others did as well.

He had an idea, but they had to hurry. As Latimer moved from the stall, the mechanical Ehrich followed with ominous, wooden steps.

In the study, Emma stood facing Maurice D'Auberge with her sword still pointed towards him.

Ehrich, Alain, and Ralph held their attention on her, snickering until the creak of the floor behind caught their attention. They jerked around to be met by three sword-wielding men.

Ehrich tried to eliminate his opponent, but his side bled so much it sapped his strength. Weakened, he collapsed on the floor with the man on top of him, pushing the sword to his throat. Never had anyone had him at such a disadvantage. At that moment, his life flashed before his eyes, beginning with the time he heard the prophecy of Shylah, his first meeting with Serena, the birth of their son, seeing their lifeless bodies lying in a pool of blood, his attack on the soldiers, Cerise performing on stage, and finally being held in the arms of his beloved Emma.

Alain jumped and sidestepped the advancing swordsman, but his judgment wasn't precise, as the blade slit his arm open. Wincing, he grabbed his wound.

Ralph moved about with agility, using his rapier to block the enemy's sword. For the brief moment while he and the other man crossed their sword hands, pushing hard against each other, Ralph looked to Ehrich on the floor with his attacker pushing the sword to his throat. But his attention soon went back to his own fight as his attacker pushed him back hard, tangling their swords. At this, the man whipped the sword out of Ralph's hand. Like Alain, he appeared defenseless as he backed into a wall, the point of a sword at his chest.

Meanwhile, Emma still faced down D'Auberge.

No matter the rumors, D'Auberge had never been a brave man. As a pirate captain, he won his battles by trickery, lying, and cheating.

"Sign the contract and pay my Ehrich and Alain what you owe them. Do it willingly or not, makes no difference," she spoke with a cold, hard voice. "If you haven't noticed, you don't have many men left. I've killed six tonight and two of your assassins, not to mention everyone in the men's quarters. You would only be one more notch on my hilt."

Suddenly, he called out. "Jean, Antoine, and whoever else is out there? Have you killed them?"

The sounds of a struggle and some grunting were the only reply.

Slowly, he straightened himself, and an evil smile spread across his face as he moved slowly around the desk as if to sit down. With lightning speed, he snatched up the rapier, vaulted over the bureau, and charged Emma.

D'Auberge used all of his best fencing moves, but Emma either sidestepped or blocked him with her sword. After about five minutes of this and hearing nothing from her men, her heart began to race; small pearls of perspiration beaded on her forehead.

"Ehrich! Ehrich, are…are you all right?" Emma called out with a faltering voice.

No answer.

Trying not to show her terror, Emma quickly wiped away the sweat streaming down her face. The silence was anything but comforting. Would this be her end? To die at the hand of man without morals or conscience?

"Sign the stinking papers. I'm tired of your games." In what could turn out to be a final act of bravery, she lunged toward him, but he sidestepped. All confidence fled her. D'Auberge tangled her sword and flipped it out of her hand. She couldn't believe she had allowed this. It became harder to breathe as fear swelled up in her while D'Auberge backed Emma against the wall with the tip of his sword.

Outside the study, Ehrich lay on the floor, still pushing the sword away as it began to draw blood.

Hearing his wife call out to him stirred what little strength he had as he pushed back hard, cutting his hands in the process. Ralph wanted to intervene or call out, but the tip of the sword to his chest stopped him.

Alain and his opponent danced around the room until Alain finally caught the man off guard and disarmed him, pitting the two against each other using only their hands.

From inside, they heard Emma screaming, "Ehrich!" This startled the man holding a sword to Ralph's chest. Distracted, he looked in the direction of the study. Ralph took the opportunity and kicked him then moved away from the sword and finally gave him a right cross to the jaw. The man went down.

Also hearing Emma's cry, the man trying to kill Ehrich looked up long enough for Ehrich to push him off, sending the sword clanging to the floor. Quickly, Ralph moved to the weakened Ehrich. When the enemy tried to recover, Ralph grabbed the sword and ran him through.

Gaining the upper hand against his assailant, Alain managed to roll him over, putting his weight on top. Then he grabbed the man's head and twisted quick and hard, snapping his neck. Quickly, he got up and moved to the gasping Ehrich where Ralph was starting to tend to his wounds.

In the study, D'Auberge laughed at Emma, who was still calling out for her husband.

"Where is he?" D'Auberge taunted. "Perhaps he's gone home. We've worn him out. Now you are mine!" Just as he advanced toward Emma, a voice interrupted the scene.

"You never could fight fair, could you, Maurice?" Ehrich sputtered, standing in the doorway as he held a handkerchief to his throat.

Hearing that voice, D'Auberge's head jerked toward the door.

"Still alive?" he gasped.

Emma lunged for her sword. Jumping back, the cowardly man dropped his weapon. Ehrich moved to the desk and opened a drawer. After pulling out a metal box, he opened it. Then he removed a bunch of papers and spread them across the desktop.

Emma forced D'Auberge to the desk as Ehrich stepped back.

"Sign the paper and end our partnership," came the order.

With a quivering hand, D'Auberge signed the contract, releasing Ehrich from his business ties. Emma tapped the tip of the sword on the desktop as a reminder. Even with his life at stake, D'Auberge still wanted to cling to the almighty franc.

He reached into the metal box. Money, money, money! Paper currency filled the rest of the metal box. Ehrich counted out exactly what was owed to Alain and him then he slammed the lid down on the rest.

"I only want what's mine." Ehrich moved away from the desk, leaving the shaken man where he was.

D'Auberge glared at his nephew peering into the room, holding his wounded arm.

As he and wife reached the door, Ehrich looked back menacingly at his former partner and warned, "If you follow us, I *will* kill you."

Emma added, "What's more, I'll let him." Then they both left the sniveling coward shaking and nearly hyperventilating, calling for his menservants.

Swallowing a hastily mixed potion to assume the appearance of D'Auberge, Etienne dressed in a smoking jacket and trousers and chatted with Brianna in the bedroom upstairs.

"I have the most delicious wine for you to taste, my dear," said the fake D'Auberge as he checked the label of the wine bottle in hand. Carefully, he sniffed the uncorked bottle then he turned his back to her and drew a small vial from his sleeve. Uncapping it quickly, he dumped the fine, white power into a glass. Then he poured out the wine, filling it halfway. After filling another glass half full, he set down the bottle and picked up the two glasses, gently moving the drugged one to make sure the powder dissolved.

"A new wine? You know I love tasting different types of wine." Brianna smiled, accepting the glass. Before tasting, she sniffed it and then drank it down like water.

Just as the commotion started downstairs, Brianna passed out, with Etienne catching her and laying her gently on the bed.

Meeting Emma and the others as they approached D'Auberge's room, Etienne said,

"Don't worry about Brianna. She'll be out for a while. I've seen to it."

Ehrich looked upstairs and said, "I believe the girls' room is on the second floor.

Etienne stated, "I've drugged the new guards to make the rescue easier. Go quickly. Landru and I will attend to the sorceress should she awaken."

"How can we thank you?" asked Emma, clinging to her husband's strong arm.

Etienne smiled. Emma moved on with her husband and the others to find the girls.

Quietly, Ehrich removed the sleeping guards who had fallen in front of the door and tried the doorknob.

Locked.

Softly, he called through the door for the girls to move back. A rustle and murmur of high-pitched voices grew distant.

With one swift, deliberate kick, the door caved in. The girls screamed and moved toward the walls. Some tried to run past Ehrich. Catching them, Emma pulled them back, speaking quietly. "No one will hurt you. We're here to help."

Emma and Ehrich ushered the girls into the corridor as Alain and Ralph led the way to the staircase.

Landru met them at the foot by the main entrance, "Latimer and James are waiting at the main gate with the caravans."

"You're welcome to go with us," invited Emma.

"Thank you, but no. The sorceress will never allow us freedom as long as she can use her powers."

With all the magick he could muster, the demon, Dyonacalus lifted the veil of sleep from Brianna, causing her to stir. In moments she began to rally. She felt groggy but tried to force herself awake. Keeping watch at her bedside, Etienne began to panic.

Quickly, he opened the door and ran to the head of the stairs. He could see Landru speaking to Emma and the others.

"Landru, hurry. She waking up," softly called Etienne. "I can hear D'Auberge moaning and howling in the study."

Landru bade them farewell and hastened to his friend and confidant. Emma, Ehrich and the others hurried the girls out into the night.

Just as Landru had said, Latimer and James waited outside the main gate, driving two caravans with the reins of their horses tied to the rear of each.

The rescuers only hesitated a moment at the gut-wrenching sounds before mounting the caravans and heading out. The girls had to be taken away quickly. If they went back, they might get caught. Landru and Etienne must have known what they were doing when they agreed to stay behind.

Upstairs in the *château*, Brianna, almost fully awake, staggered about, holding onto a chair or wall.

"D'Auberge! Where are you?" Called Brianna.

Etienne returned to the room, appearing like the nobleman. The ruckus downstairs rang throughout the castle. The automaton tore the place apart. D'Auberge screamed, scrambling to get out of its way.

Brianna tried to leave. Etienne blocked the door.

"My dear Brianna, darling, please take some more wine," said Etienne in the guise of D'Auberge, pushing another glass of nectar in her face. Shaking her head, she shoved him aside and flung open the door. Seeing the automaton, she waved her hand, slamming it into the wall.

As the wheels turned in his mind, Landru hid in the shadows, trying to think how he could stop her. Even though he and Etienne had become seasoned warlocks, their powers had never exceeded hers.

Brianna wanted to explore the *château* and the grounds more than she wanted to examine the mechanical vandal. With a gesture of upward arms, she changed into a gauzy, ebony-colored gown with a plunging neckline. Then she chanted an incantation and disappeared.

The caravans lumbered down the path away from the chaos at the *château*. Ehrich and his wife were in one wagon, while Latimer and James drove the other. Ralph and Alain rode their horses, while the other horses followed with their reins tied to the wagons.

Trying to settle their nerves from the battle, some time passed before anyone spoke. Emma grew so tired she closed her eyes and laid her head on her husband's arm as he steered the horses.

Dawn arrived as baby rays of sun peered over distant hills and tenderly caressed the trees.

Finally, Ehrich called back to Ralph, asking if he still bled. Taken aback at his concern, Ralph expressed his gratitude for asking and assured him he bled at a minimum. Before they had left, Latimer had found some herbs on the *château* grounds, which he had used to complete its dressing.

"I understand Alain and Ralph saved your life in the battle," Latimer stated with a wry smile as he glanced at Ehrich.

No comment.

Emma's ears perked up.

"I saved his life twice," added Ralph, who also gave a wry smile.

Emma lifted her head and tugged at her man's cloak. "Did you thank them? Ehrich, did you thank them?"

Then Emma whispered something which sounded like "I'm getting a headache," making him say his thanks so quickly it nearly sounded incoherent.

Alain chuckled. "Did you say something, Ehrich? Sounded like thank you."

Emma nudged Ehrich, who muttered, "Yes, Alain, thank you for saving my life."

"And me?" ask Ralph with a grin.

"Yes, Ralph, thank you for saving my life, twice," Ehrich answered gruffly. "However, this does not make us friends."

"Of course not."

"I still don't like you," Ehrich stated.

"Nor I you, sir." Ralph chuckled.

Ehrich listened carefully to the sounds around them as the others engaged in idle chatter. Latimer explained how he had animated the automaton to give them more time to escape.

The girls relaxed and drifted off to sleep.

"Do you think D'Auberge will follow us?" asked Emma in a whisper.

"Yes, he will follow us if he has any men left." Her husband put an arm around her and gave a squeeze. "In fact, he should have showed up by now. I'm going to backtrack a ways."

"No, Ehrich. I'm scared for you." She slipped both arms around him. "How is your wound?" Gingerly, Emma fingered the bandages through his tattered shirt.

"I believe you'd say, I'm good. Just tired. Not bleeding. I can still use my hands."

"Are you smiling under that hat?"

"Of course not."

With one last squeeze, he handed her the reins and motioned for Ralph. So as not to disturb the girls, he whispered his plan and asked him to pass it on to the others.

Then Ehrich jumped from the slow-moving caravan and melted into the sleepy shadows of daybreak.

Ralph relayed Ehrich's message to the others. Latimer looked behind them. Ehrich had vanished from view. The road behind looked clear and calm; maybe too calm.

Because he felt a little uneasy, Latimer handed the reins to his servant and checked his pistol. Ralph and Alain followed suite.

With the caravans being so large, they took the same road they had taken to reach the *château*.

The main road spread far and wide, making them and the wagons obvious targets.

A thicket of bushes edged the road with the sun fully awake, smiling through the foliage.

A clump of trees loomed up ahead, with the silhouette of a man standing under its lower branches. Latimer motioned for James to steer the caravan away from the trees, but it was too late. Maurice D'Auberge popped out in front of them, a pistol in each hand.

The caravans came to an abrupt halt. Aiming the guns directly at Emma and Latimer, he stood too close to miss.

"At last, little demon girl, I have you. How dare you challenge me! I am the most feared of the seven seas. I am Maurice D'Auberge!" shouted the crazed nobleman with his hand and leg wrapped in blood-soaked bandages. The pistols quivered as he tried to steady his hands.

"What kept you?" Emma piped up with sarcasm. Latimer caught her eye and shook his head. Taunting the insane was not wise, especially with loaded pistols aimed at your heart.

"I will teach you some manners, little girl, after you watch your friends die."

"You presume to kill us alone? You will have to reload after two shots," Alain smirked.

"I'm not alone. I brought four of my best men with me," justified D'Auberge. He appeared to want to look around but didn't want to turn away from his targets.

"What men?" Emma scanned the area.

D'Auberge broke into a nervous sweat..

Instead of looking around, he called out to each one.

No answer.

Not only did his hands shake but also his legs. He had definitely signed his death warrant when he defied Ehrich de Natois.

"I was fairly certain my husband said he'd kill you if you followed us," Emma gave a knowing look. She and the others saw a dark shadow jump down behind the terrified man.

"Y…y…you're his wife? *Mon Dieu*! *Le Mort a une femme*!" he cried. At that moment, two strong hands clenched around his throat. He dropped the guns and clawed desperately to remove the vice-like fingers which crushed his esophagus.

"Yes, Death has a wife," grimaced Ehrich. In seconds, they heard a gasp and a sickening crack. D'Auberge fell limp. Ehrich loosened his grip, and the body hit the ground with a gruesome thud.

"Ehrich, are you hurt?" asked Latimer as Emma leaped off the wagon and ran to him.

"I'm good," he chuckled softly, holding his wife close.

"And the men who came with him?" Ralph asked looking about.

"I have done the deed on all of them," rang the deadly reply. Ehrich resumed his place as the driver, next to his bride. Taking the reins, he gently flicked them and the journey continued.

~ * ~

Amid the ruins of the *château* grounds, the gorgeous Brianna milled through the debris, surveying death and destruction. She threw back her head and let out an ear-piercing, earth-shattering shriek. Dyonacalus would certainly punish, if not kill her for failing him; even one failure might be fatal. She could try to secure France with magick alone, but she still needed mortal means to move things along, to command, to induce mortals to worship her and the demon. Power was at its core.

Hysterically she screamed for Maurice D'Auberge. When no answer came, she teleported herself back to the *château*, where she searched the study.

Landru and Etienne would not approach her in this state of mind. Instead, with all the magick they possessed, they reanimated the automaton.

Just as Brianna discovered the bloodstains on the carpet, the automaton silently rolled up behind her. Like a streak of lightning, the metallic hands caressed her delicate neck and caught her off guard. Frantically, she clawed at the iron grip charged with some of the most powerful magick in history. Etienne and Landru drained her power through the hands of the automaton.

Brianna shuddered involuntarily as her eyes rolled back in her head. Soon, blackness engulfed her, and she lost consciousness. Landru and Etienne entered the study as the automaton loosened its grip and it, too, collapsed on to the floor. From unseen realms, mournful cries of defeat echoed throughout the room as the body hit the floor.

CHAPTER TWENTY-FOUR

As Ehrich and his group rolled into Paris, the clock struck early afternoon. They left Alain at the theater where he found Laurette.

The only place that could accommodate seven little girls was Latimer's flat. So Ehrich left Latimer and James with the task of looking out for them and giving them temporary living quarters.

Latimer brought Ralph and Ehrich into the apartment so he could attend their wounds properly. As Emma washed and dressed his wound, Ehrich watched poor, tired Latimer fumble with cleaning Ralph's injured shoulder.

More of the Chinese powder completely stopped Ehrich's bleeding.

"Emma, attend to Ralph. Latimer is not a very good nurse," Ehrich whispered.

She hesitated.

Lifting the hat just a bit, Emma kissed Ehrich, who eagerly claimed her lips. "I love you, Emma. I'm glad you're here," he said, holding her to him for a moment.

"I love you, too, Ehrich." She didn't want to go, but he pushed her toward Latimer and Ralph.

Gently, Emma offered to take the cloth and finish cleaning blood from the deep gash in Ralph's shoulder. Happily, Latimer relinquished his duty.

"Ehrich, why do you allow her to attend the young Duchenois? You know he's..." started Latimer, but Ehrich cut him off.

"Latimer, I know he has fallen in love with her, but I trust my wife, and he is growing on me. He did save my life twice. You know he didn't have to. He could have let me die or killed me himself. By the way, how do you know how he feels?" Ehrich looked his old friend in the eye.

Latimer just smiled and said nothing.

"Tell me the truth. You're hiding something," Ehrich prodded.

"Remember Emma and Ralph still need to go to the mirror in Cerise's dressing room. Then all of your questions will be answered," Latimer reminded.

That's right. He'd forgotten.

"Thank you for saving me and my husband," Emma murmured to Ralph as she finished cleaning the wound and began to apply the salve and bandages.

"I would do anything for you, Emma. Anything. I know some sort of enchantment brought you here and makes me have feelings for you, but I can't help it…" his voice trailed off.

"Ralph. It's okay. I understand. But we must return to the mirror. We've neglected that. You need Cerise."

Coming over to check Emma's progress with the bandages, Latimer smiled and patted Ralph on the shoulder. "Fighting beside you tonight was a privilege. We work well together, but remember the mirror. You and Emma must return to the mirror in Cerise's dressing room."

"You are right. Emma keeps reminding me of Cerise. I can't imagine why I keep forgetting," Ralph hung his head, ashamed he only thought of Emma.

"This I will tell you: if you do not go, both of you will forget Cerise for good," Latimer ticked a look from Emma to Ralph.

"What? How so?" Ralph frowned.

"All I can say is that it is urgent you do so. Brianna and Maurice D'Auberge have already caused enough delay." Latimer grew tense.

Ehrich moved closer. "What was this with the witch? Maurice always had a streak of treachery, but I never thought he'd form an alliance against

Paris. I overheard them discussing a coup and something the witch worshipped."

Latimer shivered and drained of color. "The demon," he gasped.

Ralph and Emma puzzled. "The what?" Ehrich grabbed his friend's arm and spun him around. "Did you say demon?"

"Listen to me, all of you. You can rest a while, but before nightfall Emma and Ralph must go to the mirror. Ehrich, no more questions and don't discuss what Brianna worshipped. When people speak of evil too much, it comes for them." Again Latimer shuddered. The others exchanged looks.

Ehrich had never seen Latimer so upset. He thought he understood about his wife and Ralph going to the mirror but what about this demon? Not being a religious man, he gave no thought to heaven, let alone demons.

Looking to Emma, Ehrich bowed his head. Realizing he wanted her to say nothing and finish bandaging Ralph's wound, she returned the bow.

The bandages secured, Ralph put on his bloodstained shirt and moved to Ehrich and apologized. "I take back all of the evil things I've said. You have my sincere apologies, *monsieur*." He bowed graciously.

Taken aback, Ehrich frowned. *Ralph apologized? Not so.* Had he dreamt it? His entire life felt like a sweet dream since his beloved wife had come to him. Maybe he still dreamed; if so, he never wanted to wake up.

Hesitating a moment, he stared at Ralph in surprise. Then he accepted the apology by returning the bow.

"This still doesn't make us friends," Ehrich retorted. "I'm just accepting your apology."

"Of course. I understand."

"Ehrich!" Emma shot him a look.

"What? I accepted his apology." Emma smiled at him. Old habits die hard. At least they didn't go at each other's throats; or rather, Ehrich didn't go after poor Ralph's throat.

Ralph Duchenois departed to his *château* while Ehrich and Emma returned to the dark wing, leaving Latimer to his concerns and James in good spirits.

155

Ehrich felt tired but not as tired as one would think. How invigorating. It had been a long time since he'd engaged in such a battle—and with allies. He'd never had allies before.

"What did Latimer mean about Brianna and the demon?" Emma asked.

"I'm not sure, but something doesn't feel right. I am not sure if I believe in demons, but perhaps all this nonsense will end once you and Ralph return to the mirror. Latimer seems consumed with this, and I don't know why. He'd never been cryptic before, so I don't know what's different now." Ehrich slipped into bed next to her.

Emma cuddled with her husband and soon fell asleep.

So, for a long time, he watched the sleeping beauty lying in his arms. Each movement of the rising and falling of her breast excited him.

Gently he nuzzled her, kissing her tenderly. Even half asleep, Emma returned his kisses. Once again, she surrendered to the man she loved. Their love had indeed become eternal.

Unbeknownst to Ehrich and Emma, dark clouds formed in the mirror attached to the dresser adjacent the bed. Angry, red eyes appeared through the clouds, glaring down at the couple with hatred.

CHAPTER TWENTY-FIVE

At noon the next day, Emma and Ralph opened the door of Cerise's dressing room. All seemed quiet. They entered and closed the door behind them then moved to the full-length mirror. At the moment, the glass showed their reflections and nothing else.

Ralph and Emma exchanged looks. "What is supposed to happen?" he wondered.

Emma shrugged.

Suddenly, roiling white clouds appeared in the mirror then parted. Twanda stared back at them with Doone and Cerise behind her.

"Where have you been? We've been coming here every day at noon," Twanda asked. "Are you guys okay?"

"Yes, we're fine. Sorry we worried you," Emma replied, trying to hide the tremor in her voice.

~ * ~

At the same moment, somewhere away from the theater in the semidarkness of a laboratory, the silhouette of a tall, slim man moved about. Jars of herbs and minerals lined the shelves braced against one wall. Musty, ancient tomes cluttered another group of shelves, facing the jars. Minimal light emanated from the two candles sitting at both ends of a long table cluttered with opened jars of odd-smelling powders and liquids.

A full-length mirror stood in the far corner of the room, between the books and dried herbs. Two other such mirrors lay scattered about the room to form a triangle with the first.

In one, the images of Emma and Ralph stepped forward. In another, Cerise, with Twanda and Doone at her side, moved into view.

"Ancient gods, hear my plea," murmured the man. "Bring forth what is meant to be. Words of a seer foretold, of two intertwining destinies." He hurled a bottle of potion at each looking glass.

In a moment, smoke seeped from all the mirrors and fogged up the room, making the spellcaster splutter and cough. When the smoke dispersed, he lay on the floor, exhausted and half-conscious. Before actually passing out, he saw Emma and Ralph appear in one mirror then disappear. Cerise did not move. *Where had Emma and Ralph gone?*

~ * ~

After the haze dissipated, Emma and Ralph found themselves outside, lying on the ground. Confusion hit them head-on when they looked about, the gloom unfolding before them. The entire world looked gray. Clouds overcast the sky, blocking out even the tiniest ray of sunlight. Gaunt, barren trees surrounded the beaten path of dirt and rocks from which they arose. Silence hung so heavy, they could hear the rhythmic beat of their hearts. No birds chirped, no animals stirred; there wasn't even a breeze.

Clouds muddled Emma's mind. She didn't belong in this gray world. Images of Twanda and Ehrich wandered back to mind, but their names and how they figured into her life escaped her.

Ralph turned to Emma. "Are you all right?"

"I think so," she replied. "Do I know you?" asked Emma.

His eyes widened and he shook his head. "I don't know. I think so." For a fleeting moment, he felt like leaning in for a kiss but didn't. "Who are you?"

"Maybe I hit my head, because I don't know that either. And you?" Ralph rubbed his head.

Emma shrugged. "Can't remember. What's going on? Where are we? You look familiar." As Emma moved her hand to straighten her dress, Ralph caught sight of the gold band.

"You're wearing a wedding ring. Are you and I...?" he started.

"Married?" Emma finished. For a moment, they both stared at the ring. *Why would we be together if we were not married?*

Ralph called out into the abandoned woods. "Who's there? Show yourself."

No answer.

He and Emma exchanged looks. Again Ralph called out, this time a little louder.

Silence.

Ralph shuddered at the hazy atmosphere. Something rustled in the ashen bushes from a distance. A small pool of water stood nearby. They looked at each other. The rustle grew louder and closer.

Ralph couldn't stand the suspense any longer, so he grabbed Emma by the hand and pulled her down the path, away from the sound. Faster and faster they ran. The rustle behind them turned into pounding footsteps, racing to catch them.

Nowhere to hide.

The barren trees melted away into ash, and a bright spot opened before them. The footsteps came faster and closer. Once again, Ralph and Emma debated whether to stay in one spot or go forward through the light.

The light? With a horrible sense of realization, Emma swallowed hard.

The footsteps ceased. Ralph didn't want to turn around.

Ralph tried to move toward the light, but Emma pulled him back. As he turned to her, he saw the owner of the footsteps.

In a dark cloak and Victorian dress stood a man. He stretched forth his hand toward Emma. An air of command and self-assurance radiated from the stranger, and his ruggedly handsome features could certainly tempt any woman. Ralph looked to the bright spot and pulled Emma backward, but she protested.

Looking to the stranger, Emma asked, "Who are you? What do you want?"

No answer.

The stranger just stood with outstretched hand, beckoning to her. The bright spot began to dim and waiver. Ralph urged her toward it again, but still she refused. The stranger moved a step closer, still reaching for her. Gradually the bright spot grew dim. When it vanished, the ground quaked and the trees swayed. Emma and Ralph embraced each other to keep from toppling to the ground, but the other man stood unshaken, as though the tremor did not affect him.

When the shaking subsided, Ralph noticed a cottage in the distance, beyond where the bright spot had opened. This time, Emma moved with him and quickly put space between them and the beckoning figure, who did not follow.

Upon reaching the cottage, they found it void of human life but filled with furniture, food on the table and a blazing fire in the fireplace. Quickly they entered and barred the door and windows. For some reason, they couldn't tell day from night. As gray as the sky and world looked, it could be either one.

"Why are we running?" Ralph asked. "Shouldn't we find out who the man is?"

"No, he frightens me." Emma cringed and huddled in the corner of the room.

Emma didn't know if she felt completely safe, but not seeing the stranger or peculiar lights, did calm her down.

"Are we dead?" Emma looked Ralph in the eye. Taken aback, the poor man could say nothing.

"You would know better than I, since it appears you time travel," he replied, hoping she'd understand. Why he said it, he didn't know. Did she travel from one period of time to another by means of a mirror?

A knock at the door broke her train of thought. It persisted and started to move from the door to the window then to the walls.

Ralph and Emma moved about the room away from the knocking. When it moved, they moved.

Finally, Ralph called out, "Who are you? What do you want?"

No answer.

The knocking persisted, again moving around the cottage, knocking on the walls then finally on the roof.

Huddled together, they tried to ignore the knocking.

CHAPTER TWENTY-SIX

In the dimness of a room filled with mirrors, herbs, and books, a silhouette rallied to consciousness and slowly scrambled to his feet. Shaking his head as if to clear his mind, he recalled the mishap as he looked from one darkened mirror to the other. He had mixed the potions properly; this he knew for sure as he removed a well-worn book from the shelves and reviewed selected pages. The instructions called for seven potion bottles, and he had used seven.

As he reviewed the spell, the terrible truth hit him hard. Magick of this magnitude called for two incantations instead of one. First, to call forth the powers and the other to give clear directions, binding what lurks between dimensions, what some texts called the *"in between."* Some religions preferred the word "purgatory."

The old conjuror cursed himself for his folly. In the name of the gods, how could he have been so stupid and careless? Anyone could mix potions, but finding the correct ingredients became the difficult task. With these incantations, the contents of the potion had to be exact, no substitutions. The last two batches had taken quite some time to gather, some to grind and mix, then boil and bottle. Generally, any type of bottle would do, but not in this case. This spell called for special bottles imported from Egypt, since the high priestess of Amon Ra had woven certain magicks into the glass before forming the bottles. At least, that was the justification for their high cost.

Whether Emma and Ralph lived or not, he didn't know. He hoped he could at least return them to their original plane of existence, even if he couldn't do what he had intended.

~ * ~

The knock persisted, moving along the cottage roof. Even with all the strange goings on, Ralph felt a warm tingle of desire for the young woman in his arms. Truly, he only meant to comfort and protect her, but the feel of her soft curves next to him carried his mind away to more pleasurable, intimate matters. For a moment, he nearly forgot the persistent knock as the need to caress her face and hair demanded his full attention. His hand moved to her flawless face, but then suddenly the knock changed directions.

The floor vibrated with the incessant knocking, breaking the spell of desire. Did a cellar lie beneath the floor? The two moved backwards away from the knocking. All at once, the knocking moved back to the door.

Noticing a peephole in the door, Ralph felt the urge to see who or what wanted to come in. Emma pulled him back, but he motioned for her to remain in the corner while he ventured a look. Gingerly, he stepped toward the door. The knock persisted.

Another portal appeared like a door in the center of the room.

By now Ralph had reached the peephole, and with much hesitation and trepidation, he peeked through it. In seconds he jumped back in horror, jamming his knuckles between his teeth to keep from crying out. His face distorted in fear and anguish while his body shook vigorously.

As she moved toward the portal, Ralph tried to speak, but the words caught in his throat, so he followed her. A flash of light struck the two, and they vanished as the cottage door caved in under the continued assault of knocking.

In a dimly lit tunnel Ralph held Emma as they braced their backs against a wall that echoed with howling and screeching.

Both sides of the tunnel felt solid, as did the ground, but in the hazy, surreal light everything looked transparent. Ralph helped his young companion to her feet.

"Where are we?" questioned Emma.

As they moved through the tunnel, Emma's mind recalled misty memories of forgotten tales describing spirits caught between life and death, trapped between heaven and hell.

They moved along when two transparent females emerged from the dimness coming toward them. The women, dressed as seventeenth-century barmaids, wept and wailed.

The tall, thin woman cried and complained. "It was all my fault he's gone. Why, oh why did he have to leave me? I loved him so much. He didn't have to go to war. Oh, Paul, can you hear me? Now we can be together."

The short, heavyset woman moaned and screamed out. "I don't belong here. There's been a mistake. I'm too young. It's not my time. What will little Marie and Jean do without me? I need to go home. I don't belong here."

When Ralph stopped them and asked where they were, the women shrieked and wailed, saying they'd died too soon and life didn't seem fair.

As the mourning women went on their way, Ralph's face drained of color. He declared that they now walked the path between life and death.

Emma stared Ralph in the eye and asked, "Are we dead? If we walk the path between life and death, then this must be purgatory…"

"No!" he cut her off. "We are not dead and certainly not in purgatory. I seem to recall a mirror, and I believe it made something happen, but we are not dead." His words seemed final and resolute, but not convincing.

Then he thought about where they had been. The ashen sky and barren trees could have been hell. Certainly they didn't want to follow the transparent, grieving women, so they continued in the opposite direction. Several shadowy figures flew past, headed in the direction of the grieving women. Weeping and wailing echoed throughout the tunnel while something up ahead lumbered toward them, shaking the ground with each thumping step. The stale air around them smelled like a match had been struck.

Sulfur.

"What's coming toward us now?" Emma hugged Ralph's arm.

"I don't know, but whatever it is must be enormous," Ralph whispered back.

The two moved against the wall, back into the shadows.

The musty, stifling stench of smoke and sulfur, sometimes called brimstone, permeated the air. Emma buried her face in the young nobleman's chest.

At that instant, an extremely tall, sinewy creature moved into view. Its face appeared human-like in a distorted, leathery way with short horns on its head. From the waist up it looked like a man. Below the waist it had the hind legs of a goat and bore cloven hooves. Its orbs glowed like red iridescent embers. Ralph closed his eyes at the sight as he shielded the young woman in his arms. The sinewy beast lumbered past them into the next passageway.

A moment later, two young rowdies dressed like thieves and pickpockets from a Dickens novel burst into view, and they halted at the sight of Ralph protecting his female companion.

"What 'ey?" cried the tallest one in a cockney accent. "Yer 'eaded the wrong way. All the dead 'ave to follow 'im, the beast."

"There's been a mistake. We're not dead," insisted Ralph. The tall rowdy moved closer.

"They all say that, guv'nor. But if yer 'ere, yer dead. Just like us." Then he and his friend burst out laughing as they grabbed Ralph and Emma and tried to force them to go with them.

Both Ralph and Emma kicked and fought the young rowdies. From a distance, the howling and wailing continued and moved closer as the fight ensued.

"Even if we were dead, why do you think we belong to the beast?" screamed Emma. The rowdies stopped short and exchanged looks with one another.

"All the dead belong to 'im," declared the short, stocky one. Emma gave him a defiant look. Ralph stood his ground.

"The beast'll come for ya if ya don't go with us."

"If you're dead, why aren't you transparent like the two women we just saw?" Ralph glared at the men with hate and disgust as he stepped back and took a fighting stance.

In confusion, they fled in the direction of the beast, leaving Ralph and Emma alone again.

Quickly they moved in the opposite direction. Emma knew they had to get off this path and leave the tunnel before something stronger than the two rowdies forced them to be dead.

Silently, they pushed their way past all sorts of staggering creatures, more transparent people, and a great number of beings with horns on their heads and leathery skin but without the red iridescent glowing eyes.

Up ahead, the darkness began to dissipate, and a tiny spot of light broke through. The closer they came to it, the brighter it grew. Ralph and Emma looked around to see a beautiful spot with rolling meadows and lacy trees scattered about, granting shade from glorious, golden beams of sun.

Where had the tunnel led them?

This place appeared to be the exact opposite of the ashen land they had visited earlier. Birds chirped and twittered in the trees while bees hummed from flower to flower. Butterflies flitted about while a gentle breeze caressed their faces, carrying the sweet scent of assorted blooms.

Emma touched a tree and it didn't turn to ash. The trunk felt rough and rugged, as it should.

"Where are we?" puzzled Emma. The murmur of a brook drew her in its direction, with Ralph in tow.

The brook looked astoundingly clear; the detail of every rock covering its bed could be described. Moving too fast to show a reflection, the water tumbled over bumpy surfaces and sped downhill.

At the end, the rushing water emptied into a pond filled with lily pads and little, green, croaking frogs.

As Ralph and Emma stared into the pond, roiling clouds cluttered its surface, and a vaguely familiar voice spoke to them.

"Well, if it isn't Ralph and Emma. Are you lost?"

Puzzled, Emma asked, "Who is speaking? Why can't we see you?"

"You're looking at me. I'm the mirror guide. Only in water, I'm just a guide."

No answer.

"What's the matter? Cat got your tongue? Come on, you guys, you do remember me, don't you?"

With a slight tremor in his voice, Ralph asked, "Should we?"

"The mirror in Cerise's room…forget it. I see you're caught in the *'in between.'* Figures. What do you expect from me?" boomed the voice of the guide.

"You're in the pond? Mirror guide," Emma mused.

"I'm in mirrors and all reflective surfaces. Now you're really in a mess. What happened? Was someone in the eggnog?" snickered the voice.

This couldn't be home. What did the guide mean, stuck in the *"in between"?* The two exchanged looks.

"You two really don't know what happened, do you?" The guide snickered again.

According to the voice, alchemy had brought them there, and alchemy should get them back.

"If you don't have the power or knowledge of alchemy, you at least know some magick, don't you?" the guide questioned. The two stood speechless.

"So, you came by the spell of another. You are caught between dimensions. That's what some call the *'in between.'* What you see around you will not last. Another portal will soon open. There is a trick to walking through dimensions. However, if you are caught in between, then you stand in jeopardy of dying and going to either heaven or hell. I could say 'follow the yellow brick road,' but it wouldn't be funny in a place like this."

"Huh? Please, we don't know where we are, or…or who we are…" Emma's voice trailed off.

"Oh, no. I forgot," the guide replied. Suddenly, he became sober.

"By the laws of magick, I cannot tell you your names or anything about your past. These laws I must obey, or I'll lose my powers and be banished to an endless void."

In seriousness, the guide went on, "Some may be tricked into going to the lower realm without ever dying. Beware! Things aren't always what they seem."

As the last word drifted from the pond, the world around Ralph and Emma shimmied and began to blur as another bright spot rolled up before them. Even the pond disappeared. As they contemplated passing through the bright spot, a new voice called out, "Don't go!"

When they turned around, they saw what looked like a young maid of fifteen or so dressed as a street urchin from nineteenth-century England. Her smudgy face stared back at them from beneath a ragged bonnet as she drew the discolored shawl about her thin, frail body.

"It's not what you think," the child continued in an English accent. Emma and Ralph exchanged looks. The bright spot began to grow dim. It appeared to represent a portal. The child did not look transparent, so they hesitated and asked her name and how she knew so much.

The maiden explained, "I walked into a bright spot where demons lived and they tried to eat me."

In a moment, the bright spot vanished and the meadow filled back in around them

Without another word, the maiden turned and walked away; Ralph and Emma followed her. They had to know where she intended to go. A number of questions spouted from them to which the girl only replied, "Things are not always what they seem. You don't always know what you want."

According to the child, she barely remembered having a fight with the local constable for stealing warm chestnuts from a stingy vendor. Then she had found herself wandering the tunnel where the beast had appeared. She had not seen the barren, ashen land or the cottage, but like them, she had little memory of her prior life. Only a strong will to survive kept her going.

Gingerly, Ralph touched her arm.

Solid.

No spirit stood before them. She looked and felt as alive as they. While the three walked, the bright sun and lush, rolling meadows fell away, replaced by a thick darkness. An eerie, dim light glowed from the path beneath their feet.

As they asked her more and more questions, the girl only answered with a grunt or another question. Finally, Ralph blurted out, "Are we dead? Have we gone to hell? I demand to know." The girl stopped and turned to him in the dimness, laughing. The laugh only agitated him more, and he repeated the questions.

"What did the pond tell you?" The maiden tried to contain her laughter.

No answer.

Then she gave a half smile and replied, "We're caught between dimensions. This happens a lot. Whenever someone goes missing, you'll find them here. When the family dog or cat doesn't come home, it's the same. They all end up here. Should the lady lose a comb or brush, it ends up here." Then she turned abruptly and began walking away. In astonishment, Ralph stood with his mouth agape, but Emma pulled him on before they lost sight of the girl.

CHAPTER TWENTY-SEVEN

As they followed the young street urchin, no one said much. Most of Ralph's mind centered on leaving this creepy place, but he was distracted by the deep attraction he felt for Emma. Her soft, warm hand in his delighted his heart and made him flush with desire. He glanced at the gold band now and again. *Did I give it to her? It doesn't feel familiar.*

As they walked, the path suddenly seemed suspended over a vast ocean of black nothingness. Emma stumbled and might have gone over the edge if Ralph and the girl hadn't caught her.

"We're crossing into another time and space. Between dimensions, time is different, and so is the space you stand in. I've been here before. Unless you can go into a dimension, you will move in circles while you're caught between," explained the maiden.

"Who are you?" Emma had to know.

Again, the girl just laughed. "Names don't matter here. Do you even know your own?"

"How long have you been walking in circles?" Emma clung to Ralph's arm.

"Here, time can't be measured. Can't say I mind it." The girl turned to move on when a bright spot rolled up ahead. Abruptly, she stopped and turned to the couple. "I won't go through it. Your choice."

"If you won't go through the light, where will you go?" Ralph's fear returned, and now he had a knot in his stomach as well. The path began to quake, and the bright spot flickered like a dying campfire.

The three couldn't remain on the path. If they didn't move into the bright spot, they would go over the edge. However, before they even tried passing the girl to reach the portal, the narrow path caused them all to lose their balance and tumble over the side into the void of nothingness.

Thick darkness engulfed them as they felt the horror of gravity sucking them down fast. No walls around them, no floor beneath, just the continuous feeling of falling, endlessly falling.

Finally, Emma found herself on the ground but still swallowed in a black void. Feeling around in the darkness, she touched a strong arm and hand that responded to her.

Light—they needed light. Emma called to the girl.

No answer.

Then she began talking to Ralph, but he didn't answer, either.

"Sweetheart, say something." Emma shook the man she clung to. Strong arms wrapped around her.

From a distance, a faint voice replied, "My darling, I'm over here. Are you hurt?"

"What?" she puzzled.

From overhead, a shaft of light broke through the void and shone down upon Emma and the man who held her. It looked like the same one she'd seen beckoning to her in the barren, ashen land. Struggling to free herself from him, she screamed and kicked. Laughing maniacally, the man tightened his grip and wouldn't let go.

Even though he appeared easy on the eyes, the wonton cravings in his red illuminated orbs frightened Emma. Then suddenly, the warmth of his body mingled with his scent overcame her senses. An insatiable desire to surrender washed over her, but instead she pushed back against the desire and fought harder.

~ * ~

Ralph struggled to move, but found his foot held tight by something rope-like connected to the ground. The shaft from the heavens began to widen and cast its light over him as well. Again Emma screamed, then the sounds became muffled and trailed. The scrapping sound of Emma's shoes on the earth faded as the man dragged her farther and farther away.

With all his strength, Ralph pulled at the roots entwined around his ankle. It looked like he couldn't save her or himself. Removing his sword from its sheath, he hacked away at the twisted roots. But it was no use. The more he hacked, the tighter the thing gripped, as if possessed.

In frustration, he cursed himself and the roots as he rammed the sword into the tree trunk. With a mighty moan, the tree expelled its prisoner. Confused, but glad for freedom, Ralph scrambled away from the groaning tree. The sound was agonized, like the cry of a dying man.

After pulling himself up, he grabbed the sword and yanked it from the trunk. Dark red, fluid-like blood spurted from the wound. Shaking his head, Ralph wiped the dripping blade on the grass and sheathed the weapon.

By now, his environ had lightened up all around, and the shaft of light had vanished. The world seemed gray again, but not as barren and ashen as the first place they'd seen.

Without further delay, Ralph hurried in the direction of Emma's screams. As he came closer, the trees and shrubs fell away, and a long winding corridor appeared, lit by candles held by sconces along the wall.

At last, he came to a tall, plain-looking door at the end of the corridor. Emma's screams sounded from the other side. Upon bursting through the door, his eyes met with a most horrifying sight. Standing near a large bed with a canopy of red silk drapes, Emma struggled with the man who had carried her away. From behind, he had his arms wrapped around her waist as he put his mouth close to her ear. At times, he appeared to whisper to her, and on the other hand, it looked as if he were forcing his kisses to her ear and down to her neck. She fought in vain to pull away. Try as he might to move, Ralph couldn't. His feet seemed stuck to the floor. He froze and could do nothing but watch.

All of a sudden, he and the man swapped places, and Ralph found himself struggling with Emma while the man looked on. He needed to make her understand how he felt for her.

"Leave me alone," begged Emma who apparently didn't realize that Ralph had not been struggling with her previously. She appeared afraid, but Ralph responded to nothing but his desire for her as the voice of the man urged him on.

In Ralph's mind, she was his wife, but she didn't seem to comprehend how much he cared for her. Why did she struggle? He would never hurt her. His arms tightened around the slender waist, as his lips pressed hard against her smooth neck and face. Her scent intoxicated him. Feeling the woman against his body excited him, and his kisses grew fierce and feral.

Emma screamed and pulled at his hands, trying to unlock them. Then she began trying to kick back at him, stomping the floor then brushing his trouser legs as he moved quickly to keep from getting kicked. Fear of being forced to surrender her body made her gasp for air.

Regardless of the heat from Ralph's body, she turned ice cold and fought even harder to get away.

"Take her now!" urged the man in a charming, French accent. "You want her. You've wanted her for a long time. In this world there are no consequences."

Suddenly, Ralph released the quivering Emma who moved away quickly, a horrified look darting from Ralph to the man.

In an instant, the young street urchin walked through the wall and the man vanished. Ralph shook his head as if awakening from a trance.

"Time displacement," said the girl. "That happens when you move through space. I don't believe I've ever seen him before." She referred to the man who had been egging Ralph on.

"This is hell, isn't it?" Ralph again asked.

"What is hell? A state of mind. A place man creates so he can punish himself." The girl spoke like a recording.

"*Madame*, you've got to believe me. I'd never do anything to hurt you." Ralph stepped toward Emma and tenderly caressed her beautiful, long hair. "Especially if you are my wife."

Emma said nothing.

"She wants to believe, but she knows what she felt. Given the chance, you will hurt her," the girl explained.

"Stop it! Stop it!" screamed Ralph. "Who or what are you? How do we get out of here?" He glared at the thin, frail girl who stared back at him innocently.

"I've been looking for the tunnel. If we go back through it, we'll be free. You will return to where you came from. Find the tunnel, go in the direction of the beast." The girl looked sad.

"What? Go in the direction of the beast? No!" protested Ralph.

"Things aren't always what they seem." The child turned and walked through the wall. Ralph and Emma tried to follow, but the wall turned solid and they bounced back.

More than anything, Emma wanted to trust him again, but she questioned his actions. Did he truly mean to express his love? How could she be sure?

"Something about the man forced me to act like that. Please forgive me. *Mon Dieu*, I don't know your name, but I do know you, don't I? Truly, I would rather die than hurt you." Poor Ralph knelt before her with bowed head. Finally, he admitted his amnesia, and he just wanted to die.

With much hesitation, the shaken woman forgave and nodded to him.

"Somehow I seem to recall someone calling me Emma, and you…Ralph. I know I'm married," she flashed the gold band. "But are we…?"

"I want to think so then I could justify my emotions," said Ralph trying to make her look at him. Emma said nothing to this.

As they looked about the room, various paintings appeared and lined the walls and murals covered the ceiling. Fire and smoke filled one painting when they moved closer to look. Wind and dust could not only be seen but also felt from another. The last showed the leathery-faced demon with the red glowing eyes.

After Emma finally calmed down, she and Ralph tried to reason through their ordeal. *Things aren't always what they seem.* There had to be a clue in those words. The quaking always occurred just before something changed. Was this a dimensional shift? If they now existed between dimensions, and freedom lay in the tunnel, then how could they find the tunnel? And would they definitely return from whence they came? Who was this young street urchin who kept popping up to give them instructions and clues? Who was the man trying to hurt Emma?

The street urchin had said time displacement happened when one traveled through space. What did this mean? Emma had a vague idea, but it was only with much difficulty that she managed to explain it to Ralph. As long as he didn't try to express his feelings for her, he made pretty good sense.

Existing in a dimension should be less confusing than the *"in between."* There should be no strange earthquakes, weird men and beasts, or the fear of what should be real. If they truly walked between dimensions, what would set them straight? Another dimension could not be so chaotic.

CHAPTER TWENTY-EIGHT

As they stared into each painting trying to decide what to do, the one of a garden filled with flowers and a fountain started to feel familiar to Ralph. Gradually, he remembered the story his father had told him of the family dog getting lost for many months. At least now he recalled he had a family, a very wealthy one.

"My father had trained the animal to sniff out truffles, tea, tobacco, and a few narcotic herbs used as substances for illegal pleasure. However, the dog had never been lost, gone missing, or been stolen. One spring day, my father recalled seeing the dog playing with the children, my cousins and me, in the gardens one minute, and then *poof,* gone the next. No one could verify where they'd last seen him other than the gardens. No one saw him wander away. That garden was surrounded by a high wall and wrought-iron gates; how could the dog escape, and why would he? Percival, as we called him, couldn't have been more loved.

"That autumn, my cousins and I finally found Percival in the gardens; the poor dog was stumbling as if he would drop. He seemed so exhausted. The pads of his paws looked worn and cracked as if he'd been in some dry, desert country. The once shiny, reddish-brown coat appeared dirty and matted. As poor Percival reached us, he fell at our feet and passed out. Besides exhaustion, the poor thing suffered from lack of water and food. It took a month or so to restore his health. If only the poor creature could talk. What a tale he would tell."

"Did you notice any water around? A pond, pool, or fountain?" questioned Emma.

"We had a rather large fountain running both days. Why?" Ralph tried to understand.

"A shift must have occurred and sent him though a reflective surface. If not a mirror, then water," Emma reasoned. "There is something scientific and a bit magickal about traveling through dimensions. If the dog returned, so can we."

The two looked back at the paintings. More visions popped up into various ones. What caused a portal to open?

As they viewed the last painting, the frail street urchin came through it. "Stay away from the light and find the tunnel. Things are not always what they seem."

Puzzled, the two exchanged looks. This made no sense. The girl kept repeating the phrase. What did she mean?

But the moment they viewed the painting depicting a storm at sea, the floor shook and the room swayed back and forth. In an instant, a vortex appeared. The movement of the room threw them into its center. In a moment, they found themselves on a dirt road outside of Paris. This really jogged their memory. They had been here before.

The two looked at each other in wonderment. Strange things happened when portals and vortices appeared, but quaking and shifting occurred when a reflective surface presented itself. Could a painting of a stormy sea bring about such a thing?

Slowly, cautiously, the two walked into the bustling city. Everything looked normal. Ralph had hazy recollections of the butcher carrying out packages of meat to a rather common looking carriage. Emma watched without a word.

When a former business associate popped out of a fancy brougham, Ralph vaguely recognized and hailed him, but the man went on as if he didn't hear or see anyone. Again Ralph called out and even moved close enough to touch the man, but his hand went right through him. Did they yet travel between dimensions? Or were they dead? They looked and felt solid to each other. The former business associate and everyone around them looked solid, but no one could see or hear them.

As they moved on, Emma tried to make herself known, but everyone ignored her, too, as if she did not exist. Trying to pick up an apple from a fresh air market, her hand passed right through it. She gasped and jumped back. Ralph tried to comfort her but couldn't. How could he when he found no explanation or solution to this horrible, ridiculous situation?

In their wanderings, they finally found themselves at *le Théâtre Ranier*. They were drawn to it, and each continued toward the front without consulting the other. Obviously, opening the door was impossible since their hands passed through everything, but walking through it presented no problem.

Again, no one saw or heard them. Once or twice, some young actresses and stagehands flinched and whispered something about feeling cold and sensing an unseen presence, but they blamed it on the ghost of the Master of Arts as usual. After all, everyone had plenty of stories of seeing the ghost.

One morning, just before rehearsal, two young actresses giggled and laughed as they made their way downstairs to the main stage.

"I don't believe in ghosts. Stories like that are made up to scare children into obeying their parents," stated the redhead.

"You shouldn't say that. Should the ghosts hear you, they will take off your head," warned the blonde.

Suddenly, a dark shadow darted in front of them and a faint whisper floated on the air: "Leave while you can."

The ladies stopped short and huddled against each other. "Did you see that?" asked the tall one.

"Did you hear that voice?" questioned the young blonde.

Again the shadow darted in front of them. The women flinched and gasped aloud. "It's him. The Master of Arts!" they cried in unison, and took off running like their dresses were on fire.

On another occasion, three stage hands were hoisting a rather large backdrop of mountain scenery when a distant breeze zipped by them. The men stopped short.

"What was that?" asked the skinny, lanky stagehand, trying to steady the scene and make it straight.

"If felt like someone passed by. But I don't see anyone here but us," said the short, stocky built one, standing on a large crate with his hands wrapped around the thick rope attached to the backdrop, looping it over a pulley.

"There! There! Look, a shadow darting among the seats," cried the eldest of the three, his hair speckled with white and black like salt and pepper.

Then all at once, a tall, black mass stood up in the center of the seats. With the lights only on the stage, the black mass took on an eerie appearance.

The three stagehands all screamed at the same time, as if rehearsed.

"The Master of Arts!" was all they could utter before dropping the backdrop and stumbling over each other for the exit. Maniacal laughter grew in volume, causing the chandelier to sway as if were about to fall.

At last, Emma and Ralph found themselves on a dimly lit stage with Ehrich speaking in whispers to Latimer. As the ghostly pair moved closer, Latimer looked their way, and for an instant they felt certain he met their gaze. Instead, he seemed to look right through them then turned back to Ehrich.

"You must know where she is. I can't believe she'd leave me. I'm going out of my mind without her," cried Ehrich with anguish in his voice.

But then he stopped speaking when Emma reached up and kissed his cheek. She didn't know why, but she felt she had to. She actually felt the softness of his skin. The scent of sandalwood, his favorite oil, filled her nostrils.

Ehrich turned deathly pale as he touched his face and whispered, "She's here. I felt her kiss."

Latimer blanched white as he looked around them. Tears welled up in Ehrich's eyes as the words escaped his lips, "She's dead."

Ralph and Emma now realized the men knew she was there. Finally, a connection to reality! They did everything they could think of to make noise. They screamed and jumped up and down. Trying to pull back the curtains, their hands passed right through them. Finally, when they attempted to turn the gaslight up or down, they found the closer they moved to the flame, the dimmer it became. When they withdrew, it grew brighter.

Latimer perked up and moved quickly to the gas lamp mounted at the rear of the stage with Ehrich not far behind.

"Emma, is that you? Dim the flame once for yes and twice for no," he instructed. In a moment, the flame dimmed once then grew bright. Ehrich wiped away his tears and asked if she was hurt. The flame dimmed once. Then it dimmed again and grew bright.

Why was this man crying, and why did he care for Emma so? Emma felt a loving, familiar feeling about Ehrich calling her by name and expressing his concern. She watched tears run down his cheeks as his hands trembled. Automatically, her hand reached out, even though it went right through him. This had to be her husband and the other his friend.

"Are you dead?" Ehrich had to know. Latimer shot him a look of disdain, but the flame dimmed once and grew bright then dimmed a second time before growing bright.

"She's alive! My God, she's alive!" he sputtered with joy and looked to Latimer.

Emma thought quickly. They needed more than yes and no answers, but how could they communicate?

Emma nudged Ralph gently to get his attention and rambled something about how non-corporeal beings contact the living. He frowned, trying to understand. Even a ghost moved things, but they could do nothing but dim a flame.

"We must go to him. Somehow we have energy to affect fire, so we should be able to move an object like a pen," Emma reasoned. Ralph still frowned in confusion. "If we move like ghosts, maybe we have to communicate like ghosts," she continued.

"Emma, are you here?" Ehrich called out. "If you're here, can you move something? Move a chair or put out a candle."

"Are we speaking scientifically? I rather hope so, as magick baffles me," Ralph answered, watching as Latimer and Ehrich waited for another sign.

Suddenly, Emma remembered that she had done very well in science, and many of her experiments and reports popped into her head.

"Scientifically, we must be moving slower than they are. It's easy to affect a flame because we use energy. Now to use movement." Emma looked about her and spied a chair. Quickly, she moved to it and pushed fast and hard, sending it sliding across the stage. Startled, the two men jumped and ran to it.

"So, we have to act very quickly to move things?" Ralph verified as he pulled down fast and hard on the cord to draw the curtains. And did they move! He jumped up and clapped his hands like an amused child. Latimer and Ehrich exchanged puzzled looks.

"We have to communicate," declared Latimer as he rushed his friend backstage in search of pen and paper.

After acquiring them, he called out to Emma and asked if she could write. She tried to pick up the pen, but even with speed, her hand passed through it.

"Draw a spirit board," suggested her husband. Latimer shook his head. "It's the only way," continued Ehrich.

"This is not a game. Perhaps she can move an object to spell out a word, but so could something else. Something you don't want to summon. Boards like this are typically used to speak to the dead, but generally evil spirits answer instead. Trust me, I've had it happen to me." Latimer looked serious. His face appeared strained, and his hands shook a bit.

"I don't care. I need to know where my wife is and how we can get her back," Ehrich said, determined. "No matter what, I have to save her." Knowing he had no choice, Latimer wrote the alphabet on a large sheet of paper and the numbers from one to ten, as well as the words "yes" and "no" in the center.

Then he called out to Emma and asked where she was. The first few tries to move the pen almost seemed useless. Then she pushed a little faster and shoved the thing off the table.

Confused, Ehrich picked it up and placed it back on the paper. Ralph looked to Emma, silently asking permission to try it himself, and she nodded. In a moment, the pen began to move and Ralph spelled out the words, "between dimensions." Latimer again paled like he'd seen a ghost, for he clearly understood. Ehrich looked to his old friend for an answer. Then Ralph spelled his own name. Again, a puzzled look crossed Ehrich's face.

"Ralph is with you?" asked Latimer. The pen moved to the word "yes."

"We have to get them back. What do we do?" Ehrich tugged at his old friend's sleeve. Latimer didn't know what to say.

Suddenly, the pen moved freely, spelling out a number of words. When Latimer completed writing the message, he handed it to his friend and shook his head. "This is what I warned you about."

The message read: "They belong to me, they've come too far to be free."

A moment later, the pen went sailing through the air and rammed into the back wall.

Knowing they hadn't moved the pen, Emma and Ralph looked about fearfully, trying to discover who had sent the message. Ehrich shrieked in agony and vowed to destroy whatever held his wife captive.

Latimer bit his lip, trying hard to think of what more he could do. At least he knew where Ralph and Emma had gone. Latimer still had a handful of herbs to collect then he would prepare the potion.

Hoping to communicate more, Ralph attempted to remove the pen from the wall, but an invisible force held him back.

CHAPTER TWENTY-NINE

Whatever wrote the foreboding message had to be the one restraining Ralph. Though they couldn't see anything, it either existed on the same plane or had a powerful influence.

Latimer looked to Ehrich. "I will do everything I can to find out where she is and how to bring her back." Then he lowered his voice, hoping he wouldn't alarm Emma if she was still there. "I can't promise anything, but I will do my best."

"What do you mean, you can't promise? Let me help. What can I do?"

"At the moment, nothing. I need to look through some books and some of my notes. Please go home and rest. If she contacts you, try to find out where she is."

"I can't just go home," Ehrich protested, but Latimer insisted.

Looking around the room, Latimer's gaze fell upon a book lying on the table. He picked it up and handed it to his friend. "Look through this book. See if you find anything that will help."

"I can do that here." Ehrich took the book.

"But I need to be alone to think and research. You know I do my best work alone." Latimer's words sounded final on the subject. Ehrich could have stayed anyway, but he reconsidered.

Ralph and Emma wanted to remain in the company of Latimer and Ehrich, whether they could see them or not, but since the two parted company and went separate ways, Ralph followed Latimer offstage, and Emma followed her husband to the dark wing.

Both knew they should stay together, but wanting to remain in contact with the men outweighed all other thoughts.

~ * ~

In the dark wing, Ehrich returned to the broken creature he had become when his beautiful Serena had died. In a fit of anger, he threw the book then he picked up everything in sight and hurled it all against the wall, cursing himself for such misfortune. Apparently, true love and happiness would never be his to keep. The pain of losing his beloved Emma nearly killed him. His heart ached and his blood ran cold. Without her, he didn't want to live. Again, life had dealt him a losing hand, and it claimed his sweet bride in the bargain. Even though she had verified her existence, it still felt like death to him. He couldn't see her, and she moved things like a ghost.

Red illuminated eyes popped up in the mirror hanging on the wall in the corner of the room. But Ehrich was too occupied to notice.

He paced the floor. At times Ehrich could hear Latimer's voice: *I will do everything I can to find out where she is and how to bring her back.* This felt reassuring, and he tried to calm down, but then *I can't promise anything* echoed over and over in his mind.

He put his hands over his ears and tried to shut out the echo, but it got louder.

So deep and loud came his lament, the entire theater heard it echoing within the walls. The moaning and wailing proved to many that a ghost truly haunted the theater.

~ * ~

Ehrich's grief pained Emma. She wished he could see her.

"Emma, are you still here?" asked Ehrich with a tremor in his voice. "Do you remember the time we went to the park and watched the puppet show?"

"Yes, yes. It was the first time we saw a show together," Emma said, smiling as the memory suddenly came back to her.

"It was our first time watching a show together," Ehrich said almost the same thing.

"Ehrich, can you hear me? I'm right here, in front of you," she said, still trying to touch him.

"Please, Emma, if you can hear me, try to remember what happened before you arrived at wherever you are?" Ehrich said as he reached out for her, but his hand passed through her as if she were a spirit.

At first, Emma said nothing. She stared hard at him as if trying to remember. The corners of her mouth pulled into a smile.

"The mirror! It was the mirror!" she and Ehrich exclaimed in unison.

Turning to the mirror on the wall in the corner of the room, Ehrich ran to it, touching it gingerly. "Are you in there? Is this the way to find you?" The mirror remained solid. Ehrich gave an anguished cry.

"Perhaps I must die in order to see you again, my sweet."

Even though he couldn't see her, Emma shook her head and screamed, "NO! NO! THAT'S NOT THE WAY!"

If only she could embrace his manly form to let him know how much she loved him. Seeing him left no doubt in her mind. She loved him. Knowing she lived, even between dimensions, should comfort him, but obviously it didn't. What could she do?

The grieving man wept and wailed for a long time, calling for death to take him. Existing on another plane only meant death to Ehrich, regardless of Latimer's explanation.

~ * ~

At Latimer's flat, Ralph watched the Englishman busy himself in the library/laboratory off of the sitting room. There, Latimer read over ancient tomes and fiddled around with various jars of smelly herbs and strange-colored liquids. Peering over Latimer's shoulder, the young nobleman read the potion recipe and shook his head in confusion. He wished the man would stick to science instead of rituals pertaining to heathen beliefs.

As Ralph looked around the room, he noticed something hidden and shoved against the far wall. As he drew closer, sheets covered something about his height. With a quick jerk, the sheets tumbled to the floor revealing two full-length mirrors. Each one displayed scorched edges of glass.

Then it dawned in him. *Smoke seeped from the mirror before Emma and I appeared in the ashen world...Latimer! Latimer must be the spellcaster!*

Quickly, the Englishman whipped around in direction of the mirrors. Seeing the sheets on the floor, he called out, "Emma? Is that you? Or is it Ralph?"

He moved about, searching for more signs of someone in the room besides himself, but Latimer still could not see Ralph or hear him.

"I'm here," cried Ralph in vain. Then his look wandered back to the scorched mirrors.

He needed one more element to complete the recipe, so Latimer left the simmering mixture on the stove while he trotted off to get it. Ralph hurried to catch up, and Latimer turned to see if anyone was behind him. No one!

"Whatever or whoever you are, get away from me," Ralph shouted, turning around and around trying to see through the darkness.

A wicked laugh echoed in the near distance; a man's laugh. Who or what followed him?

The last ingredient needed for the potion came from an obscure shop hidden between a *boulangerie* and a produce vendor.

Upon entering the tiny, dingy shop, Latimer spied the array of jars filled with powders and whole herbs. Among them sat one filled with peacock feathers. Their bright-colored pattern resembling eyes seemed to stare back at him. One feather, that was all he needed he told the shopkeeper, but he had a personal emergency and wanted to close early.

Latimer insisted, but the shopkeeper rudely pushed him outside and locked the door. Muttering and cursing under his breath, he could not control his anger and frustration. He pounded fiercely on the door until a *gendarme* came and threatened to lock him away if he didn't keep quiet. Then the *gendarme* ordered him to move away from the shop door. At this, Latimer wheeled around and sauntered back toward his flat as the law enforcer watched him carefully.

However, Ralph had heard what Latimer was after and would not give up so easily. Quickly and silently, he slipped through the door and moved to the shelf where the jar of feathers sat. As quickly as possible, he grabbed the jar and set it on the counter. Now to unscrew the lid. After several failed attempts, he huffed in exasperation and contemplated the problem. He could pass his hand through the jar and grab a feather, but existing in the current dimension, the feather would probably not pass through the jar, or would it? If he held the feather really tight, making it part of the plane he existed on for a brief second, he might achieve his goal.

Easily his hand passed through the jar. Quickly he grabbed a feather, but as he tried to pull it through, it hit the side of the jar as he'd feared, popped out from between his fingers, and settled back on the stack of feathers.

By nature, patience did not come to Ralph often or easily. He felt like smashing the glass container, but he stopped himself; that might incriminate Latimer, since he might have been the last person seen leaving the shop. After a few more failed attempts, Ralph closed his eyes, gripped the feather really tight, and pulled his hand through as fast as he could.

Success! This time the feather passed through the jar with his hand. He jumped up and down, clapping like a child cheering a marionette show.

After replacing the jar, Ralph stuffed the feather into his coat pocket and passed through the door with great speed. He felt comfortable and confident in his newly discovered knowledge and skill.

Back at the flat, the potion still simmered, and Latimer continued to mumble and mutter as he read from one of his musty books. He couldn't find anything to substitute for a peacock feather, and his face distorted in frustration as he cursed under his breath. Over and over he read the same text stating the ingredients had no substitutes. After screaming out insults and profanities, something caught his eye—a feather! To his surprise, a peacock feather wafted from the ceiling and settled on the book before him. After blinking several times, he gingerly touched it.

Solid! He hadn't dreamt it.

Quickly, he grabbed the feather and looked about cautiously. Certainly someone brought it. Whoever had written the threatening message wouldn't help; therefore Emma and Ralph had to be there.

Without further delay, Latimer dropped the feather into the simmering mixture. A small *poof* sounded, and a little white puff of smoke flashed from the pot. After a few minutes, he removed the hot liquid and set it aside to cool.

"Thank you," he spoke out loud and smiled.

When Ralph said, "You're welcome," it was faint. His eyes widened.

"Ralph? Is that you?" Latimer peered about the room.

Ralph said excitedly, "You can hear me! I'm right in front of you." By now he was waving his hands about as he jumped up and down.

For a moment, Latimer paused, listening. He heard it again. "I hear you, old chap, but I can't see you. Allow me to finish what I'm doing, and with the help of the gods I shall see you in a moment," he said, looking around the room with his right arm extended in hopes of being able to touch and feel the young man.

Latimer poured a small portion of the hot liquid into a cold flagon. Ralph tried to help by attempting to pick it up, but his hand went through the flagon and touched the hot liquid. He drew back quickly and gasped—odd, since he hadn't felt sensations like this for some time. An instant later, he found Latimer staring him in the face.

Both men were shocked. What had made Ralph visible? The only logical possibility was that touching the liquid must have triggered something. Not that it mattered. He just felt happy someone could see him in the real world.

"Ralph! It's so good to see you. Are you all right? Where is Emma? Is she well?" came the queries as Latimer grabbed the man and embraced him.

"You can see me? I'm back?" After Latimer released him, Ralph touched his face then his arms. Latimer patted his shoulder. Presently, all his memories came rushing back to him like the waves at sea. Without a doubt, he now remembered his family and friends, and they called him Ralph Duchenois.

"Yes, my good man, you are back. But where is Emma?" Latimer looked around in confusion.

"She followed Ehrich," Ralph replied. "We returned to the mirror as you requested, but strangely enough, we were somehow transported to an eerie, gray place. What happened?" Ralph looked Latimer in the eye.

At first, Latimer said nothing and tried to avoid answering.

"I have never been so terrified in my life," Ralph said taking a deep breath. "I'm certainly happy you found a way to bring me back. I can't tell you how relieved—"

"It was my fault," Latimer blurted out. He patted Ralph's shoulder and moved away, shaking his head as he cast his eyes to the floor.

"What do you mean?"

"I am the spellcaster. Let's find Emma first and then I will explain my reasons to all."

Ralph didn't want to let the subject go, but finding Emma took priority.

~ * ~

The dark wing would truly become a haunted one after all the wailing and mourning from Ehrich.

"I have no other thought but to be with my loved one," he said out loud as he drew out a sharp letter opener from his desk drawer and prepared to plunge it deep into his aching, beating heart. He had no idea Emma would disapprove. Surely, she'd welcome her husband when he joined her in death.

Standing unseen nearby, Emma screamed in horrible realization. Pushing him backwards quick and hard, Emma screamed again, causing the letter opener to go flying. She could not stand and watch him take his life.

Startled, Ehrich stumbled back. "Emma, are you here?" he looked about. Suddenly, he could see her standing before him. "Emma?" But within a split second of seeing her, the total absence of memory hit him hard and wiped away his past and present.

"You can see me!" Emma ran to him, threw her arms around his neck, and covered his face with kisses. Slowly, he took in the sweet taste of his beloved as he moved back to the sofa. Yet in the attempt to sit back with his wife, they both passed through the sofa and crashed to the floor hard.

No man could ever summon such emotion as the man she called husband. In her poor, muddled mind, Emma now clearly recalled Ehrich. But he didn't seem to understand. Memory loss occurred when they crossed from one dimension to another, even in the *"in between."*

For a moment, he pulled back from her as they sat staring at each other. When she flashed her wedding ring, he appeared to recognize it.

"I do remember what happened just before I came to this gray, surreal world," said Emma. "The other man…yes, Ralph, now I recall his name. Ralph and I returned to the mirror as Latimer suggested. We stood there a few minutes then the entire mirror clouded and began to seep smoke from the corners. Soon the room filled up with it and when it cleared away we found ourselves on the ground of a world of gray trees, gray skies, just gray everything." Emma strained to remember, but it made her head throb in pain. She placed a hand on each temple as if to make the pounding stop.

Ehrich gathered her up in his arms to comfort her. He closed his eyes and held her tight as she continued to explain.

"Then we were chased by a man, a tall man, like you, but not. He kept following us and then strange, confusing things began to happen, and I found myself trying to fight this man. I didn't want him to touch me." Emma finished her explanation and reached for him, but Ehrich pushed her back.

After hearing her explanation about the mirror seeping smoke, the ashen world, and her struggle with a strange man and then Ralph, his demeanor changed in concern for Emma's safety overriding the worst of the memory loss.

Ehrich howled a few obscene words and realized he now abided in another dimension, as did his wife.

"I recall who I am! I can see you," he looked around in wide-eyed amazement. "Am I dead? That's it. Finally, I've taken my own life. It was the only way to see you again."

"I'm not dead. You're not dead. Latimer was trying to tell you—"Emma tried to explain but Ehrich cut her off.

"What else can it be?"

"It seems there's a temporary memory loss then slowly things come back to you," Emma said, trying to make sense of things.

"Memory loss is death, or part of it. Where are we? Nothing alive can exist here. Could this be hell? The plane around me feels dream-like."

"I don't truly understand the concept of dimensions and what lies between them, but I know there has been a lot written about it by some very learned men," Emma remarked thoughtfully, trying to find comfort in what she said.

"What does that have to do with our plight? I am just as confused as you."

"Latimer! He must have an answer to this," Emma thought out loud as she clung to Ehrich.

For a brief moment, he stared at her, "Who is Latimer?" he asked, but her urging pulled him onward.

Once again, Ehrich had cheated death. Deep inside herself, Emma dwelt on a familiar feeling of love and caring for this man.

"Why?" she looked up into his sweet face. "You knew I was alive. Why would you consider killing yourself? Why?" Tears streamed down her face.

"I suppose I assumed the worst. Where are we? We belong together, don't we?" He barely recalled the question even as he replied, holding her close and tight.

"Oh, how I rejoice in feeling you next to me. Tasting your sweet lips make me tingle and tremble from the passion. Many things seemed lost from my mind, but the feel of you next to me brings back such emotions," he said lovingly.

"Latimer! He must have an answer to this," Emma thought out loud as she clung to Ehrich.

For a brief moment, he stared at her, "Who is Latimer?" he asked, but her urging pulled him onward.

As soon as Emma said Latimer's name, they materialized in his flat. They arrived so quickly, the realization that Ralph stood corporeal took a moment to soak in. Then came the dawn. For whatever reasons, he and Ehrich had traded places. But how and why?

Emma looked for a pen and some paper but found nothing but dusty, old books, jars of herbs, bottles filled with liquid and a hot, smelly mixture cooling in a flagon.

After a quick explanation from his wife, Ehrich tried to move the book on the table, the one his friend had been reading earlier. When the book slid across the surface, Latimer and Ralph realized Emma must have found them, and Latimer ran about his flat gathering up a sheet of blank paper and a pen. After recreating a spirit board, he explained that somehow Ralph had returned to his own dimension. Then he asked Emma to speak.

Without hesitation, she began to spell out, "My husband is with—" but then something yanked her backward.

"I grow weary of your games, Emma. Time to claim what's mine," echoed a distorted male voice. She looked around but saw nothing.

Latimer called out, asking her to complete the message, but the unseen entity would not permit it, and Emma was distracted from trying when another bright spot rolled up before them. Ehrich puzzled at it. Emma shook her head and pulled him back.

"Something prevents her from speaking. I think Ehrich may be with her. Why you traded places is a mystery." Latimer frowned.

"Careful what you say. Something evil may hear," Ralph warned.

CHAPTER THIRTY

In his years of travel and brief time with the gypsies, Latimer had learned to rely on research to explain the inexplicable. Bringing Ralph back to his laboratory was the result he wanted, but things still seemed foggy to both men.

"Come, my good man." He beckoned to Ralph. The two walked closer to the shelves of books lining the walls.

"I know I've heard of dimensional travel and time travel, but there is also something called a time pocket where people and other things fall now and again. This time pocket is in between dimensions. Some consider it a void, some religious zealots call it purgatory, and yet others call it the *'in between,'*" Latimer said aloud as he closed in on a section of books behind a large table, with a few scattered, straight-backed chairs set around it. For a moment he thumbed through the pages.

Ralph asked, "Are these all books on magick?."

"Not just magick, but legends, myths, and things…" answered Latimer.

"Things?" questioned Ralph.

Latimer pulled out another book and handed it to Ralph.

"What are we looking for?" Ralph asked as he sat down, book in hand, still looking at Latimer, waiting for a reply.

"Anything that mentions what lies between dimensions."

As Ralph and Latimer researched dimensions in several ancient texts, Ehrich and Emma remained nearby. The tiny laboratory made a nice library as the two men discussed the possibilities of how a portal could open to the wrong place.

"Listen to this," began Latimer. "In a book called *Time and Space*, the description of a dimensional plane appears. There is also a reference to a section called 'Beyond Eternity,' which tells of an evil entity referred to as Dyonacalus, a creature that dwells in the dark of the *'in between.'* This malicious shape-shifter not only collects the souls of unwary victims but also appears as an impending threat to all dimensions. It holds the key to the seven deadly sins: avarice, lust, slothfulness, pride, rage, gluttony, and envy. These seven sins could bring down countries, empires, and continents. Dyonacalus is said to control the sins. It knows the weaknesses of mortals and which sin would fit best with each person."

Ralph got up and went behind Latimer to read over his shoulder.

"Once freed from its unholy prison, it could leap from plane to plane, wreaking havoc wherever it went, releasing all of the deadly sins until it destroyed the entire universe. A beautiful woman with a pure heart must willingly give herself to the dark lord in order to free him from the bonds that bound him to the plane between dimensions." Ralph stopped reading. "What does this mean?"

At hearing this, Emma flinched. Now she knew why the demon had tried to convince her to give herself to it. She closed her eyes and shuddered at the thought.

"I assume it means what it says," replied Latimer as he glanced up at Ralph then back to the book.

"Certainly sin has touched the heart of most everyone in our world, but imagine an entire dimension plagued with all seven deadly sins at once, having no reprieve. With such rampant evil, there would be no one left on the face of the Earth or any planet. The true appearance of the demon has been disputed. Some say it had leathery, scaly skin and glowing red eyes, with horns on its head and cloven hooves as feet. Yet others described it as a handsome man with impeccable manners and dress. Both descriptions note the glowing red eyes." Ralph stopped reading.

"What's wrong?" Latimer inquired.

"It's both," said Ralph. "It can appear both as a horned devil and as a man."

"You saw it?"

"Yes. We've got to get Emma out of there."

"Keep reading and we'll find a way," Latimer tried to sound reassuring. Ralph's mind began spinning with visions of a leathery-skinned devil with horns on its head that stood up on hind legs like a goat only with cloven hooves then the dark-haired, handsome man who had tried to make him hurt Emma.

After hearing all this, Emma said, "Ralph, Latimer, we are both here, Ehrich and I. The demon lurks in the mist and in shadows," she said. Reaching out, her hands went through them.

Ehrich said, "I hear them but can't say anything to the men. It's like I'm watching my home as if through a window. I feel like a ghost; being able to see and hear the mortals, but they cannot see or hear me."

Latimer reached up, took the book from Ralph, and began reading again. "A warning to all: should an inexperienced alchemist or spellcaster attempt to open a portal or vortex to another plane of existence, Dyonacalus may take advantage of the situation and pull the subjects into the *'in between'* as a desperate attempt to find a pure-hearted maiden to release him.

"Should Dyonacalus escape the *'in between,'* death and destruction will soon ravish the unsuspecting dimension.

"The use of divination almost always opened channels to Dyonacalus and not to the dearly departed—a common mistake most people made. Unfortunately, the demon could not be controlled, and in the end, these people almost always died horribly." Latimer stopped reading for a moment to set the book down on the table and shot a look to Ralph, who turned white and swallowed hard.

"This demon must have spelled out the foreboding message on the spirit board. It had stopped the communication between us and Emma."

"What can we do to combat this beast?" Ralph asked, trembling.

Latimer stared at Ralph. "No potion ever affected the demon. No spell ever slowed it down or stopped it."

Ehrich vaguely recalled, "I seem to remember hearing such tales in the gypsy camp but viewed them all as the product of overactive imaginations. To me, these were just stories parents told children to make them obey. Stories children told to scare one another on cold, wintry nights by a blazing fireplace."

Something brushed against Latimer and Ralph as they stood up, trying to make sense of all they had discussed. "Did you feel that?" asked Ralph.

"Yes, I did. It felt like someone touched me as they passed." Latimer visually searched the room.

No one.

Seeing a shadowy figure pass by them, Emma screamed, "He's right there beside you!" But they didn't hear her, no matter how much she waved her hands and stamped her feet.

Ralph and Latimer appeared to be alone, even if the hair on the back of their necks stood up on end. They both shuddered at the thought that some evil had slipped into the real world when Ralph reentered.

Latimer picked up the book *Time and Space* and continued reading. "In order to walk through dimensions without being trapped in the *'in between,'* one needs potions, spells, and above all, a pure heart.

"Smoke seeping from the mirrors you used earlier as a conduit for magickal teleportation showed evidence of Dyonacalus' interference. Unless we bind the demon, we can never use the mirrors again." Latimer paused. Ralph glared at him.

"This is your fault." His look pierced Latimer like a sword.

When he opened his mouth to reply, whatever he said became inaudible to Emma. Confused, she turned to her husband to ask if he could still hear what was being said.

Alone.

Ehrich had vanished, and suddenly, she could no longer hear Ralph and Latimer.

Around and around she whirled, looking for Ehrich, but he was gone. She had never felt him go away.

Leaving Ralph and Latimer at the moment did not seem wise but neither did losing her husband.

After listening to Ralph's account of the veil of forgetfulness clouding his and Emma's minds while they were in the *"in between,"* Latimer reached for a worn book from the shelf. Because the mortal body can endure only so much stress, passing into another period of time, dimension or reality challenged the human brain. After all, the fragility of mortals was what distinguished them from a higher being, like Deity.

The paper spirit board still lay on the table before them. Suddenly, the pen began to move again from one letter to another. Ralph saw it first and began to jot down the letters.

The message read: "Ehrich gone how find how return."

"It's Emma!" Ralph gasped.

"He must have gone somewhere, and she needs to find him. How return? What does that mean?" muttered Latimer as he thumbed through the book. "Emma? Emma, if you can hear me, don't move. Stay where you are. If you move about too much, you may slide into another dimension or fall into the *'in between,'*" he cautioned, praying he would find a way to free her from her invisible prison.

From a distance, someone called out Emma's name. The call seemed desperate and urgent. Who called her? Ehrich? Or this creature called Dyonacalus? She had to turn away, tune it out. Responding to the call might result in her destruction. Then again, if the call came from Ehrich, she'd never forgive herself for not going to him.

Latimer shoved the book he was holding at Ralph, pointing to the top of the page.

"Read!" he insisted. Then he walked around the room furiously, calling out to Emma.

Ralph looked at him. He read aloud, "Dyonacalus could mimic the voice or sound of anyone or anything. Two ways to escape him lay in finding the tunnel between life and death where one could return to their own dimension—oh, just as the little street urchin said!—or dying in one life to return to the other."

Ralph frowned. Even Latimer shivered and reached for the book. What seemed like death in any dimension would definitely bring life in another, but how could they know for sure if this action would bring Emma and Ehrich back to them?

The rest of the account seemed just as vague as the part about dying to reach another dimension.

With more urgency, Latimer called for Emma again.

Ralph and Latimer read on, turning page after page. Based on a list that ran on for some thirty pages, planes coexisting with ours existed beyond eternity; intertwining and yet separate, like Ehrich's destiny foretold by Shylah the Celtic seer.

"This makes it clear." Latimer gave a lopsided smile. "Ralph, do you believe in predestination?"

"What? Predestination? You mean having a future you can't change?" Ralph puzzled.

"Crudely put but yes," Latimer agreed. "This passage says, 'Planes coexisting with ours existed beyond eternity, intertwining and yet separate.' Many years ago, a seer gave Ehrich a prophecy which sounded much like this. She told him he had two separate yet intertwining destinies. Imagine a person having two destinies that intertwine." Latimer smiled.

Ralph scratched his head and stared blankly at Latimer. "That doesn't make sense. A person would have to be in two places at once, or at least live like that, which is not possible. Unless two people assume the same identity."

"I was thinking the same thing." Latimer nodded.

Emma listened intently. The prophecy was talked about in some of Ehrich's journals, but was this what it meant? Two people sharing the same identity, having two separate but entwining destinies? *That was the only explanation, but who could share Ehrich's identity? Who?*

As the men continued to talk, Emma felt helpless and alone. She wished her husband had not disappeared. Tears ran down her pale cheeks as she contemplated her and Ehrich's fate. Again, her name drifted through the air, and she felt pulled toward the voice.

"No," she told herself. Covering her ears, she tried not to listen. If only she had a clear memory. Maybe something she'd forgotten would help her now.

Quickly, she spelled out a message to the men. Latimer looked to Ralph.

The message: "siren calls help find Ehrich."

"Siren calls? What does that mean?" Ralph puzzled.

"What is a siren?" Latimer thought out loud.

No answer.

Flipping through another one of his books, Latimer looked up the term. "'A magickal being possessing the power to hypnotize with its voice.' Someone is trying to entrance her." Latimer looked around the room as if he could visually find the woman. "Emma, think only of survival. Think of your husband. Ignore the voice."

Ignoring the voice was harder than it sounded. The voice caused a surreal state where movement grew difficult and speech nearly impossible.

Latimer jumped up, as if a light bulb had gone off over his head. He took the cool potion and poured it into seven vials. Now he realized where he had gone wrong last time. "The two incantations would bind all evil to the *'in between'* and give the spell proper direction to the location of transport. The vials of potion warded off the seven deadly sins."

Ralph's eyes narrowed. "Maybe you should have read this passage before going all Merlin on us," Latimer said.

Emma was still in despair. Her mind whirled, trying to block out the tantalizing voice while listening to the men's discussion. She now believed

Ehrich had been tricked into leaving her. Possibly, he had slipped between dimensions. It had to be Dyonacalus. Now he wanted her.

She gasped as the voice persisted and grew louder. Ralph's ears perked up.

"Latimer, did you hear that?" He turned pale, as if he'd seen a ghost—or heard one.

Latimer put down the empty flagon and cocked his head from side to side.

"I hear a low humming sound," replied Latimer.

"A voice. A man's voice calling Emma," replied Ralph, not knowing he looked the young woman in the face at that very moment. Emma tried to touch him, but her hand went through his body. He shivered.

"I take it she's still here?" Latimer arose from the chair and moved to Ralph. "You hear it clearer than I. Probably because you've been where she is. It makes you a bit different from those who haven't. You've become sensitive."

"Like being dead?" Ralph looked him in the eye.

Hesitantly, he nodded. "Like returning to life." Latimer sounded grim.

Suddenly, the pen went crazy and spelled out: "it's coming what do I do."

Latimer held the book tight and stood his ground as if to brace himself for a collision. "Don't move, Emma. Please don't move. If you move, it can pull you into the 'in between.'"

The more she resisted, the louder the voice grew, and her guilt increased as well. Her husband couldn't be too far. Maybe she could help him. Staying put might save her, but did she want salvation without Ehrich?

She was slipping. The men could feel it.

The two men screamed for her to ignore the plea for help, but she could only endure so much. She had been trying too hard for too long. Turning to the voice, she reached out, and right away something grabbed her wrist and pulled her back into the *"in between."*

CHAPTER THIRTY-ONE

Icy cold air stung Emma's arm and hand. Wailing and moaning filled the air, and one last great tug on her wrist pulled her back between dimensions. A dark mist engulfed her as a man stepped into view, the same one who had tried to hurt her earlier.

The window that allowed her to see and hear Latimer and Ralph rolled up and disappeared.

"Welcome back, my dear. For a moment, I thought we'd lost you," the man said in a light French accent and bowed, as a gentleman should before a lady.

"Who are you? Where is my husband?" demanded Emma, her face distorted in fear and anguish. "Stay away from me. You tried to hurt me!"

"I will do nothing you don't want me to do. Who am I? Please forgive my rudeness. I thought you knew. Call me Dyonacalus." Again, he bowed. "At your service, *mademoiselle*."

Emma stumbled back as panic washed over her. Her hands felt clammy, and her mouth grew dry as cotton.

"Why do you address me as *mademoiselle*? Where is my husband?" Emma bit her lip to keep composure.

"What makes you think he's your husband? In this plane, there are no husbands and wives. There are no marriages," came the startling reply.

Emma didn't know what to say. Dyonacalus was a demon, after all. He deceived and played tricks on the living. Now he wanted her to free him.

"Where is Ehrich?" Emma demanded again.

"Who? Ehrich? Ah, the man you assume is your husband. Is that what you returned to the *'in between'* for? Ehrich? He no longer wants you, my dear. Here, he can enjoy many pleasures that you cannot be a part of. Here, you can do anything you want with no consequences. I am your destiny, my dear Emma." Dyonacalus moved closer.

The man's voice brought peace to her heart, and his dark eyes flashed with cravings. The crisp, white shirt he wore unbuttoned, gathered at the bottom and tucked into his dark-colored trousers.

She tried, but she could not look away. "Come with me, and I will bring you pleasure that no woman has ever known." Closer and closer he moved to the half-resisting woman. The sensuality of the creature became overwhelming. His face displayed the most handsome, chiseled features she'd ever seen. A sweet, yet masculine scent enveloped her. The slim, muscular body tempted her, and she found herself wanting to touch him. That voice, laced with an unmistakable French accent, sent shivers up and down her spine; it was like the first time she'd ever heard Ehrich, whom she almost couldn't remember now.

"No," she protested as she turned away. "No! I love Ehrich. You are a demon!"

"Am I?" came the soft question. "Look at me."

Reluctantly, she obeyed. Those dark, piercing eyes penetrated her very soul. Cravings for his touch increased, and it took all her strength, mentally and physically, to resist the temptation of giving herself to him.

"Do I look like a demon? Here, there is no heaven or hell. I have lived all these centuries waiting for you. Waiting for the moment I could have you all to myself. We can dwell here together beyond eternity."

Walking through dimensions and in between had exhausted the young woman, and the desire to give up was suddenly overwhelming. If she indeed spoke to a man and not a demon, then perhaps he told the truth. This dimension might exist without heaven or hell, without a deity or a lower being. The thought was appealing. There would be no consequences, no chastisement, and no punishment.

When her guard dropped, Dyonacalus moved in, wrapping his arms around her, claiming her lips like a hungry beast. She fell into a trance.

From a short distance away, a man's voice called her name. Emma felt as if she were slowly waking from a dream. Soon she realized the voices of three men called her name. Her body froze, and the demon stopped the kiss with a growl of displeasure. Emma listened harder. One voice she recognized as Ehrich's, and the other two belonged to Ralph and Latimer. All gave variations of the same warning: *things are not always what they seem.*

The demon fought back. "Open your heart to me, Emma. I can give you anything you want," the evil one lied and feathered kisses from her ear to her heaving bosom.

In a moment, her husband stood before them in the dark mist. Only a faint glimmer of light from an unknown source illuminated the environs. Ehrich's blazing orbs glinted like tiny, angry embers.

He moved closer, with arms outstretched. "Come, my beloved. Don't leave me alone. You saved me more than once. Don't let this demon take you from me. Save me again."

The sweet, loving voice of her husband pushed away the evil feelings stirred by Dyonacalus. Emma's eyes flew open, and she pushed away from the man, but his grip grew tighter and his touch scorching hot.

"So you know me, do you? Why, Ehrich, I'm flattered. Or have you just been eavesdropping on two men through an open portal? The woman is mine. Her heart is pure, and she came to me of her own free will." The man laughed wickedly, and the red glint in his eyes revealed his true nature.

"I had hoped, coming here, you'd completely forget everything and allow my world to remove the depression. Kill yourself. Remain here. You are a challenge," he continued, taunting Ehrich. "You are very strong. Every moment, you fight to remember. Why? Give in to your surroundings. Enjoy lust, hatred, and anger. All of your life these sins have plagued you so. Give up trying to please anyone but your own wonton desires."

"Why do you come as man?" Ehrich moved closer, and the evil hissed, stepping back with a squirming Emma in his arms.

"I am a man," declared Dyonacalus. "The general thought that demons are hideous monsters is not true. Besides, I can look like whatever or whoever you want. Had I appeared as anything other than a handsome man, would she have willingly come to me? No, of course not. And you would not converse with me as you do now." The evil one laughed maniacally and pressed a kiss on the cheek of the weakly struggling woman.

The toll of walking through dimensions fell upon Emma as if she had been hit by a ton of bricks. Her body felt drained of energy, and the will to resist weakened. Existing within the *"in between"* felt even more draining since she'd returned from a dimension coexisting with her own.

Emma's struggling became even weaker, and Dyonacalus laughed again. "Why do you fight me, Ehrich? Long have I waited to bring you here. Why do you shun death? I am here to relieve you of the life that has tortured you all these years. You freely admit you were not meant to be happy, not meant to love. Die knowing you will no longer have to suffer mortality."

Did death no longer interest Ehrich? How could he willfully leave the woman who had stopped him from killing himself only moments ago? Yes, this all came back to him. He felt it deep inside. Something no dimension or demon could take from him: love, true and unconditional love.

Looking around, Ralph appeared agitated. Had he heard something?

After Ralph repeated all he'd heard, Latimer called out to the evil and demanded it manifest itself.

Dyonacalus looked surprised and searched for the whereabouts of the voice. Emma passed out in his arms, and he held her fast, making sure Ehrich would not pull her from his grasp.

The laws of the *"in between"* forced him to answer Latimer. Therefore, he carried his trophy through the mist to a portal, which returned him to where Ralph and Latimer waited by the paper spirit board. He didn't walk through the portal but rather looked in like one would through a window.

By telekinesis, Dyonacalus moved the pen and asked why they called.

Latimer demanded that the demon release Ehrich and Emma and leave them in peace. Dyonacalus gritted his teeth, hating to respond, but he had no choice. Still, he had one more idea in mind.

Again the pen spun around and then wrote: "The woman came to me willingly and the man must now go with the grim mistress."

"It means Death. This makes me feel ill. I see disturbing scenarios flashing through my mind as if I were going mad. We've pitted ourselves against something we can't see." Latimer looked away.

CHAPTER THIRTY-TWO

Dyonacalus didn't get a reputation as a trickster for nothing. Grinning like a Cheshire cat, he telekinetically spun the pen around and wrote another foreboding message, albeit a lie.

Latimer and Ralph sat with a morbid fixation for the paper spirit board. The message read, "What death claims no one can retrieve what once was can never be again."

It laughed with hideous pleasure. Soon the chains that bound him to the *"in between"* would be broken, and Ehrich would be his forever.

"Perhaps you will enjoy the show, knowing you will never be with her again. You can see I am not without feelings. After I destroy love and your wife, I shall go forth and remove all mankind. You hate humanity as much as I, *mon vieux*. This should delight you, knowing I shall destroy the humans, all the world and all its people. *Au revoir, mon vieux. À bientôt.*"

As Dyonacalus passed, dragging Emma from the room, Ehrich hissed and reached out in vain to restrain him, but he couldn't move. The thought of losing his love tormented him. His prayers for aid rose to the heavens.

Suddenly, hearing everything clearly, Latimer rose from his chair and strode about the room, jabbing his finger into thin air from time to time seemingly to search of an open vortex or a forgotten portal.

Ehrich believed some things between dimensions could be accomplished mentally. In his days with the gypsies, he had learned to move little objects, bend spoons and other small, metallic things. The memory seemed cloudy, but selected visions flashed before him. Right now, he needed to move himself. Closing his eyes, he exerted all his mental power to move his feet and legs. He had to move. His wife's life as well as his own depended on it. If the demon could move through the *"in between,"* then so could he.

Meanwhile, Latimer was still searching his laboratory. "Somewhere, somehow, there is an opening. I heard what you heard, which means a portal is open somewhere. If we can find it, perhaps we can pull them through and close it."

Ralph faced Latimer and said, "I can imagine the confusion Ehrich and Emma must be experiencing in such a plane. Dyonacalus didn't want me. He wanted Ehrich all along. But how did he get the power to switch me for Ehrich, when he can't free himself?"

"It was my bungling magick he took advantage of," cried Latimer, cursing himself for his stupidity and neglect.

"Ehrich, I know you can hear me. Emma can only be in one of two places for the seduction to work. She's either in the place resembling a boudoir or the gardens near the tunnel. Do you understand?" Latimer called out.

From a distance, Emma's faint cry for help pierced Ehrich's ears and drove him mad with hatred. In more urgency he pushed his mind to move his legs. Agonized by not having a clear memory of who he was, or whose voice prompted him, Ehrich's breathing changed to near hyperventilation. But the hazy, surreal existence of the *"in between"* caused him to doubt the voice and the emotions that choked him.

After the third cry for help, Ehrich closed his eyes and strained even harder to move until he broke free of his invisible bonds and took off in the direction of his wife's voice. Emma's plea for help as well as the sound of Ehrich breaking free sounded in the atmosphere.

The portal had to be somewhere close. They tested all of the mirrors and everything with a reflective surface but to no avail. Ralph took to poking at the air around him for a hidden portal or vortex as Latimer did. The sounds rang so crisp and clear, as if he and Latimer stood in the *"in between"* as well.

Without warning, a vapor of gas took shape before them, near the table bearing the paper spirit board. Distracted once again from his conquest, Dyonacalus had made the mistake in leaving the portal open, but for some reason he couldn't close it. His power seemed to be growing weaker, and the plane between dimensions wanted to expel the intruders. If he didn't complete the seduction, the *"in between"* would find a way to remove Emma and Ehrich, and he would lose his last chance for freedom.

Above the spirit board, the gaseous vapor took the shape of a familiar, handsome man and spun the pen around until it touched the tip of the letter "w." Again the writing instrument pointed to letter after letter, spelling out the same foreboding message, "What death claims no one can retrieve what once was can never be again."

Latimer looked to Ralph. When their jaws dropped and eyes widened, Dyonacalus knew they saw him. Quickly, he melted back into the shadows. Ralph wanted to follow, but Latimer held him back.

~ * ~

As the darkness of unconsciousness lifted to an eerie orange haze, Emma laid in the arms of the man beyond handsome. From a great distance, a faint male voice called her name. A familiar feeling stirred, but Dyonacalus quickly shot it down by forcing her to look at him. Again, the man's voice broke the trance and called the young woman's name, reminding her how much he loved her.

"Ehrich!" The name slipped from her lips.

"You want only me," hissed Dyonacalus. "My touch is all that will satisfy you. I alone am all you will ever need or want. I will lead you to a place women only dream of. I will take your passion to incredible heights."

Suddenly, Ehrich stood in horror in the doorway. Dyonacalus was clearly trying to seduce his wife; the evil raised a hand, evoking a surge of energy, blasting Ehrich across the room. Had there not been solid wall to stop him, he would have been hurled out into the great unknown. His back ached and his head spun.

"YOU CANNOT HAVE HER. I LOVE HER!" screamed Ehrich.

The word "love" seemed to prick Dyonacalus, and he slowly turned his head and glared at Ehrich with red glowing eyes.

"Love does not exist between dimensions, *mon ami*. I rule the plane between heaven and hell, between life and death. Here, only sin prevails. You mortals are so gullible." Then the demon taunted him by imitating Emma's voice. "Ehrich, help me. Please help me." Dyonacalus laughed maniacally.

Ehrich's face flushed crimson as the heat of hatred flamed within, but the power of the demon held fast, and he could not pass through the invisible barrier holding him back. Watching Emma struggle jogged his mind. He remembered nothing clearly, only vague emotions, but still she belonged to him, and he would not let anyone or anything take her away.

"Emma, come back to me. I love you," Ehrich found himself calling to her as tears rolled down his face. "You are part of my two destinies. Remember, you cannot change history." These words fell from his lips as if someone else had put them there.

The words rang true but try as she might to free herself, she couldn't. The grip of the demon felt stronger than that of any ordinary human.

She fought for freedom. He wanted to help, but still could not move his feet. As his mind pushed for freedom, his head felt like someone had split it open, and something wet and warm ran from his nose.

"The great Dyonacalus has to cheat in order to win. How cowardly!" he needled. His eyes flashed with resolve.

At this, Dyonacalus stopped short and turned his glaring, red eyes toward Ehrich. "I, cheat? This is an insult. Dyonacalus does not have to cheat. Victory is already mine. She comes to me willingly."

"Hypnosis takes away her free will. She comes to you by command. Hardly playing fair, I'd say." Ehrich drove the verbal knife in hard. The feeling akin to needles in his head increased, and so did the dripping from his nose.

In spite of this, his words seemed to aggravate the demon.

"I have no need for hypnosis." The evil released Emma and faced his rival. "I am the great Dyonacalus! Women flock to my side. They vie for my attention."

Emma tried to run, but the demon turned to her and raised his hand. She froze. No matter how hard she strained to move her feet, they felt like cement.

"They cringe at the sight of you. Most would rather die than surrender to you," Ehrich retorted. With flames in its eyes, the demon advanced toward the Master of Arts.

At last, Ehrich's feet moved.

Darting forward and wrapping his arms around Emma, Ehrich pulled her away from the advancing evil. His voice roared like a lion and threatened total annihilation in revenge for Ehrich's mockery and disrespect.

"Really now, old fellow, you have been trapped here for how long and not one damsel has offered herself to you? You're not the irresistible lover you claim to be." Ehrich stared the creature in the eyes as his wife buried her face in his warm chest. Emma trembled a little, and a prayer fell from her lips. By now, a few drops of red fluid dripped from her nose.

"Seems like your seven deadly sins are consuming you. Anger leads you now," called Ehrich.

The demon's face distorted with rage as it advanced on the two with murder in its eyes. They needed to find the tunnel.

Dyonacalus pushed them around the room. For the moment, they found no way out. Not a single door or window came into view.

"Why do you come as a man, Dyonacalus? Why not come in your true form?" cried the frightened Emma.

"Ah, *ma cherie*, as I have said before, if I came as beast, could I convince you to covet what is not yours? I think not. If I looked less than a man, would a woman allow me to seduce her, or would the revolutionaries of great nations listen to my plans for a *coup d'état*? *Mais non*! I think not. It is a shame I must destroy such beauty, but in the end all mankind will be annihilated, *n'est-ce pas*?" mocked the demon.

With wooden steps, Dyonacalus closed in on his prey. The fear in their eyes fed his lust for death and stoked the furnace of anger.

"Your memories fade in and out. A much better challenge. Too bad you couldn't have been more submissive and just sat back to watch the master at work."

"It looks to us like all you can do is create illusions and fear, in hopes your victims succumb to your lies. You rule nothing. God rules everything. You can do nothing to us unless God permits it." Ehrich stuck in the proverbial knife and twisted it. Dyonacalus flamed with rage, and his red eyes shot out small fiery darts, which missed them by a hair's breadth.

An open portal or vortex existed somewhere in the boudoir, but where? The advancing evil would eventually back them into a corner then what? Every wall he and his beloved Emma touched felt solid, and so did the floor. Circling the room backward in a vain effort to escape the advancing demon seemed like complete insanity. They did this over and over and still found no way out.

The atmosphere grew hot and humid, while the air no longer smelled of lavender but rather like sulfur or brimstone. Gradually, the two grew weaker and weaker from the strain of abiding this plane. Streams of sticky fluid trickled from their nostrils, and their heads felt like bursting.

"Prepare to meet your maker, *mes amis*. And by the way, *mon vieux*, you have no destiny. Shylah the seer lied." The evil being broke into hideous laughter. "For you, tomorrow never comes."

CHAPTER THIRTY-THREE

Ehrich and Emma seemed doomed to a damned existence between dimensions. The demon raging before them shifted through myriad forms in an effort to scare and confuse. The glint of its glowing red eyes seemed like the only thing that remained constant.

As feared, Ehrich and Emma ended up with their backs against a solid wall when the shape-shifting creature returned to the more agreeable form of a man.

Dyonacalus drew closer and held his hand out to Emma where she trembled in her husband's arms.

"You cannot escape. If you want to return to the plane where the dimensional slide occurred, you could find the tunnel or just kill yourselves as lovers often do," stated Dyonacalus in a loud, distorted voice.

They both considered this choice. Death could lead them to another dimension, freeing them from Dyonacalus and perhaps returning them to the original point of transport. At this moment, all they knew of religion and God seemed to wash over them. Should that fail, suicide would make them murderers in sight of God and they'd be damned for all eternity.

Walking around seemed effortless until Ehrich reached the area where vines and bushes grew in abundance, as if hiding something. The closer he drew, the more difficult it became to move, as if in a dream. His arms grew heavy and no longer could he carry his wife. So he laid her on the grass and again tried to move his weighted-down legs. If the tunnel they sought lay behind vines and bushes, they might find their way back to their dimension. Then his wife would regain her strength and memory, and so would he. A glimmer of hope showed through the bleakness of their ordeal. For now, he and Emma could rest a little.

~ * ~

Latimer and Ralph lost the sound of movement for a brief moment, but as soon as Ehrich and Emma reached the garden, they once again heard everything. Ralph would know the fear they had experienced in going through bright spots and following the beast and the strange assortment of other characters through the tunnel. Choosing the opposite direction had led them in a twisted circle of mayhem, compliments of Dyonacalus. Ralph's eyes looked from side to side as if confused.

"I'm afraid you should have remained in the tunnel and followed the beast and others back to the here and now," Latimer confirmed his fears. "Walking through dimensions can be a tricky thing, as you have seen. I feel responsible for the mishap in trying to make my old friend happy."

"What do you mean? What were you trying to do? Send me and Emma to her time? That's absurd!" Ralph waved a hand as if to dismiss the subject.

Latimer didn't explain but instead replied, "It's no more absurd than you and Emma getting trapped by the *'in between'* in the first place. As you very well know, things aren't always what they seem."

CHAPTER THIRTY-FOUR

Setting the chairs around the table, Latimer put the paper spirit board in the center and moved the potions aside. He and Ralph stood helpless, unless they could find something in the musty old books lining the shelves.

As they sat at the table thumbing through some ancient texts, Latimer noticed the frown on the young noble's face as he stared at the book before him.

"Ralph, is something wrong? You're just staring." Latimer's brows knitted together.

"Will we ever get her back? Emma, I mean." Ralph sniffled a bit.

"Are you crying?"

"No, of course not," Ralph sniffled again and looked away.

Latimer reached over and patted the young man's arm. "We'll find her and Ehrich. I feel it. Trade books with me," he said, shoving his toward Ralph. "Time is of the essence."

During their research, Ralph made a frightening discovery. A book called *Endless Todays* took the reader through the personal experiences of a young scientist turned alchemist, named Faulker von Heissler.

Latimer began reading. "Born in Heidelberg, Germany in 1829, young Faulker began conducting experiments in 1854 in which he ingested large amounts of bourbon as a depressant before transporting himself to another dimension. The most dangerous aspect of the journey was Faulkner's experience within the *'in between,'* where short-term memory loss occurred.

"After various attempts to enter another dimension, two ways proved most successful: one involved the use of mirrors, potions, and spells, and the other used a peculiar energy later known as electricity, which caused the body to vibrate at an abnormal rate of speed. The intoxication seduced the mind into drifting to the point of believing the faster rate of living as normal and added to the temporary amnesia. Physically, the damage to the body would happen regardless. However, if the body did not vibrate at just the right speed, the subject would slip in between dimensions.

"According to the *Book of Prophecy* penned by an unnamed Christian, a prophet of God traveling from the moors of Scotland to the shores of northern France healed seven brothers plagued by the sins upon which all sins are based: rage, avarice, slothfulness, pride, lust, gluttony, and envy. Theology later referred to them as the seven deadly sins. After making the last brother whole, the prophet faced the demon. From the waist up it resembled a man, but the lower half resembled a goat with two cloven hooves. The face looked leathery, and the thing sported tiny horns upon its head. The red, piercing eyes glowed like tiny, stray embers from a dying fire.

"The prophet described the place as one of earthly pleasures, later to bring the mind to ultimate regret and torture from all seven of the basic sins; an endless torment where the suffering never ends."

Ralph shuddered at the last words. Now things seemed clear.

Latimer continued reading the prophet's words. "Being of a cunning nature, the demon again tried to bargain for freedom before the portal closed. Here the prophet declared that if a woman with a pure heart willingly gave herself to the creature, he would regain his freedom to roam the earth and distribute the seven sins, which he ruled.

"'Willingly' and 'with a pure heart,' became the key terms in the prophet's declaration. The creature could not use any form of trickery or deceit. A pure-hearted woman had to see him in his true form and know full well what he was, and then willingly give herself to him. This sounded virtually impossible, dooming the thing to be trapped 'beyond darkness' for all eternity." He set down the text.

"There is one last book to look in. I feel we are close to a solution, regardless of some of the things we've read." Latimer stood up and moved to a shelf of books.

"And the potion you used to bring me back? What about using it somehow?" Ralph picked up the cooled flagon of liquid. Latimer smiled and nodded.

"You just may have something." Latimer's eyes lit up.

~ * ~

In the heavenly garden, near the vines and bushes, Ehrich continued struggling to move his feet. Nearby, Emma lay in a dreamless sleep. Their survival depended solely on him. As he leaned in and reached out for the vines, a transparent girl passed between them and through Ehrich's body. Something like a sudden gust of strong wind seemed to rush through him, as he gasped and tried to move backward. The girl never acknowledged him but continued on her way toward the brook.

Again, Ehrich leaned in and reached for the vines; this time, his feet moved as another transparent person rushed through him. Finding himself on the grass next to his unconscious wife, he quickly got up and ripped the vines apart. The tunnel lay before him. Inside, it looked dismal and gloomy. Sounds of people moving echoed quietly from the walls. With one swift movement, he scooped up his wife and melted into the vines, dissolving into the strange world of transparent people, shadowy shapeless masses, and the skittering of whatever slithered under foot.

The length of the dismal tunnel seemed endless, echoing with distant screeching and occasional howling. After walking for some time, Ehrich moved to a wall where he sat cradling his beloved wife. Though he appeared to have more stamina than she, he now suffered the consequence of existing in this weird plane. Ehrich's head pounded and throbbed from the base of his skull to its center. The pain felt worse than before. His eyelids fluttered as if to close, but he fought to stay awake. If he blacked out, who would protect his beloved? Who would fight Dyonacalus when he came for her?

Ehrich's breathing became labored, and he again noticed a few drops of red dripping from his nose. Not sure what to make of it, he tried to force himself to get up.

Suddenly, a form moved toward him. A thin, frail girl dressed as a street child from a Dickens novel stood before him, cocking her head from side to side in examination of the young woman in his arms.

"She don't look well. I'd say it's her time, guv'nor." The street urchin moved in for a closer look. Ehrich eyed her suspiciously and wanted to say something, but more and more red dripped from his nose, and his head felt like it had split open.

"Best leave her behind if you want to make it to the other side in time."

After taking a deep breath, Ehrich asked, "What do you mean?"

Then she explained, "The plane will shift and spit you out. The unconscious woman will die, and no one can stop it. If you want to live, leave her and go to the end of the tunnel."

Nothing would make Ehrich leave the woman he loved. The pain of being alone rushed back to him, and he knew he could not live without her. If she died, so would he.

The child did not appear to understand. She had been there too long, like them. A small trickle of thick, red liquid oozed from the corners of her mouth.

"Come quickly, before we both die. The woman is dead already," declared the girl without emotion.

With all the strength he could muster, Ehrich gathered up his wife and dragged her past the street urchin. He would not leave his beloved. Whether or not the girl told the truth, he didn't care. Nothing would make him leave Emma behind. With or without a clear recollection, the heart never forgets. And his heart validated their bond, for love cannot be hidden or forgotten; it is eternal.

As he half carried, half dragged Emma along the path, the street urchin chattered away about his stupidity, and how he'd die uselessly if he didn't drop his burden. The strength ebbed from his weakened body.

Images of a woman's blood-soaked body in the arms of a grief stricken man loomed up before him. Losing one wife had destroyed his life. Losing another would end it. Mentally, he struggled for a complete memory as his head throbbed.

Though not a religious man, Ehrich mustered up enough strength to gather Emma up into his arms and mumbled, "God, I know I've never asked you for anything. I've blamed you for a lot, but now, there's only one thing…I ask…please don't let my Emma die. You've taken everything else away. Please don't take her." Tears rolled down his cheeks as the red fluid of life ran from his nostrils.

When he looked up, he saw the light at the end of the tunnel. Not only could he see the sunshine, but he could smell the scent of the city, a mix of bread from the *boulangerie* and vegetables and herbs from the marketplace. The scent of horse droppings combined with dust from carriages and coaches going to and fro permeated the atmosphere.

"You are more stubborn then I thought," growled Dyonacalus, whose voice grew louder and more distorted. When Ehrich turned, he saw a tall black mass shape-shift into many different forms until finally into that of a man, the diabolical Dyonacalus. The street urchin ran into the shadows and vanished.

"No one can be more pig-headed then a man in love. Did you really think I would let you leave so easily? You are even stupid enough to fight to remember a past life. Why? Do you crave pain and misery that much?" Dyonacalus moved toward him with outstretched arms to relieve him of his wife. Ehrich moved away, dragging her with him.

"As soon as you reach the light, the woman will die anyway. Give her to me and save yourself. Look at you! You can barely stand. Your nose is bleeding, and I'm sure your head gives you much pain," goaded Dyonacalus as he flashed those red, beady eyes.

"I am surprised at the strong mind and will you possess. By now, I would think nothing would allow you to even remember her. Don't fight the veil of darkness. Forget the life you left behind," continued the demon.

Ehrich only had a few more steps to reach the light of day. The demon held up a hand, and Ehrich froze. Once again, his feet and legs could not move. His head

pounded and began to spin like a top. Images and sounds from the real world became distorted. A strange sleepiness washed over him, making his eyelids grow heavy. He needed to close them. If he dropped the burden in his arms, then he would make it to the sunlight where he could sleep. All pain would leave him, and he could sleep a sweet, peaceful sleep.

As the demon attempted to pull Emma from his grasp, Ehrich heard his wife rally and whisper, "Ehrich…I love…you. I will…always love you." Somehow, deep inside, unconditional love yet existed.

When he turned and looked into her sweet face, her eyelids fluttered to stay open, and again she gasped for breath.

"How touching but stupid!" exclaimed the angry demon. "Leave her and save yourself!"

Ignoring the evil rantings, Ehrich gently, lovingly pressed his lips against Emma's, holding her close and tight. Over and over Dyonacalus shrieked, "With me she lives, with you she dies! Make your choice!"

But before Ehrich could move on, the demon appeared in front of him, blocking the light and the exit. He raised his hand and bolts of energy shot forth, slamming Ehrich and Emma back into the tunnel. The blast sent them sprawling to the ground several meters in, farther away from their escape. Maniacal laughter echoed all around them. Barely conscious, it looked as if death drew near. A dark, shrouded figure stood in the shadows, holding its trademark scythe. Death seemed the only answer. No longer could she speak.

Ehrich struggled to gather her into his arms.

A few capillaries in Emma's arms began to pop one by one. Blood oozed from the ruptured pores, and it seemed she'd lose the battle to live. Ehrich's eyelids fluttered, trying to focus on his wife. *My prayers to God seem in vain. Would making a deal with the demon be better?* The thought sounded appealing.

The back of Ehrich's head felt numb. Sharp, excruciating pain shot through his nervous system. The sticky red substance spotted his clothes and the ground. Silently, Ehrich closed his eyes, holding Emma tight in his arms. He forced himself to focus on the deal offered. If he didn't do something, they would surely die.

While his body strained to live, his mind strained to heal his wife. A bright spot opened before them. Ehrich felt warmth from the light and forced his eyes open. Something about the brightness gave him promise of escape and safety. Suddenly, he made his choice.

Ignoring the offer from Dyonacalus, Ehrich staggered toward the light, knowing full well he took a risk that could kill them both. He and his precious Emma melted into the bright spot and vanished.

CHAPTER THIRTY-FIVE

At Latimer's residence, peering through the mist in a cauldron of simmering herbs, Latimer chanted something akin to prayer instead of an incantation. White mist rose up from the hot liquid and opened the vortex wider so Ehrich and Emma could pass through.

As he continued chanting, Ehrich dragging Emma within the liquid of the cauldron, moving toward the brightness at the end of the tunnel while Dyonacalus tried to bargain with them.

In a few minutes, they found Ehrich and Emma in the streets of Paris, amid the center of a busy marketplace. As soon as they returned to the nineteenth century, all of Ehrich's memories rushed back to him.

"I remember us," Emma whispered. "We are married and in love."

Ehrich's head calmed and he felt relaxed, even sleepy. He touched his nose. No more trickling. Still weak from the experience, Emma fainted in his arms, but at least he had the strength to the carry her. Blood stained her arms, but only a few pores still oozed. Apparently, Latimer's intervention with his potion and prayer had stopped the progressive deterioration of her health.

When Ehrich turned the corner to leave the marketplace, Ralph and Latimer rolled up with a carriage.

The two jumped down and ran to the couple. Latimer caught Ehrich just as he collapsed, releasing his wife to roll onto the ground. Ralph ran to her, tears in his eyes at seeing the blood smeared on her face, neck and on her arms.

"Ehrich, speak to me. Thank the gods you and Emma are alive!" Latimer hugged his friend.

Ehrich tried to speak, but he barely had the strength to lift his hand and touch Latimer's arm.

Then supporting him, Latimer helped Ehrich into the carriage.

"Emma, Emma, speak to me." Ralph held her close. When he pulled back, her eyelids fluttered as if trying to force them open.

Scooping her into his arms, Ralph carried her to the carriage and laid her next to her husband.

After closing the door, Ralph and Latimer mounted the carriage.

"She's alive! I thought we'd never see her again," Ralph wiped away the tears.

Latimer flicked the reins and the horse began to move. "I thought we'd never see either of them. But they're still in danger of succumbing to their injuries. We must hurry."

In a few minutes, the carriage brought them to Ralph's home, *le Château Duchenois*, where a family physician attended both Ehrich and Emma.

Emma's condition stabilized after the good doctor gave her a spoonful of two different types of liquids. Then he left the bottles with Ralph and gave instructions to keep her warm and feed her a spoonful of each liquid every four hours until he emptied the bottles. Fortunately, her stage of dehydration seemed easy to remedy with medicine and water, but Ehrich's dehydration began to worsen. Bedridden for the time being, he had to take orders from Ralph since he was too weak to stay in his dark wing alone.

Entering the bedroom where the bedridden Ehrich lay, Ralph carried a tray filled with a glass of water, a spoon and a bottle of the concoction Latimer had simmered earlier.

After setting the tray on the end table by the bed, Ralph opened the bottle of this smelly, thick, unappetizing liquid. Sniffing it, he wrinkled his nose and picked up a spoon from the tray.

"What's that?" growled Ehrich.

"Sounds like you're feeling better. This is something Latimer brewed. He said it will help you get well." Ralph poured some of the liquid into the spoon.

"You're not feeding me that," Ehrich protested in a quiet voice, still weak from his ordeal. When the spoon came closer, he turned away.

"This will stop the dehydration. Please open your mouth." Ralph set the bottle back on the tray and moved the spoon closer.

"No," again Ehrich kept his head turned away.

"Ehrich, please." Ralph would have to force the medicine down the patient's throat. Therefore, he grabbed Ehrich by the shoulder farthest from him and tried to pull his face toward him. The spoon shook out some of the liquid.

"Please stop resisting. I'm only trying to help." Ralph continued to pull at him.

Finally, he released Ehrich and set the spoon on the tray. Pulling a handkerchief from his inside jacket pocket, he mopped at the spots of medicine that splattered on the bed and on his trousers.

Suddenly, Latimer appeared in the doorway. "How goes it?"

"Just fine, if I can get this stubborn man to take a spoon full of this liquid." Ralph sputtered.

"Ehrich, are you giving Ralph a difficult time?" Latimer smiled as he moved closer.

"Make him go away," mumbled Ehrich. "I don't need his help."

"You sound better, but you have to take the brew I made. Do you want to see Emma?"

Quickly Ehrich's head snapped around to him. "Then take the medicine from Ralph," Latimer smiled. "If you don't, the dehydration will get worse.

"You give it to me," Ehrich sounded determined, even in a quiet voice.

"I cannot be everywhere at once. If you want to get well, you will have to obey Ralph. He will not hurt you," Latimer reassured him.

Ehrich looked sharply at Ralph who picked up the bottle and poured a little more liquid into the spoon. Then Ralph set down the bottle and turned to the stubborn man.

This time, Ehrich opened his mouth, and Ralph put the spoon in.

"That wasn't so bad, was it?" said Ralph and he put the empty spoon on the tray.

No answer.

Latimer smiled and patted Ehrich's arm. Then he turned to Ralph.

"Thank you." With that he left the room.

~ * ~

Gathering her strength seemed a long and arduous journey for Emma. But with the help of medicine and knowing her husband fared better and better each day, the time didn't seem so stressful.

Ralph read stories to her every day. When she asked about the *"in between,"* he'd read sections of the text he and Latimer had researched.

The religious account intrigued her more than any, especially the part where the prophet of God had banished the creature to "beyond darkness" with the keys to the seven sins.

At one point, when Emma recalled her encounter with Dyonacalus as he tried to force his kisses on her, Ralph could not control his feelings.

So he leaned in and kissed her gently on the lips, surprising her.

Emma pushed him back hard, just as Latimer entered with a tray of tea and sweets. He stopped short with surprise.

No one said a word, and things went on as usual. Hanging his head, Ralph quickly left the room. But Latimer never put it out of his mind.

Toggling from one bedside to the other wore out both Latimer and Ralph, but having their friends back alive and on the mend felt like one of the greatest gifts they could ever receive from the Almighty.

No matter how much Ehrich snapped or refused to speak, Ralph greeted him with a smile. Not once did he lose his temper or become impatient.

While Ehrich slept, Ralph and Latimer discussed dimensional shifts, time travel and alternate realities.

"No matter what we've read, heard, or felt, who could say we clearly understand how a body travels from one dimension, time, or reality to another?" Latimer sat back in an overstuffed chair in the parlor in front of a cold fireplace.

"I agree. I was actually there, and I still don't understand. Something apparently evil dwelled in the dark plane between dimensions. And now I realize everything and everybody must pass through the *'in between,'* but should not linger," Ralph stated as he sat on the sofa and sipped his tea from a china cup. "Isn't the *'in between'* another name for hell?" he puzzled.

Latimer shook his head. "According to what I understand, part of it is like heaven and another part like hell. That's what makes it the *'in between.'*"

"Perhaps a demonic being calling itself Dylon, Dyonicas, or Dyonacalus lived there, or perhaps it was a mere figment of the imagination. The further away from the incident, the less they will remember." Latimer smiled. "Except for me. I have recorded everything in a journal. I want to recall precisely what happened so as not to make the same mistakes again." Seven Egyptian bottles filled with a potion lay in reserve for the time when he would use them. Seven bottles filled with the potion, two incantations, and three mirrors. "Nothing can change if I want to succeed in making an old friend happy. Magick has to be exact, accurate. No substitutes allowed."

"What do you mean by that?" asked Ralph.

"Magick has to be exact?"

"No. Before that. What do you mean, 'If you want to succeed in making an old friend happy'?" Ralph's eyebrows knitted together as he tried to comprehend.

"Go back to the mirror with Emma and you will understand."

When the bride and groom felt strong enough to leave the *château*, Latimer returned them to their home in the dark wing of *le Théâtre Ranier*.

Emma smiled at Ehrich as they entered the dark wing. "There really is no place like home."

CHAPTER THIRTY-SIX

Three weeks later, things had returned to the normal routine of rehearsals, performing plays on selected evenings, or just being wife to the renowned Ehrich de Natois. Emma tried to blot out the unfortunate incident of the *"in between."* Even though she and her husband had not been gone for long according to the real world, it seemed like forever to her. No one in the theater questioned her whereabouts, since Ralph had written a letter to the theater manager excusing her absence for a family emergency.

However, nightmares haunted her sleep, though she tried to ignore them and said nothing to her husband.

As Emma lay next to Ehrich, she slept fitfully, tossing and turning as flashing, red eyes loomed up before her from a black void. Vague scenes of gray, ashen trees, barren and dreary, flashed before her and then blurred as if she were running. But the hot breath of Dyonacalus as he held her tight around the waist felt crystal clear. She felt herself struggle for freedom, tugging at his arms and hands tightening about her waist. At one point, the demon tightened his grip so that she awoke, bolting straight up in bed, gasping for air. She shook from head to toe in fear of her life.

This awakened Ehrich. He gathered into his arms. "What's wrong? Did you have a bad dream?"

Emma hugged him, burying her face into his neck, and said nothing.

"I'm here. Nothing will harm you. If you don't want to talk about it, that's all right." He held her until she fell back to sleep.

Whenever she looked into a mirror or even the bath water, the grinning face of the demon seemed to mock her and promise to come for her when she least expected.

Evening found Emma sitting out the night's performance. The understudy, an actress with less talent, took her place to the displeasure of the theater manager. But he could say nothing if his star felt ill.

Ehrich entered the sitting room with Latimer.

A kiss from her dear husband always cheered Emma's heart and brought a smile to her face, but would nightmares of the demon haunt her for the rest of her life?

Latimer noticed the drawn, sallow look on her face and the dark circles around her eyes.

"What's the matter, my dear? You seem troubled. You are unusually quiet and seem lost in your thoughts."

At first, Emma said nothing as she stared at the open window across the room. Sunlight flooded the chamber and birds chirped merrily, but she showed no response to the lovely day outside.

Gingerly, Latimer touched her shoulder. She looked up at him.

"Talk to each other. No matter how you feel, talk about it," he said.

"It's difficult," Emma tried to smile.

Latimer grinned, "The key to a successful relation is communication."

She nodded in agreement and her countenance brightened.

CHAPTER THIRTY-SEVEN

Twanda and Cerise wanted to stop for the day. They had been sitting in Cerise's old dressing room for a couple of hours now.

"I'm exhausted. Let's go back to the hotel," grumbled Cerise, head in hands as she sat leaning on an end table near the mirror. "I don't know why we keep coming back here. Nothing ever happens."

"We need to, like, get our friend Emma back," Doone replied in his valley-boy way. "I hope she's okay. Twanda, when you talked to her, she was, like, okay?"

"Yes, for the umpteenth time, she was good. Both of them were good," replied Twanda as she sat on a nearby tapestry chair, fidgeting with the shoulder strap of her purse. "I'm getting tired too. Maybe we should go back to the hotel."

"Like, what do you mean, both were good?" Doone's brows knitted together as he narrowed his eyes at her.

"Ralph was with her. You saw him the last time when the mirrors smoked up," Twanda explained. "I told you that he came with her the first time."

Doone made a face as he recalled the man standing next to Emma.

"Why are you making a face?" Twanda cocked her head to one side, as if to study him.

"Nothing."

"Let's go," Twanda rose up from the chair. Cerise perked up with the prospect of leaving.

Doone stood in front of the mirror and tapped on it gently. "Hello! Hello! Is anybody there?"

Cerise sat with a smile on her face as she stared at Doone.

Twanda leaned in to her and whispered, "Are you crushing on Doone?"

"Huh? Crushing?"

"Do you love Ralph? You're supposed to, but you seem to spend a lot of time looking at Doone." Twanda tried to understand.

This jolted the pretty blonde back to reality. "Of course I...I love...you...you know," Cerise blushed and stammered as if caught doing something bad.

"Ralph. We were talking about you loving Ralph," Twanda puzzled at her reactions.

No reply.

Talk then dwindled to a minimum.

Doone began to yawn and stretch when the mirror grew cloudy. Everyone's attention turned to it.

As the clouds dispersed, there before them stood Emma and Ehrich on one side of the mirror and Doone, Cerise, and Twanda assembled on the other.

"Who are you?" Cerise asked, staring at Ehrich.

"I am Ehrich de Natois, the Master of Arts."

Turning to Cerise, Doone stretched forth his hand. "It is time." For a moment, she hesitated. Doone pulled himself up to his full height and his demeanor changed. His voice and actions were those of Ehrich de Natois.

Softly, gently, Doone began his sweet recitation of eternal love, hailing Cerise to him.

"No painting could ever convey your beauty. No words could utter what's felt in my heart. Only the seraphim from heaven would know, The ecstasy my Cerise can impart."

Those velvet tones seemed to seduce the girl, wrapping themselves around her like grapevines entwined in a trellis.

Again came a flash of white light, like the one that brought Emma through the mirror. As Cerise melted into the glass through the watery vortex, Emma and Ehrich stepped forward and emerged simultaneously into the present.

"I remember!" exclaimed Emma. "I recall my life in the nineteenth century and this one!"

This time Ehrich remembered all. Unlike Emma losing her memory when she entered his time, he still remembered his former life.

Twanda embraced each one, though she grieved at the loss of Doone.

Sadly, they watched him lead Cerise deep into the dark recesses of the hidden passage inside the walls, with Ralph following behind. The three never looked back.

"Will we ever see Doone again?" Twanda groaned.

"I don't know. I hope so," Emma blinked back the tears, but as she looked around, a smile spread across her face. "I'm home."

"So, this handsome thing here is your husband. Shame on you, girl! Keeping a hunk like this a secret," Twanda grinned and gave Ehrich a welcome hug.

"Handsome thing?" Ehrich puzzled.

"Do you know who you are and who I am?" Emma smiled.

Gathering his wife in his arms, he claimed her lips and held her close.

"How could I forget the woman who saved me so many times, whose love pulled me from the grave and led me to heaven?" he smiled.

"Look in the mirror," Twanda and Emma chimed in at once.

When Ehrich turned around, the reflection he saw astounded him. He beamed with happiness and contentment. His eyes looked bright and alert. Even the expression on his face appeared soft and kind. Laugh lines increased as his smile widened.

When he looked down, he found himself wearing the tattered jeans and sandals Doone had worn before entering the vortex. He even wore the odd-looking tie-dye shirt Doone loved.

Gingerly, he touched his face and chest as he stared in the mirror.

"You're so gorgeous, you may not want me after a while," teased his wife.

"Don't ever say that." He smiled and kissed her tenderly. "I will love you beyond eternity."

"Hey!" Twanda playfully interrupted. "Kiss later. We've got a plane to catch."

"That's right. Check your pockets, Ehrich. You're wearing Doone's clothes. See if you've got his boarding pass." He obeyed, and sure enough, he had it.

Twanda raced out of the dressing room, leaving them alone for a moment. As they turned to leave, a voice called from the mirror. Latimer's form appeared through the mist.

"Latimer? How?" asked Ehrich in surprise.

"Just want to say goodbye for the moment. Happiness is yours."

"Why and how have I retained my memory when Emma and the others lost theirs in the shift between dimensions?" Ehrich puzzled.

"I used a little Celtic magick. May God smile upon you."

"Did you send me through the mirror?" Emma questioned.

"Yes. It was the only way I could have you meet Ehrich and get him away from here. Ehrich, if you had stayed, you would never have found happiness. Shylah's vision of the young woman from another time was you, Emma. Her description was unquestionably you."

"Will we ever see you and Doone again?" Ehrich felt saddened at the thought of losing his friends.

"Who knows what God has in store for us?" As the last words fell from his lips, Latimer's image grew dim. Ehrich and Emma called out, but he vanished before they could thank him.

The two Ehrichs finally found their destinies. After all, they'd been through, Ehrich and Emma enjoyed one more kiss before moving on to their new life together.

Meanwhile, long ago, in the depths of the walls of *le Théâtre Ranier*, Cerise wept as she followed the bright red drops splattered on the floor leading to the entrance of the dark wing. *Only the seraphim from heaven would know the ecstasy my Cerise can impart,* echoed in her head

FRENCH GLOSSARY

Cerise-Cherry

"Mon Dieu, ma petite!"-"My God, my little one!" - s'il vous plaît-please.

M.-Abbreviation for monsieur (mister).

Boulangerie-bakery.

Mon vieux-old friend (m)

"Au revoir, mon vieux. À bientôt."-"Goodbye, old friend. See you soon."

…n'est-ce pas?-… isn't that right?

Ma bien-aimée-my beloved (f)

tête-à-tête—face-to-face (informal)

About the Author

Born and raised in Salt Lake City, Fay E. Simon nurtured and developed a love for writing from an early age. She started out writing short stories for an English class, and took first place in several local short story and poetry contests. In high school, she served as a member of the editorial staff of the creative writing magazine and wrote a number of short skits for her acting class. Fay tried her hand at writing several different screenplays (still in progress), only to return to her first love, writing novels. Today she lives near Los Angeles where she continues to write and coach new writers online.